SEEING SOUND
BOOK ONE OF THE TASTING MADNESS SERIES

ALBANY WALKER

Copyright © 2020 by Albany Walker

All rights reserved

No part of this book may be reproduced in any form or by any electronic or mechanical means, including information storage and retrieval systems, without permission in writing from the author. The only exception is by a reviewer, who may quote short excerpts in a review.

This book is a work of fiction. Names, characters, places, and incidents either are products of the author's imagination or are used fictitiously. Any resemblance to actual persons, living or dead, or events is entirely coincidental.

Albany Walker

Cover art done by Opulent Designs

Editing done by Elemental Editing and Proofreading

Proofreading done by Bookish Dreams Editing

❀ Created with Vellum

ALSO BY ALBANY WALKER

Coming soon

Touching Oblivion Book Two of Tasting Madness

Tasting Madness Series

Seeing Sound

Completed Monsters Series

Friends With the Monsters

Some Kind of Monster

Completed series Havenfall Harbor

Havenfall Harbor Book One

Havenfall Harbor Book Two

Completed Series Infinity Chronicles

Infinity Chronicles Book One

Infinity Chronicles Book Two

Infinity Chronicles Book three

Infinity Chronicles Book Four

Completed Series Magical Bureau of Investigation

Homecoming Homicide

Creeping it Real

Perfectly Wicked

Dollhouse World can be read as standalone novels

Amusement

Diversion

Standalone novels

Beautiful Deceit

Becoming His

Stone Will Obsidian Angels MC Shared World MC Syndicates

DEAR READER,

This novel is a work of fiction and contains content intended for a mature audience only. Due to explicit language, mental heath issues, misdiagnoses, drug and alcohol use/abuse, graphic depictions of sex, and other triggers it may not be suitable for all readers.

    Thank you,
    Albany

THE SOUND OF RAIN

Without a doubt, I've grown accustomed to sterile walls and soft edges—a result of spending too much time in treatment centers and therapists' offices—but watching the rain trail down the pane of the large, thick glass window, I can almost forget I'm locked in my room for the last night.

I'm tired of trying to get better, it's much more exhausting than pretending I'm well, so even if this next round of medicine stops working like all the others have, then I'll never tell.

"Hey, Way," Alexis rasps, her voice still hoarse from yelling at group earlier.

"Mm-hmm." I don't look away from the window. I'm afraid she'll see the sympathy I feel for her if I do. I know from experience that's the last thing she'd want. Rooming with her always makes my heart heavy.

"Do you think we would be friends if we weren't in here?"

No. I don't have a lot of real friends. I pretend to fit in, and nobody really pushes it beyond that surface level friendship. "Yeah, we would have bonded the first time we met. I wouldn't have been able to resist your killer bunny shirt." The lie slips off my tongue with ease.

From the corner of my eye, I can see Alexis plucking at her light green uniform shirt. Her parents are going to be pissed. She drew all over her clothes again, and we're not permitted anything that's individual, so she'll need a new set, which isn't cheap. You'd think they'd have a designer label or at least be comfortable for the price, but nope.

"How long before you think you'll be back?" The longing in her tone is only amplified by the sadness emanating from her. I can't tell if it's because I'm leaving or because she's locked in the same rinse and repeat pattern I have been for the past few years and doesn't see any hope for herself.

"These new meds have been working really well," I answer noncommittally.

"That's really awesome." She tosses herself back on the bed with a huff. "I wish they could find a cure for my fucked-up parents."

"It won't be long until you age out. You'll be eighteen soon." I try to sound encouraging.

"They are already talking about a conservatorship." She rolls over on her side, facing the wall. Well, damn.

I don't know what to say to that, so I keep my mouth shut.

While my parents have put me into facilities a few times, their intentions are always to help me get better. Not so much with Alexis' parents, if I can believe what she says at group. They think she's "unbalanced" because she draws dark shit and likes to accessorize with sharp pointy things, and that's not acceptable to most UHNW families.

I think about telling her that maybe if she just toned it down for a little while and let her parents think they converted her into the perfect scion, she could be herself when she moved out, but I keep my lips sealed. I can't risk her wondering if I took my own advice and then telling someone.

When Alexis' breaths even out, and I know she either cried herself to sleep again or ran out of tears for the night, I slip down from the wide windowsill. My butt is numb from sitting for so long, but the ache fades fast as I crawl into my bed and pull the covers up to my chin.

It's hard to will my eyes closed. I have so much crap running through my mind. I wish I could have music to help with the silence, but that's not permitted. I squeeze my eyes shut and begin one of the few useful techniques Dr. Tobin has taught me. Locking my lips, I inhale for four seconds, then hold my breath while counting to seven. Exhaling, I count to eight before I repeat it over and over until I lose track of the numbers and fall asleep.

3 MONTHS LATER

"Are you sure you'll be comfortable here, Waylynn?" My mom rests her hand on the granite island, trying to look casual in her Chanel pantsuit and loafers.

I want to tell her I knew this house was mine the moment I saw it, that it spoke to me, but I'm afraid she will think I mean something else, so I sigh out an indulgent, "Yes, Mom."

"You don't think it's too…" She doesn't finish her sentence as she glances around, but I can fill in the blanks—too small to have a separate wing for staff, not in a gated community, and, the most important, far from home.

My dad enters from the sunroom off the kitchen and wraps his arm around my mom's waist before tugging her in close to his body. "Do you remember our first place, Cordy?"

My mom tries to fight a smile when she mutters, "I try not to."

"Oh, you loved it," he taunts.

Her eyes go a little unfocused when she defends softly, "I thought it was charming."

"It was just a little bigger than this." Dad sends me a wink to show his support.

"Yeah," Mom agrees faintly. "The garden *is* lovely, even if it is a little small."

I glance out one of the lead glass windows to the meticulously manicured backyard, seeing the hedges creating a tiny labyrinth that's only as high as my hip. The house and grounds look like a perfect English cottage, while the interior is a mix of old and new.

"And it's within walking distance to campus," I offer.

Mom gasps. "I don't want you walking, Waylynn Graff. If you don't want to drive, then hire someone." I bet she doesn't even know how snooty she sounds. My dad rolls his eyes but quickly wipes the look off his face when Mom turns her head like she senses he's mocking her.

I'm actually going to miss them. The realization hits me hard and fast. My face must register my thought, because Dad asks, "Is everything okay?"

I'm able to mask the emotion on my face just as quickly as he did, and instead I smear a wince on my features. "Just thinking about my orientation tomorrow." It works as a good cover. I am a little nervous about spending the day on campus tomorrow. I should have taken Mom up on the offer to request a private tour, but I was feeling brave at the time and wanted to mix with all the other freshmen. Now all I can think about is how the huge group of us are going to stand out clear as day as incoming freshmen.

"You'll fit right in," Dad soothes, trying to make me feel better. The problem is, I don't know if I want to fit in. I think I'd rather not get noticed at all.

"What can I help you with? Have you unpacked the things we brought today? Do you have something picked out to wear?" Mom brings her hands together in a clap under her chin, so she looks like she's praying.

"Umm..."

"Waylynn," she chastises. She hates stammering. "Come on, let's go find something nearly as fabulous as you. We want to make a good first impression." Her annoyance is short-lived, like always.

∼

I stand in the open rear doorway, waving to my parents as they back out the brick driveway separating the house from the garden. There are tears shimmering in my mom's eyes, but she's smiling so broadly, I bet her face hurts. I flick a tear off my own cheek as the red glow of their taillights disappear down the street. I'm only a few blocks away from sorority row, but I'm not surprised by how lonely the street feels. With my house situated on a corner, it feels entirely separate from the neighborhood, especially considering how large the lots are and the nature park across the street. I doubt I'll ever interact with my neighbors, but that's fine with me—the couple I saw next door looked older than my parents.

Fucking hell, whispers through my mind the moment I engage the deadbolt. My breath catches before I moan out a weak sounding, "No." That was too clear, and it's too quiet to pretend that was something other than it was.

My hands shake when I pull the zipper on my bag open and fist the orange bottle of pills. It has been a busy few days, so maybe I forgot to take my medicine this morning. I know

I'm lying to myself. I never forget to take my pills, but I dump the bottle out in my palm and start counting them just in case.

Seventeen, sixteen... I pop one in my mouth and swallow it down, dry as a bone. There are exactly how many there should be in this bottle, damn it. I stand at the island, listening for the deep voice again, but nothing comes.

It's a relief to hear silence, but a small part of me missed the voices. They have been with me for as long as I can remember, up until a few months ago that is. This is the longest I've gone without hearing them.

Maybe Dr. Tobin can up the dose of my current medication. I shake the bottle. Maybe I can up the dose myself, but I already feel a little fuzzy some days and I don't want to walk around like a zombie. *It's better than being crazy*, I think to myself.

"Give it a few days." I'm trying to calm my nerves. There's been a lot going on the past few weeks, and starting college is stressful for everyone, but none of it makes me feel better.

After setting the house alarm, I tote my purse upstairs to my bedroom and leave it on my nightstand, pretending it's normal for me to haul it around, when really, having my pills closer is my true motivation. Even though I have no intention of taking more, it's just comforting having them nearby.

I power on the television, then turn on a favorite movie, something I've seen twenty times but could never get sick of.

A snort leaves my lips when I walk past the chair, artfully

draped with the clothes my mother picked out for me to wear. There's nothing wrong with the jeans and Gucci cropped cardigan. It came from my closet, after all, but it screams trying too hard, not to mention it's going to be almost ninety degrees tomorrow. I would be a red-faced sweat hog just from walking across campus.

When I enter the bathroom, I hit the music icon on my phone and select an album before turning on the shower. I've become so used to using background noise to drown out the voices, it's become more of a habit than anything else, but it feels important now.

By the time I'm climbing into bed, Keanu is picking up his new car and I've successfully avoided the only part of the film I don't like, but in truth, I'm not really paying much attention to it anyway.

I glance around the room, surprised at how comfortable I am, considering it's my first night here. Being in a new place isn't all that unusual for me, since my parents moved us around our fair share, but being alone is new. Even when I was in Netherwood, I always had a roommate, so this may take some getting used to.

As I settle against my pillow, it gets really hard not to think about all the what-ifs. What if I hate it here? What if I can't handle my class load? What if I eat alone every day like a loser? What if I hear something in my head and respond to it? Now I'm really just giving myself anxiety, because that hasn't happened in years. Even then, it was just the abrupt nature that would have me quickly responding to things only I could hear. The voices never interacted with me. It's more like I'm hearing random snippets of someone else's conversation, but when I was younger, I would try to talk back to them to see if maybe they could hear me too. I got very familiar with a few of the voices, like the one I heard tonight. Even though it's changed so much over the years, I know it's one of the same boys I grew up hearing all the time.

When I close my eyes, I see the image of him I created in my head. He's vague and faceless, but still familiar to me somehow. He feels big in a sense, as if there's so much inside him, it would be hard to contain in a small package—if he were real, that is. I've never given the voices a name, because that would make them too real, when they already feel more solid than the world around me.

One of the theories my parents have, or that my therapist implanted in their minds, is that I created these identities as a coping mechanism when my brother died, but I don't even remember my brother. Still, they tell me I changed after the accident.

I don't have theories as to why, and I gave up trying to figure out what goes on in my head a long time ago. It's easier that way.

With my eyes still closed, I pick up the eerie music from the movie, and something about it seems to fit with the surreality of the moment. Does that mean I think the voice is like the boogeyman?

YOU DON'T ALWAYS NEED A PLAN. SOMETIMES YOU JUST NEED TO BREATHE

Even though I'm early—a horrible habit I developed in a bid to never be late—I linger in the back of the group. There are not as many students as I thought there would be, but considering I did an online orientation two months ago, it shouldn't surprise me. I wonder if I could have skipped this altogether.

I glance around, trying to take everything in without looking like I'm staring at people. Several have already formed small groups and are chatting in a way that makes me think they already know each other. Maybe they do from the dorms and such.

For a fleeting moment, I think that was a missed opportunity and I should have taken a room with the other freshmen, but the thought is gone before it's even fully formed. I didn't ask how I escaped the requirement to stay in a dorm as a first year, instead I only offered a grateful thank you to my mom after she arranged it before we started house hunting.

I'm not the only one milling around by myself either. There are more of us than them, but it doesn't feel that way when you're alone.

"All right, guys, I think we're all here. Are we ready to get started?" a guy with way too much enthusiasm, or caffeine, asks loudly enough that I see people fifty yards away turn their heads to look in our direction. The smug, indulgent smiles say so much. I can't wait until I can just stroll past too and act like I wasn't ever this green.

The group as a whole moves a little closer to the four people in university T-shirts. From there, we're broken up into smaller, more manageable groups. I somehow get stuck with the loud guy, even though I was inching my way toward the pretty girl with blonde hair who seemed much more subdued.

"I'm a fast talker and walker," Chad warns, already moving backward. "We won't get to see everything, but I really want you guys to get a good sense of the campus. How many of you are coming from a small town or school?" He peers around, and I do too. My town wasn't small, however my school was tiny, but I'm not going to admit that. Several hands start to lift but don't rise fully into the air. That seems to be good enough for Chad, though, because he comments, "It can feel overwhelming at first, but you'll be golden after the first few weeks."

I don't necessarily believe his promise of being golden, but I trust we won't be getting lost at that point.

"Since you guys all did the virtual welcome event, I'll just point out a few places of importance that we'll pass on our tour." Chad does, in fact, walk and talk fast, but that means this might be over sooner, right?

When we enter the first building, I let out a pleased sigh. Michigan is hot in August. I'm going to have to peel my jeans off when I get home. I'm so glad I went with a pair of slides, at least I'm comfortable and my feet aren't sweating like the rest of me.

"We're going to get a chance to meet a few other students. Feel free to ask any questions you have" —Chad looks down at his phone— "for the next twenty-three minutes."

"He's an RA in my dorm," a nearby girl mutters. "Every time he looks at me, I feel like I should be doing something more. He has like five jobs and a double major."

"I just want to get through my first year without being placed on academic probation," the girl she's chatting with replies.

"Hey, guys," a much more restrained voice calls out, but they still manage to be heard. I lean around the group and spot four students, all in the same university shirts, seated at the front of a stage with their legs dangling over. My eyes are drawn to a wide set of shoulders exiting the stage to a curtained off area. The light-headedness and slightly woozy feeling that follows comes without explanation and only lasts long enough for me to question what the hell is happening.

A flash of heat runs from my head down to the backs of my calves, and I pluck at my shirt a few times, trying to get air. I'm convinced I'm overheated. The guy next to me gives me the side-eye and takes a few steps away, which is fine by me. When everyone else meanders toward the front of the auditorium to take a seat, I linger halfway back at the end of a row all by myself. This is probably making me stick out more, but I'm not feeling so hot, and I'd rather be closer to the exit if I need to run out and puke. Spilling my salted caramel cold brew down the aisle would be much worse.

Once everyone is seated, Chad announces, "This is Kayleigh, Carmelo, Ethan, and Mia. They are going to tell you a little about themselves and answer any questions you have."

The first girl waves to us. She's pretty, with a perfect smile and long dark hair that looks silky and soft, even from far away. "Hi, I'm Kayleigh. I'm a third year, and I'm in the nursing program. I'm also in a couple of our one thousand, five hundred, and twenty-seven student led organizations."

"I'm Carmelo. I study sports medicine, and I'm on the lacrosse team." His build is similar to the guy who left the stage, and I wonder if he was one of his teammates.

"Hey, guys, I'm Ethan." He smiles wide, like he's actually happy to be talking to us. "I'm a political science major. I head up a few of the student organizations Kayleigh mentioned, and I'm a senior. You picked a great place to start your future."

Ethan isn't nearly as handsome as Carmelo, but he certainly makes up for it in charm.

The last girl is in a cute set of paint splattered jeans, and her hair is styled in pigtails. "Hello, freshmen." Her voice is raspy, a total contrast with the cutesy look she has going on. "I'm Mia, an art student. It's part of my job here at school to greet the incoming undergrads. I'm a junior, and I hope at least one of you has an original question to ask." She scans the filled seats, appearing bored. I like her. She feels genuine.

"I know we're short on time, so let's get started with questions," Kayleigh says and points to the first hand that shoots into the air.

"What if you're undecided?" a guy asks.

Mia's head falls back on her shoulders. I bet if I were closer, I would have heard her groan.

The group takes turns answering our questions as if they have a predetermined order. None are what I would call original, I could literally google every question that's posed and get an answer, but I guess it's not the same as hearing someone enrolled in the school answer.

"I see there are a few more questions, but we need to head over to get your Mcards. There will be lots of opportunities to speak with your fellow students," Chad interrupts Ethan before he can call on another person.

"What dorm has the best food?" a guy shouts.

Mia shields her eyes with her hand, looking out into the

crowd. "Not original, but at least it's a decent question. The dorm the football players live in."

"Okay, let's go." Chad starts waving out the front rows, ushering them up the aisle. I stay seated so I don't end up at the front of the group, plus my eyes are locked on the stage to see if the shoulders that drew my attention make another appearance.

I'm not the last to leave, but pretty close, so I hear Ethan chastising Mia. "Everyone's question is important to them."

"Shove it up your ass, Ethan."

I'm smiling when I finally exit the auditorium and walk face-first into someone's shoulder. My nose crunches, but the embarrassment I feel is so much worse, not to mention I brushed my hand across the person's tight butt when I lifted my hands to my face after stepping back. My gut tightens as a wave of annoyance washes over me that is so misplaced, I don't understand it myself. I was the one who wasn't watching where I was going.

"I'm so sorry," I blurt out before he can turn around, then wedge myself into the slowly shuffling forward group. I make it a point to not look in his direction, but from the corner of my eye, I can see his stubbled chin shifting as he looks for the person who just groped him and put their nose print on his back.

My nose hurts, but there's no way I'm touching my face.

The rest of the tour is blessedly uneventful. We get our Mcards, and Chad walks us around a little more until he eventually drops us off at the south quad, which he mentions is the football players' dorm.

I don't notice the guy I ran into again, so he must not have been with our group, which gives me a smidgen of hope I won't run into him again—not that I even allowed myself to look at his face.

I pull up the little map of campus on my phone once most of the group disperses because I don't want to ask how to get back to the union where we started.

"You're not eating?"

When I look up, I'm surprised to see Mia, still rocking the pigtails, peering at me. "I wasn't."

"You got your card, right?" Her brow furrows.

"Yes, I just—"

"Want to sit with me?" she offers before I can finish. It would be rude to say no, even though I would much rather go home.

I slip my phone into my pocket. "Sure, thank you for asking."

Mia purses her lips. "It's mostly for selfish reasons. I saw you bump into Gravlin." I'm sure my face turns bright red, but I'm not sure she notices because she's already walking and pulling the door to the dorm open. "I felt bad for you since it seemed like a real accident, and he probably gave you an earful, but more importantly, I want to know if he smells as good as he looks."

Mia swipes her card through the reader near a small

kiosk with takeout containers, then looks back over her shoulder to make sure I'm still with her. I'm not capable of speech yet, so I just swipe my card and tag along behind her, processing what she told me. Not only do I now have a name for the guy I ran into, but I also know people witnessed it, and he must not be an incoming freshman if she knows him.

"So does he?" she urges before we even make it through the seating area to the cafeteria.

"Yes," is my one-word answer.

"I knew it." She clenches her fist. "I've never been lucky enough to have him in a class, and he doesn't take time for students not in his classes. Hell, he barely speaks to anyone. I wonder what he was doing there today." She pops her hip out and taps her card on her thigh. She's so animated and bright, she makes me feel sunny just being around her.

"His classes?" I question. Is she telling me he's a very fit member of the faculty?

"Yeah, he's in the graduate program, a TA. What do you want to eat? Newbie's pick." She does a half spin, showcasing all the different options behind her.

"What's good?" I counter.

"Most of it really. Just make sure you come here if you want fish or sushi, it's always the freshest. I'm going to grab a pizza." She hooks her thumb over her shoulder. "I need to finish my project, and I won't feel like coming back out when I'm done later."

"Okay. I think I'm going there." I point to the nearest place.

"Meet you after," she says, already walking away.

Once I have my chicken burger and fries, I spin around and spot Mia in the center of the room, waving like a mad woman. She has no problem being the center of attention. Pretending this is completely normal, I walk over to her table and place my tray down before pulling out my seat.

"They'll text when my pizza is ready," she explains after resting her chin in her upturned palm. "So, what did he say?"

"Nothing. I apologized and hid in the crowd," I tell her honestly.

Her mouth pops open in an O before she starts to snigger. "You probably surprised him. He usually makes his boundaries really clear, not that I can blame him. He's super gorgeous and doesn't really date, from what I hear, so naturally, we all want to know why and see if we can be the one to tame him. You know what I mean?"

"Yeah, want some?" I push my plate a little closer to her, and she snags a fry. I want to stop talking about him. I'm going to be reliving that moment for years to come, probably when I'm just about to fall asleep so there's nothing else to distract me. Fingers crossed I don't have any classes with him. I doubt I'll even be able to look him in the face.

"So what made you decide to become a wolverine? Oh fuck. Forget I just asked you that. It's like they are turning me into a minion. Where are you from?" she amends.

"California, mostly." I shove a fry into my mouth. It tastes like sawdust. I hate talking about myself.

Mia's mouth snaps open again, this time in clear outrage. "Why the hell would you come here from California? That's where I'm going as soon as I can get out of here."

I think about telling her the truth, that out of all the different schools I looked at, none of them called to me like this one, but I settle on the more acceptable answer, one that doesn't invite so many questions. "I wanted a change."

"Ah, your parents are assholes," she surmises.

I laugh a little. "Not really. Plus, it's a really good school."

Mia's phone buzzes on the table. "Pizza's ready. I need to run."

"Oh, okay." I realize she's not planning on coming back to the table, and I haven't even touched my burger yet. My first instinct is to throw it away, since I hadn't planned on eating alone in the center of the cafeteria.

"What was your name?" she asks as she rises.

"Waylynn."

"That's a cool ass name. I take back the judgment on your parents. See you around, Waylynn."

"Bye, Mia," I say softly to her back. I don't know if I'm relieved that we didn't share contact info or sad. I tear at my food for a few more minutes but cave pretty quickly and toss most of my late lunch in the bin before sorting my silverware and plate for the kitchen window.

THE ONLY WAY AROUND IT IS THROUGH IT

Memphis

Oswald is pissing me off, and he hasn't even started classes yet. The shithead was supposed to be with this group, but I watched the place clear out, and he wasn't in the bunch. The moment my back was turned, someone poked my shoulder and smacked my ass. I thought it was my little brother until I heard a sweet little voice apologize. By the time I turned around to give her my usual *hands to yourself* spiel, she had merged into the group of students, but I have a fair guess who it was—the curvy brunette who seemed to be smiling to herself as she walked up the aisle with her eyes on the ground. Why the hell was she sitting alone and waiting for everyone else to leave?

The next group of freshmen are already waiting to have their turn in the theater for the Q and A portion of the tour, so I search the faces entering through the doors, but I don't spot Oswald. His big ass is hard to miss nowadays, so I don't think he sneaked past me.

I shove my hand in my pocket to get my phone, then fire a text off, asking where the hell he is. Certain privileges come with my position. I was able to get Oswald a partial dependent tuition scholarship because I'm technically employed by the school, but he has to check all the boxes or they will drop his ass faster than I can appeal the decision.

"Excuse me." I lift my eyes from my phone and see a pair of tits wrapped in a tiny pink shirt nearly on top of my phone.

"Can I help you?" I meet her dark eyes, taking in her nearly white blonde hair. I want to tell her to get out of my space, but I refrain.

"Are you going in?" She tilts her head to the side, motioning to the auditorium. "I'm a little late, and I thought we could sit together if you were."

"No, you should stay with your group," I tell her in a firm but professional tone. I don't want her filing a complaint because I'm an asshole. I have no idea why I thought it was a good idea to take a position here for my graduate work and not in a different setting, not that high school would be much better. I feel like I'm constantly threading a needle when dealing with the student body. I can't be a prick, and I can't be too nice. Either choice could threaten my job, and I don't want

Oz to be in debt up to his ass when he graduates, so I remind myself why this is the best choice. Five more years, and it won't matter. The students won't look at me the same way when I'm almost thirty—at least I fucking hope not.

My phone buzzes, and I stride down the hall before looking down to see a reply from Oswald.

Oz: That shit's lame. I know where everything is.

I grit my teeth before sending him a reply, but his comes faster.

Oz: I made an appearance. No one is going to notice I left.

I did, but I don't bother texting that to him. There's no point. I'll talk to him about it tonight.

Waylynn

WHEN I CLOSE the door behind me and drop my shoulders against the cool wood, I start second-guessing walking to and from campus. My slides are kicked off right before I reach for the button on my pants.

I'm so hot, they stick to my legs as I try to drag them down. I have one knee lifted, trying to shuck the things off, when the doorbell rings. I collapse to the ground in a heap and search the kitchen windows, wondering who might have seen me butt up, shimmying out of my jeans.

Forty seconds later, the bell rings again, and I realize it's coming from the front door. The front walkway is about as long as a football field, so who the heck would traverse that to ring my bell? It must be a package or a neighbor. I flop onto my back and hike my pants up before rising from the cool wooden floor and then straighten my shirt.

There's an older woman with a knobby knuckle poised to ring the bell again when I pull open the front door. "Hello, sorry." I'm a little breathless, but I try to cover it with my short greeting.

"Oh, hello, dear. Are your parents home? I'm Eddy from next door. I wanted to introduce myself and say hello." She smiles at me with the indulgence of a grandparent.

There goes not needing to meet the neighbors. I can honestly say this is a new experience. My parents tend to prefer estates, and the gates pretty much deter anyone from stopping by. I lean my shoulder on the green door and reply, "Hello, Eddy, my name is Waylynn. It's nice to meet you."

"Aren't you a darling?" she coos like I'm a precocious seven-year-old. "Now I really must meet your parents. They have set a fine example." She leans around me, trying to see inside the house.

Telling her I live alone isn't on the top of my to-do list today. I have a strong feeling Eddy might be a little bit of a nosy busybody, and I don't need the entire neighborhood knowing my business the first week I live here. It's going to be pretty obvious I live alone soon enough to anyone who cares to notice.

"It's just me here now, but I'll let them know you stopped by," I tell her while keeping my stance firm in the doorway.

"Oh yes, you do that, dear. Tell them I said welcome to the neighborhood." She smiles at me again and shuffles down the steps then across the paver stones to a little gap in the hedges that takes her over to her own driveway. Whoever used to live here must have been very friendly with her family. I hope she's not too terribly disappointed with me as a neighbor, but I don't plan on inviting her over for tea anytime soon.

After closing the door, I turn the locks and head back to the kitchen. I need a drink, but at least I've cooled down enough so I don't feel the need to strip out of my clothes. I can wait until I get upstairs when I call Mom to let her know how today went for that.

～

I'M ABOUT to walk to my first college class, and I'm actually excited to see other people, even if I have no intention of talking to anyone. I thought I was used to being alone and that it wouldn't be a big change, but that was before I realized all the little interactions I took for granted, like speaking to Beth, the house manager, in the morning when I would make coffee, or John, my parents' longtime gardener, when I was outside. Then, there was knowing Mom was usually around somewhere if I wanted to talk.

It's not until I'm standing at the corner, waiting for the

light to change, when I allow the nerves that are making my stomach cramp to get to me. I've been pretty good at pretending this is no big deal, though my jittery hand would beg to differ.

My first class of the day is English. I wanted something I was comfortable with, unlike math, to get my week started. I wish I could skip math altogether, but I can't, so it's my second Monday and Wednesday class. At least I only have two classes today. Tuesday and Thursday I'll have three, but I was lucky enough to keep most of my Fridays clear this semester, besides a few discussion classes.

The signpost for the crosswalk beeps, alerting me and the other students waiting to cross it's time to go. I shuffle into the back of the group, not in too big of a hurry since it's only half past nine. Everyone around me is either still half asleep or too absorbed in their own worlds to engage with each other, but I prefer it that way. I would probably stutter if I tried to speak with anyone at this point.

The group splits into different directions after we cross the street. I head down the path that will take me to Angell Hall. I spent Sunday walking around a little, making sure I knew where all my classes were. Why did it feel so much easier to navigate yesterday?

Once I'm in the building, a sense of relief washes over me. There are several other students standing around much like myself. I find a corner and pull out my phone, pretending I have someone to talk to just so I have an excuse to keep my head down.

A short time later, the door to room 113 is pushed open from the inside and a tall, thin woman leans against the wood, waving us in. "First day every year, I say I'm going to remember to prop the door," she mutters to herself as we filter past, then announces, "Have a seat," much louder.

The room is massive. I've been to concert venues smaller than this. While everyone is taking seats in the middle aisle, I walk along the back wall and select an outside seat about halfway down toward the stage. I like knowing I can get out fast if I need to.

It's not long before the seats around me begin to fill in, and I have to tuck my bag between my feet so it doesn't get stepped on by the students heading deeper into my row.

The woman who opened the door for us is down by a lectern, sorting some papers. She doesn't look up or acknowledge the class at all for several long minutes. Once she does, most of the seats are full and it's a quarter past ten. "In the spirit of goodwill on the first day, I like to give a few extra minutes for everyone to find their way. On Wednesday, I expect all of you to be here promptly before class so I don't have to wait."

She takes a long look around the room. "Welcome to English 125, I'm Professor Hilbrand—just Hilbrand is fine. If you are not in the right place, I suggest you figure it out quickly."

There are some small chuckles, but everyone stays seated.

"Today, we'll go over the syllabus, discuss expectations, and I'll introduce you to my teaching assistant, who will be handling the majority of the lectures." She gestures to the front left, and my eyes follow her movement, but I have no idea whom she's looking at. "I trust all of you are familiar with your school email. That is where you'll find your copy of the syllabus and our contact info, as well as my and Gravlin's hours. If you…" The rest of what she says gets lost after I hear the name Gravlin. It's an unusual name, and one I was hoping to avoid. What kind of luck do I have if I have to run into the one person I didn't want to in a school of forty-four thousand, and on my first day no less? Thank goodness he will have no idea who I am.

It takes me a few seconds to reengage with what's happening around me, but thankfully, everyone opening up their computers pulls me out of my own head enough to push the thoughts of my embarrassment to the back of my mind.

Hilbrand goes over the course and talks about the importance of critical thinking when it comes to writing before she sinks into a short lecture about our first assignment and how it will be graded.

As she winds down, I sink lower in my seat. I know what's coming next, especially when Gravlin stands up and turns to face the classroom. There are over four hundred students in here, so it would be hard for him to spot me, even if he knew who he was looking for, but my rational brain can't convince the other half of me of the truth in that statement.

"As promised, I'd like to introduce my TA, Gravlin. He has a busy schedule, so he will not be running a study group. However, you can check out the class message boards, where I'm sure you'll be able to get a group together easily enough.

"We will both be available during posted hours for drop-ins and scheduled appointments. If you think you will need a tutor, I suggest you sign up quickly. Otherwise, you can avail yourselves of the peer led tutoring in the library. Gravlin." She motions to the guy standing up in the front row.

I try really hard not to look at him, but it's impossible, especially when I hear the students murmuring around me. I already know from Mia's response he's attractive, but I'm not prepared for just how striking he is. Tall with wide shoulders and short dark hair, Gravlin could rival most of Hollywood's young elite. His chiseled jaw is set tightly, making his high cheekbones seem more prominent. He's too far away for me to discern his eye color, but it wouldn't even matter, because I'm sure they match the rest of him.

His lips are pressed together rather tightly before he finally opens his mouth to speak. I don't know if everyone else can hear the annoyance in his tone or if it's just me reading too much into his demeanor and facial expression. "Please familiarize yourself with the contact form. That is the only way to reach me. I try to answer emails promptly. Drop-ins will be limited to fifteen minutes, so if you need longer, you need to make an appointment. Any questions?" Something about his voice is familiar, but I can't place it.

"What are the rules on dating the TA?"

I snap my head to the left to search for the girl fearless enough to shout out that question. My mouth is probably hanging open, along with half the class's.

"You'll find all the fraternization policies listed on the school website, but since you seem to be fine calling out Mr. Gravlin, I'll do the same to you. Students may not be romantically involved with TAs from the classes for which they are enrolled, however, you won't have a shot next semester either. Any *real* questions?" Hilbrand asks the rest of the class, most of which are wincing and making pain-filled utterances for the bold girl.

I sink even lower in my seat. The secondhand embarrassment is real.

"Challenge accepted," the girl states with a confidence I couldn't manage when picking my meal for lunch.

I peer to the side again to see she's staring right at Gravlin. If I thought he looked annoyed before, he looks disgusted now, or maybe that's just my misplaced indignation for him. Shit like this would not be tolerated if he were a girl, not out in the open like this. I'm glad Hilbrand called her out, but it seems like it might have just spurred her on.

I lower my eyes, trying to give the poor guy a modicum of privacy, even though it's impossible in this situation. Several people laugh and make little comments until Hilbrand brings the class back to order. "I suggest you all focus on your studies. If you thought getting into this school was hard, it was a mere precursor for what's to come. I promise that if you can't keep up, there is someone waiting to take your place. I'll see you all Wednesday. Read the assigned course material and start gathering your thoughts on the topic for your first drafts."

The sounds of closing laptops and murmurs fill my ears as I pack up my own things. If I could teleport out of this room, I would. Instead, I linger until almost everyone else has left.

Just before picking up my bag, I glance down at the stage area, not expecting to see Gravlin standing next to the professor since he wasn't before, and he seems to be staring right at me. I duck my head after meeting his eye. Just as I rise from my seat and turn up the aisle to leave, I nearly run into someone else.

He grins down at me with twinkling blue eyes.

"Sorry, I wasn't expecting anyone to be coming this way," I mumble as I take one step back down the aisle to catch my footing, and it makes him seem even taller because of the angle.

There's an awkward pause where I'm just staring up at him, waiting for him to say something back, and I eventually hear, "Do you ever watch where you're going?" The familiarity of the voice catches me off guard. Never once have the voices in my head interacted with me or been so clear. Why is this happening right now?

The guy in front of me tilts his head to the side, his

eyebrows lowering. Oh hell, he's probably wondering why I look so shocked, or maybe I'm panicked.

"Don't be a dick, Memphis," he chastises.

Now I know I'm losing my mind, because I know both of these voices, and his lips moved, so I know he's actually speaking. Plus, it's almost like he's responding to the voice as if he can hear it too. I need to get the hell out of here.

Where are my pills? I duck to the left, avoiding the guy in front of me, and try to dash out of the class as fast as I can without actually running, but before I make it to the door I hear, "You scared her away." Helpless not to, I look over my shoulder and see Gravlin and the guy I almost ran into today facing each other, but both are watching me. I almost stop to see if I can hear them speak again to see if maybe I was imagining how much they sounded like two of the voices I've always heard, but I'm too afraid, so I push my way out the door and haul ass out of the building into the sweltering heat outside.

There's not enough air, and everything feels thick around me. I glance around, wondering if everyone is witnessing my freak-out. I pull my phone out of my pocket. Should I call Maxwell, my therapist? I've never had an emergency call, so if I call him now, will they want me to come back home for in-person visits to evaluate my meds?

I tuck my phone away. That's too big of a step right now. It's my first day, and there are bound to be hiccups. Maybe it was just my mind playing tricks on me, because those voices weren't in my head at all. I have no idea why my brain processed them the way it did, but it has to be wrong. There isn't another explanation. These are all the things I tell myself as I fight to take deep, even breaths.

My fear eclipsed my embarrassment, but as I begin to calm, I remember I left them both standing there while I ran from the room. "Great," I hiss, frustrated with myself.

When I'm plodding down the walkway, I decide this is the last time I'm walking to school. If I had my car, I could escape faster and not have a heart attack while doing it. Instead of heading to one of the dorms for lunch like I planned, I turn down a sidewalk that will have me reentering the English building from the other side in another hall, far away from my class and both guys.

THE FINE ART OF BULLSHIT

~~~

It takes the entire two-hour break I have between classes to convince myself to actually go to math, and even then, it's only with the promise that I will turn around and go straight home if I happen to run into any more problems, especially the two I can't seem to get out of my head. I decided not to call Maxwell before our scheduled phone appointment. I don't want to send up any red flags.

I do contemplate dying my hair to aid me in becoming unrecognizable though, not that I think either one of them will remember what I look like anyway. Hell, their faces are blurry in my head right now.

"Anyone sitting here?" a male voice—blessedly unfamiliar—asks after a bag is dropped on the seat next to me.

"No, you're good." I barely look up from my phone.

The guy sighs as he tucks himself into the rigid chair. His

arm brushes mine, and a riot of nerves erupts in my stomach. Damn it, I thought I was getting myself under control.

"You look smart," is his opening line. I'm not really sure how to take it. Being smart certainly isn't an insult, but how does one look smart? "I suck at math," he continues. "I'm probably going to need all the help I can get."

I finally look over at him, thinking seeing his face will help me understand his intentions, because I'm getting the feeling he's expecting me to help him. He smiles at me when I look over. His bottom teeth are a little crooked, but it doesn't detract from how cute he is. His eyes are almost pale, but the blue is too vivid for that to be an accurate description. He's lean, but I can see the muscles in his arms, even while he's at rest.

"I kind of suck at math," I warn him.

"Shit, I mean darn." He winces but covers it quickly with a smile I'm sure has gotten him out of trouble many times.

"I won't be offended if you want to sit somewhere else," I tell him sincerely.

"Nah, but I appreciate your honesty…unless you really are good at math and you're just trying to get rid of me," he teases in a self-deprecating way, but the curl of his lip makes it obvious he's confident that's not going to happen.

"I'm not horrible, but it's definitely not my favorite subject, and I'll have to work to keep up myself."

"Is that your way of saying I should stay?" He lifts his bag as if he might leave if I don't ask him to stay, but I'm not going to do that. He's cute—hell, cute probably isn't a strong enough word for what he is—but I'm not looking for a hookup, and he has hookup written all over his pretty face.

"That's your decision, but you better decide quickly, the seats are filling up fast." I cast my eyes around the room.

"I think I'll take my chances with you. I bet you're smarter than you give yourself credit for." I almost roll my eyes. He's a charmer, that's for sure. I should probably tell him he would have better luck in that department somewhere else too, but it's just one class, and he helped me stop thinking about what happened in English—until now.

"I'm Liam." He extends his hand to me. I react on instinct and offer him my hand in return. The moment our palms touch, the image I have of him in my head, confident and sure, gets tarnished by the dampness of his palm and the uncertainty in his eyes. When I pull my hand away, he's back to being that same cool, self-assured guy who sat down, leaving me feeling like I'm reeling from the swift changes.

Beth mentioned she suffered from vertigo more than once, saying that sometimes the world would feel like it was moving too fast while she was standing still. I wonder if this is what that feels like. I certainly feel untethered.

"Are you going to tell me your name, or do I have to guess?" Liam prompts.

"Waylynn," I supply swiftly. Can he tell I was lost in my head?

"Cool, like the country music singer," he replies. Not many people my age get the association.

"Yeah," I agree.

"Your parents must be big fans."

I chuckle. "You'd be surprised." No one ever pegs my dad for a classic country fan, but he certainly is. Thankfully, the teacher saves me from having to explain my mirth when she calls the class to attention.

I was dreading math, but by the end of the two-hour class, I'm feeling a little better and certainly more relaxed than I was in English as I waited to be introduced to Gravlin. The TA in this class is a girl with green hair and thick-rimmed glasses. Her smile is easy, and she's even heading the study group for the first few meetups.

Thankfully, Liam stayed quiet the entire class. He seemed to be just as absorbed in the information that was given as I was.

"Do you have any more classes today? Have you eaten?" Liam asks as we gather our bags.

"No, I had English this morning."

"Want to grab something to eat with me? What professor do you have?" He starts walking forward once he has his bag slung over his shoulder.

"Um…" I am hungry since I skipped lunch, and it would be nice not to sit alone. This two questions at a time tactic is hard to counter quickly.

"Come on, don't make me eat alone." Liam gazes down at me with pleading eyes.

"Sure, where are you going?" I hope he doesn't leave me alone like Mia did. If he does, I'm going to start taking it personally.

"Wherever. What dorm are you in?" We make it to the exit with all the other students, and I stall a little. Why didn't I think that this kind of question would come up so I could have an answer ready?

"What dorm are you in?" I counter instead. He gives me a lopsided grin like he thinks I'm avoiding the question because I don't want him knowing where I live, as if I think he's going to become a stalker.

"North quad," he answers easily. "I heard south was the best."

"They have a lot of choices," I agree.

"It's not far, are you good going there?" He's walking kind of sideways so he can look at me.

"Sure, I can do that." At least I know how to get home from there now.

"So what professor do you have for English?" he inquires, reminding me I didn't answer his other question.

"Hilbrand. She seems okay," I answer.

"Too bad I don't have her then. I have Wideman, and I've heard he's an ass—jerk," he amends.

"I would trade you if I could, and cursing doesn't offend

me," I tell him, since that is the second time he's corrected himself.

"Why would you trade if she seems okay?" he asks. Dang it, I should probably think about filtering my words if I don't want to explain them.

"I don't mind a tough English course, unlike math, and that's probably why people call him a jerk." That sounds like a valid explanation to me. I'm kind of impressed with myself.

"Are you an English major?" Liam questions when he hauls the door open to the dorm. I'm surprised how much faster the walk over seemed with someone else to walk with.

"No, psychology. How about you?"

Liam winces. "Is it too late to take my question back?"

"You don't have to tell me," I respond quickly. I don't want to make him uncomfortable.

"Nah, it's okay. I'm just undecided." He scans his card and waits for me to pull mine out of my wallet.

"There's nothing wrong with that. I read somewhere that something like forty-five percent of students change their major at least once. You have time. You don't even need to declare until next year, right?"

"Is this good?" He meets my eyes while standing next to a table that's near the wall and kind of tucked away. It's a table I would have picked myself.

"Absolutely." I hook my bag over one of the chairs. This is so much better than in the center of the room.

"It just seems like everyone knows what they want and

what they are doing," he says, and I see a little of that vulnerability I first noticed in the classroom.

"My dad calls that the fine art of bullshit. People tell you what they want you to hear," I tell him. It's probably weird I mentioned my dad, but Liam just smiles.

"Yeah, he's probably right. Have you eaten here before?"

"Just once. The girl that invited me to eat with her took her food to go and left me alone," I confess, wanting to share something with him since he shared with me.

"What the hell? That's weird."

"I know," I agree. "I mean, she told me she wanted to know about someone I literally ran into, so I should have known then she just wanted tea."

"Was she the girl's friend or something? Was she trying to start beef?"

"It was a guy actually, and no beef." I'm not going to tell him she asked me how he smelled.

"Ah, so she likes the dude and she got worried he talked to you," he surmises. He's maybe half right.

"We didn't talk. I said sorry and hoofed it." I chuckle.

"I get it." He's looking down at me with a lopsided grin that makes my stomach feel funny, but it also makes me nervous.

"What are you getting?" I turn to look at the dining options.

"I don't know. Want to walk around? This place is bigger than the one in my dorm."

"Sure. Supposedly, this is where a lot of the football players eat, and they have the freshest stuff." I give him the tidbit of information Mia gave us at orientation.

"Makes sense," he remarks, and we make a slow lap around the room. It's not very busy, but it's pretty early for dinner.

"I'm going to go with that." He points to the same place I already had.

"I actually had that last time. I'm going with tacos."

"I knew you were my kind of people. Feel the vibe?" Liam gestures between the two of us.

"We vibe because I like tacos?"

"Definitely, but that's just one of the reasons. See you in a few minutes," he says, backing away like I might run the second he turns his back.

"Okay," I agree. This is familiar. Let's hope it doesn't end the same way it did the last time.

I'm already seated when Liam returns. He has two plates, one in each hand, that he places on the table. "I'm going to grab something to drink. Need anything?"

"I'll go with you." I push my chair in and tag along behind him to the drink station. He fills up a cup with soda while I opt for juice.

"So where are you from?" he asks after we return to the table.

"California, you?"

"Here." He takes a big bite out of his burger and chews it

before adding, "Bloomfield. It's not too far from here. California's far. Have you gotten home sick?"

"Maybe a little. I didn't realize how nice it was to always have someone in the house, you know?" I admit.

"Did you score a single?" His eyes are a little wide. "You're lucky. I'd kill to not have roommates."

Damn it, I brought this on myself. That's what I get for opening up so soon. "I'm actually off campus."

"Huh." Liam takes another bite of food, and I tuck into mine. "Are you a transfer?"

I was hoping he was just going to let it go, but it doesn't seem like he will. "No."

"I thought all first years had to do the room and board thing." He holds up a fry as if to drive the point home.

I could lie and chance getting caught later if we remain friendly or give him part of the truth. "I don't think they care if you actually stay in the room as long as it's paid for," I tell him and lean back in my seat to gauge his reaction.

"Oh, cool, do you have family close by then? Wait, does that mean your room is open then? Is it a single?"

"I don't actually know anything about it. I never signed up for a room, but I think I got an email about being assigned one. I doubt it would be a single."

"Man, your roommates are still lucky as hell. One less person."

"What are your roommates like?" I ask before he can

question me about who I live with. I plan to change the subject as soon as I find another topic to segue into.

"I only have one, thank fu—" He doesn't complete the word, but he might as well have. "Ben's okay. I just hate sharing the space with anyone. It's so small, and I get up early to go to the gym, so I like to get to bed early."

I wrinkle my nose at the mention of going to the gym but cover it quickly when he looks up from his plate. One thing you will never find me doing is exercising. "Does he stay up late and disturb your sleep?"

"Not really. He's pretty considerate, actually, but he does stay up later than I do. I'm hoping he will settle into an earlier schedule now that classes have started."

"Do you get up early on the weekends too?"

"Most of the year," he answers. "I play lacrosse, so we hit the gym hard for a couple of months before the season actually starts, and that goes until after the playoffs are done."

"Are you on the team here?"

"Yeah, but I doubt I'll get much play time this season." He drops his eyes from mine before grabbing a few fries. I get the feeling that's something that bothers him.

"You must be really good to make the team. Do you have any more classes today?" I toss the first comment then ask another question, hoping it will alleviate the new tension in his shoulders.

"No, I'm done for today. Do you think you'll join the study group for math?"

I push my plate to the side. Eating tacos while talking isn't easy. "I'm not sure yet."

"They made it seem like it filled up fast. I probably will, I don't want to get behind." He takes another bite. His salad, which was mostly meat and cheese with a little bit of lettuce and cucumber, is already gone, as is most of his burger.

"I'll decide by the end of the week," I tell him. I don't have much else going on in my life, so I'm confident I'll have time to study if need be, plus there's always the library peer tutoring.

I touch the screen on my phone to check the time, and it doesn't go unnoticed. "Got somewhere to be?" Liam balls up a napkin and tosses it on his mostly clean plate.

I don't want to tell him no and seem lame, but I'm kind of ready to get home and decompress a little. Even though I haven't done much today, I feel a little overwhelmed and a lot tired. "I just need to get going soon," I answer noncommittally.

"Want to grab lunch, dinner, food, whatever this is, Wednesday after class?" he asks, and scoots his chair back to stand.

"Sure," I reply, probably answering too fast.

"Save me a seat if you get to math before me." He loads my plate on his tray, leaving me to carry my cup and empty tray.

"Okay," I agree again, following him to the small hall where we're supposed to place our used dishes.

We walk quietly to the front of the dorm, and he pushes the door open for me, urging me to pass in front of him. I duck under his arm, and he follows me out. There's a small group of guys jogging up the walkway, and I step to the side to make room, but one of the guys stops short, and the guy behind him bumps into his back. There's some cursing, but the guy who stopped just ignores it and stares at me.

I know those clear blue eyes. I thought his face was blurry in my head, but the moment I see him, I remember every detail I thought I ignored—short dark lashes, bright eyes, and an easy grin on full lips. My stomach does a flip-flop, and I get that same woozy feeling I had earlier when I was in the auditorium. Could he be the shoulders I saw disappearing behind the curtain and the same guy I almost ran into in English? I stop there because I don't want to think about how his voice was familiar to me.

A touch on my arm has my thoughts scattering. When I look up, Liam is watching me with a furrowed brow. I don't have a chance to explain why I stopped and was staring at the other guy, because the other guy comes right over and steals my attention again.

"Twice in one day. And here I thought I was going to have to wait until Wednesday to see you again." His eyes roam over my face, but it's his voice that gets me—so familiar yet so foreign to me at the same time.

My tongue is glued to the roof of my mouth. I have no idea what to say to him, and I can feel Liam's eyes on the side of my face as if he's waiting too. I have the urge to run again, but then I really would look crazy, and that's something I would like to avoid.

"Did you want me to walk with you?" Liam finally says, breaking the stare off between the other guy and me.

"Where are you headed?" the voice asks.

"Home," I tell him without reservation.

His blue eyes finally leave my face, and he meets Liam's gaze. I watch the two of them size each other up the way guys do for just a blink of an eye before he says, "I'm Gravlin." My stomach does that funny summersault again. It's part nerves, part I don't know what.

"Oz Gravlin?" Liam asks as his lips curl up in a grin.

Oh man, he and the TA must be brothers, that's the only explanation that makes sense.

"Yeah. And you are?" he inquires with his head tilted to the side as if he's surprised he knew his name.

"Liam. I caught your game in Bloomfield. You guys had a fantastic night."

Gravlin is smiling now too. "You guys can go," he hollers over his shoulder to his friends waiting a few feet away.

I take one small step back, thinking this will be the perfect time to escape, but Gravlin pins me with a stare the moment I twitch. "Thanks, man," he says, but he's looking dead at me. "Mind if I talk to her about English real quick?" Gravlin gestures to me.

"Oh yeah," Liam says slowly as if he just remembered I was here. "See you Wednesday?"

"Um," is all I get out before Gravlin shifts his footing and basically shuts Liam away from us.

"I need to know your name," he says almost urgently.

"Waylynn Graff," I answer without hesitation. His mouth moves as if he's repeating my name, but no sounds emerge. "You're Gravlin?" I say his name slowly.

"Oswald, but I don't tell most people that, everyone calls me Oz," he admits. There's this stillness around us that I can't fully describe, but it feels significant.

"I'm sorry I almost ran into you," I tell him when I can't think of anything else to say. The way we're just staring at each other is starting to feel strange.

"I'm only sorry you left. My brother can be a dick," he replies, confirming my suspicions.

I wince. "I think he knows I bumped into him. I swear it was an accident, and I did say sorry." The confession flies from my lips.

"Have we met before?" he asks, and I'm not even sure he was listening to me explain about his brother.

"No, but I know what you mean."

"Gravlin, we've got to go," a guy yells near the dorm doors.

"Do you live here?" he questions hurriedly.

"No, I'm over by Hill."

"Yo, Oz," the guy calls more urgently.

Oswald reluctantly starts to back away. "Oxford?"

"No, near the park." I'm so flustered, I can't think of the cross street. In my defense, I have only lived here a short time, and I've had to do a lot of mapping to get where I'm going.

"In a sorority house?"

"No." I hike my bag up higher and shake my head.

"Gravlin, we've got to go now," the other guy yells.

"Fuck. 734-344-2100. Can you remember that? I've got to go. Text me." He says his number so fast, I don't even register it as more than a single word, plus he was trying to keep his voice down, so I'm not confident I heard him correctly.

I shrug my shoulders and shake my head again. He dashes forward and grabs my hand. A jolt passes through me, and I experience something I've only ever heard people talk about—a true sense of peace and calmness. "734-344-2100, repeat it," he demands, and I recite the number without fail.

Oz

She's staring up at me with wide eyes, and her lips are slightly parted. I want to kiss her nearly as badly as I want to punch Higgins in the side of the head, probably more, but I can't do either.

"I have to go."

"I know, he's getting really agitated," she says so softly, I can barely hear her. I get goose bumps on my arms like she's blowing across my neck. My eyes search hers again, looking for answers she doesn't seem to have.

I need to know one thing though—what was she doing with the other dude? Clearly, he's not her boyfriend if he left her with me, but how well do they know each other? I plan to ask her that as soon as she calls me.

"You need to go, people are staring," she tells me when I still don't move.

I want to tell her to let them look, but I was in a hurry before I ran into her. She pushes me with just a single finger on my chest, and I release her hand. I still can't force myself to turn around though, even when she ducks her head and turns to hurry down the path.

"What the fuck, Oz? Coach is going to be pissed you're making us late."

I don't even bother responding to Higgins. Instead, I pull my phone out of my pocket, so I'll know the moment she texts me, before hustling my ass down the corridor to the stupid team building dinner.

KISMET

Waylynn

THE MOMENT OSWALD IS GONE, the effervescent feeling that was spilling through me disappears. I start doubting any of it was real before I even make it to the next building. By the time I'm crossing Washtenaw, I'm questioning everything I said and did.

I can't believe I told him I live by Hill. I mean, it's not like he can find me from just that little bit of information, but what was I thinking? And then the crap I told him about running into his brother. A groan leaves my lips, and the girl next to me gives me the side-eye like I was complaining about her.

My name. I want to smack myself in the forehead after I remember that part. Now he can tell his brother who I am too.

He probably thinks I was trying to grope him on purpose, and I can't even blame him after the way the girl acted in class.

My fingers and toes are tingling by the time I make it to my backdoor. I just need to get inside, and then I won't feel like I have eyes on my back watching my every move.

Once the door is shut, I turn the lock and let my bag slip off my arm to the floor. It feels easier to breathe, but not like the blissful twenty seconds Oswald was holding my hand. I bite the corner of my lip, already warring with myself about him. I know I'm always going to wonder if that was a one-time event or if it can be replicated, and if it can, then how much am I going to crave it?

That night before going to bed, I actually program the number that has been on repeat in my head all evening into my phone. Feeling brave, I even put it under the name Oswald instead of a fake name like I planned.

Memphis

My door opens without a knock. I should really learn to lock the fucking thing. Oz slips in quietly, as if he thinks he can sneak in. "What are you doing awake?" he chastises when he sees me at my desk.

I spin around in my shitty computer chair and override his question. "What are you doing here?"

"I hate that fucking room." He plods over to my futon and throws himself on it. I'm surprised the thing has lasted as long as it has with his big ass dropping on it so often.

"What exactly do you hate? The bathroom you only have to share with your *one* roommate and your premium mattress, or is it the fact that you have an all-you-can-eat buffet two floors down?" I deadpan.

"It must not be that great, or you'd still be there," he retorts.

"I moved out because it's cheaper to live here for me, plus I had three roommates with no bathroom. I'd say the situation is vastly different."

"I'm more comfortable here." He has his phone out and in his face. "Why are you awake?"

"I'm going over some shit. Why are you awake, and didn't you have a team dinner? Don't tell me you blew that off."

"No, I went." He huffs and flips onto his side so he can look at me. "I wish I could have skipped it. It was just a bunch of the same shit."

"What's with the attitude?" There must be something else going on. Oswald doesn't usually rip on shit to do with his team, he takes that stuff seriously.

"I ran into that girl again, the one from class today." He didn't even need to elaborate. I knew exactly who he was talking about. "I gave her my number, but she didn't text." He still has his phone gripped in his palm, as if he's waiting for the damn thing to ring.

Why does that make me want to smile? At least now I know why he's pissy. Oswald isn't used to having to work for female attention. "Did you get her number? Just call her." I spin back around to my open laptop and close the tab with the class roster. I don't know why I thought I would be able to figure out who she was from a list of names, or why I felt the need to.

"I didn't. I was running late for the stupid banquet." Ah, another reason for why he's pissed. He props his head on his palm. "She said she lived near Hill."

"In Oxford?" That's not usually a freshman dorm. Maybe she's a transfer.

"I asked the same thing, and she said no, she lived by the park, but I don't even know of a park near Hill." He sits up.

"That's because you think all parks have swings and a slide," I tease. "Did you at least get her name?"

"Waylynn Graff," he says, and I look down at my notebook. That name is scribbled across the paper with only two others, Emily Kitch and Madison Green. I flip the cover closed on the notebook and spin back around.

"So why didn't she call? And don't tell me you're going to stalk her." This girl may have made herself damn near irresistible to my brother by not rushing to call him. Once he gets something in his head, he's like a dog with a bone, and this girl seems to be in his head, which is a first. Football has ruled his life for years, but he wanted to blow it off for her, and more importantly, why was I thinking about her before he even showed up here?

"No fucking clue. I was sure she would. Maybe she forgot my number." Oz bends down and unlaces his shoes.

I knew he was planning on staying the second he walked through the door, but this is confirmation. "What time are you getting up?" He usually hits the gym in the morning for lifting, but it's late, so I doubt he'll go.

"I don't have class until ten." He tucks his shoes under the futon and stands up.

"I'm not fighting you for my shower," I warn. "I have to be at class every day by nine, so I'll be up at eight. If you're showering, it needs to be before then."

"I'll shower now and set my alarm for eight-thirty." He walks past me to the bathroom. I glance into my tiny, darkened kitchen. Not much has changed now that he's enrolled with me, but at least I don't have to worry about feeding him all the time. He can eat on campus.

Waylynn

My stomach is churning when I approach Angell Hall. I know Gravlin will be there, but I don't know if Oswald mentioned me to him or told him I was the one who bumped into him. I left my hair down today, even though it's hot. I even took the time to curl the ends. Why did I do this when I want him to pretend like I don't exist and I didn't rub his butt? Because there's a chance Oswald did tell him about me, and he'll have something to say about it. I made it through the entire day yesterday without running into either of them. I hate to admit it, but I was kind of looking for them too.

I filter in the door with a group of other students, keeping my head down as I take an open seat on the opposite side of the room, even farther back from the stage. The girl next to me has cute bright pink hair.

I try to seem inconspicuous when I pull out my computer while looking around. I don't know if Oswald has this class or if he was just stopping by to see his brother. I don't see either right now, and that gives me a tiny bit of courage to relax.

Surely Gravlin isn't going to call me out in the middle of class. I just need to escape as soon as Hilbrand dismisses us, that way I have less of a chance of running into either of them after.

"Hey, can I ask you a favor?" I snap my head up at the sound of his voice and see Oswald standing just to the left of the girl with pink hair. She doesn't get a chance to respond before he continues. "Can I switch seats with you?" He motions to the empty seat he's standing in front of.

She looks over at me as if this is somehow my fault. I work hard to hide the panic and edgy excitement that seems to have developed with his presence and keep my face smooth. I open my mouth to tell her she doesn't have to move, that he can have my seat, but she slaps her laptop closed with a huff and slings her bag over her shoulder before scooting past me, even bumping my knees as she leaves the row completely. I jerk back my legs as far as I can to prevent my feet from getting stepped on.

"Thank you," he calls after her cheerfully.

Oswald drops into the seat she vacated, and my heart is already beating way too fast. This is strange. "So…" He curls his hand around the tiny built-in desk and leans forward, trying to catch my gaze. I'm honestly a little afraid to look at him. When I did last time, I felt the entire world shift under my feet, and I'm worried it might happen again but also a little concerned it might not. At least his voice isn't sending me into a panic. I recognize the richness of his tone, and I can differentiate it from the one I've always heard in my head that sounds hollower.

With my eyes locked on the front of the room, I notice when Gravlin stands and turns around. His eyes go right to mine as if he knew exactly where I was the entire time, and I'm locked in his stare.

I wiggle my toes to make sure I still have some control over my body, which I thankfully do, but I still can't force myself to look away from him. My entire world shrinks down to just the three of us. I'm unbelievably aware of them and only them, even the sounds from the room are muffled.

The longer our eyes stay connected, the more I start to feel calmness settle over me, like I'm practicing deep breathing exercises, and then I feel a light touch on my arm and my heart evens out, so it doesn't feel as if it's beating to explode out of my chest.

"Waylynn." Oswald says my name so softly, I'm not convinced it's out loud, but I answer him anyway.

"Yeah?" I feel his finger touch right beneath my chin, directing my head toward him. My eyes go from his brother's to his. This close, I can see the deep flecks of blue in his light eyes. I feel fuzzy, like the moment right before you fall asleep when you feel like you're tipping over the edge into darkness, but it's warm and comforting.

The loud sound of a door slamming makes me jump, and the bubble around us pops, bringing everything back into harsh focus—the murmurings of people chatting around us, the squeaking of seats as people adjust, and the tapping of keys as they sign into their computers.

"Good morning," Hilbrand calls loudly, and I blink several times before pulling my head back so Oswald is no longer touching me, and then I look toward the stage. Gravlin is seated nearly directly in front of me, but several rows down. I'm confident I could pick out the set of his shoulders anytime now, and I'm not so sure that's a good thing. Why am I so enamored by these two?

Hilbrand gives some basic instructions about what she will be discussing, then she launches into a lecture. To be honest, my mind is split. I'm trying very hard to focus on what she's talking about, but I'm still hyperaware of Oswald and every move he makes. I even catch myself staring at the back of Gravlin's head instead of focusing on the teacher, but I'm still able to take notes on my computer. I just hope I'm not missing too much. Maybe I should be recording the class.

As Hilbrand finishes her lesson, she closes up a book on the lectern and curls her fingers over the front of the wood while staring out into the sea of students. I doubt she'll know many of us by name at the end of the semester—how could she with such a large class? "I'm happy to see the activity on the class message boards." She pauses. "However, Gravlin has mentioned an issue with the email contact form. I want to take a moment to reiterate a few things. First, emails sent through these channels are not private. Neither Mr. Gravlin nor I are under any guidelines that bar us from sharing the emails with the class or even making the email available to the advisory board. I suggest you take the time to look up professional email etiquette, or you might find yourself facing a harassment committee.

"Second, let's address exactly what those emails should be. If you would like to schedule a tutoring session with myself or my TA, you may do so through the contact form. We are both very busy and our time is not free." She pauses briefly and looks around the room, gauging the group. "If you need to inform us of an extended absence for a medical issue or any other reason, or if you are dropping the class, please contact us. *Those* are things we may need to know. What we do not need to waste time answering are questions asking about our office hours and when drop-in times are available. You can find that and many other important details on the syllabus already provided to you. Lastly..."

She sighs, making me feel like she doesn't want to say whatever she is about to tell us. "This is one of the many courses required to get any degree this university offers. If you do not want to pay for this class again, I suggest you don't treat it like Tinder. Any questions?"

There are a few chuckles around us. They are not very far removed from high school, and it seems to be showing.

Feeling embarrassed by association, I pull my bag up from the floor and take out my phone so I can slide my laptop in. Oswald snatches my phone from my fingers and holds it near my face. I know the moment it unlocks because icons appear on the screen. "Hey," I protest weakly, but he just flips it to face him and taps the phone button.

"Making sure you have my num...ber," he stammers, then looks over at me when he sees his name already programmed into my contacts. "You didn't call." He sounds slightly bewildered and maybe even a little hurt.

I can feel heat rising up the back of my neck. I don't know how to tell him I didn't know what to say and there were times I questioned if it really happened the way I remember.

His lips thin as he looks down and thumbs my phone screen. I hear a vibration seconds later, and then he extends my phone back to me. When I look at the screen, there's an empty green text bubble on the right side under his name.

I feel a looming presence on my other side, and I know without looking it's going to be Gravlin. I turn slowly and peer up. "I'm sorry, Mr. Gravlin, it was an accident." It flies from my mouth in a rush, referencing the first time I bumped into him.

His lips twitch before he looks around the room and says, "Don't call me that."

I mash my molars together and swallow the question burning my lips. What should I call him then?

"Ready for lunch, Waylynn?" Oswald asks.

I would agree to just about anything to get out of this room. "Yes."

"Where are we going?" his brother interjects.

"How much time do you have before your next class?" Oswald questions, and I'm reeling from the rapidly changing events.

"I have math at two."

"Plenty of time. Let's go to Barney's." Oswald is looking over my head at his brother.

"Meet me in the parking lot." Gravlin spins and bounces down the steps back to the stage.

"Ready?"

I glance away from Gravlin's back to see Oswald already standing and holding my bag. "Um, I've got that." I reach for my bag, but he pulls his shoulder back, evading my fingers.

"No," is his simple reply, and I drop my arm. I should be worried that he has my computer, the keys to my house, and even my wallet, but I'm not and that's weird. It's not in my nature to trust so easily.

"I wouldn't put it past him to leave us," Oswald warns, and his urgency spurs me into action, even though I'm not worried about being left behind.

I back out of the row and head up the side aisle with him right behind me. When we reach the doors, I step to the side with the intention of following Oswald, because I have no idea where we are going. He passes me and opens the door, and it dawns on me that it looks like I was expecting the courtesy. "I wasn't… I just didn't know where to go."

"Come on." He tilts his head to the side, urging me to go ahead of him again. I dart out, and he quickens his step, catching up to me easily.

"I was planning on following you out," I explain, but he just slowly shakes his head as if he thinks I'm being silly for saying it again. He has both of our bags slung over one shoulder as if the weight doesn't bother him. I'm itching to take mine back, because I don't want him thinking he has to carry my stuff. "I have a car, I can drive," I offer instead.

"On campus? Are you a transfer student?" He gives me the side-eye.

"Yes and no," I answer in succession.

"How'd you get a parking pass?"

"I didn't, I used the visitor lot today. It's so far from my classes, I might as well have walked," I admit while trying to keep up with his pace.

A grin slides over his lips. "I didn't peg you for a rule breaker."

"Well, I vastly underestimated the size of this campus." I don't tell him I have my car today so I could escape faster if I felt the need to.

TWO FOR ONE

"Here we are." Oswald hauls open the door of an older truck, which squeals in protest, and then he grabs another handle on the inside of the door. It flaps open in reverse, revealing a tiny backseat, where he sets our bags. I hear another groan of metal as the driver's door opens, exposing Gravlin.

I lean forward and place my foot on the bar to get in after our bags, but I stop dead when I feel an arm wrap around my waist. "Not back there." Oswald hauls me back, and my butt bumps into his front. He slams the little door and urges me toward the front seat with his body pressed up against mine.

The calm that usually accompanies his touch is absent. I'm way too aware of his fingers near my hips and the way his arm is lingering on my waist to be relaxed. "Scoot in," he urges just after my butt lands on the seat. I glance over at Gravlin to see if he's going to object, but he's just watching me.

This is how horror movies start, with a girl making a dumb decision just like this, but I still scoot closer to Gravlin, and Oswald climbs in right behind me.

"Seatbelt," Gravlin instructs, and I look over my shoulder.

"It's down here." Oswald reaches into the small space between us, and his knuckle brushes against my side and hip, so I try to sit impossibly still while he fishes around. My dad has a few older cars with lap belts, so I know what he's doing, but I'm already thinking about when I need to lean over and plug it in between Gravlin and me. Will he think I'm trying to cop a feel again? "I don't need it," I blurt out.

"The hell you don't. Give me that." Gravlin reaches over me, snatches the silver tab from his brother, and shoves it into the slot without error. In the next second, I suck in a breath as he jerks the extra belt, tightening it over my lower stomach.

"Damn, Memphis, chill. Are you okay?" Oswald asks me.

"I'm fine." I nod, looking straight ahead, but I won't be for long if Gravlin keeps running his fingers over my tummy and sides, messing with the belt.

"She said she's good. Let's go before it gets too busy," Oswald tells Memphis. I wonder if their parents just liked their names or if there's some significance to them. I knew a girl in school named Aspen. She hated her name because her parents told her that was where she was conceived.

The drive to the smallish restaurant is short, and there's

already a line. As soon as Gravlin parks the car, he reaches down and pops my seatbelt, and I let out a thankful breath. I can see him watching the side of my face, and I know he witnesses my relief. "Loosen that again." He hands the belt over to Oswald, who fiddles with the strap.

I really just want out of the car. Being between them is making my brain go haywire. The doors groan again when they open, but the guys don't seem to notice. Oswald offers me his hand as if he's going to help me down, and I take it because I don't want to be rude. I like the sweet gesture.

I end up between them as we walk to the restaurant. "Have you been here before?" Oswald inquires.

"No, I haven't been in town long."

"Sorry about the seatbelt," Gravlin interjects.

"It's okay, I promise," I tell him in earnest.

"They have the best subs," Oswald continues as if his brother didn't even speak. "You're going to want it all the time after this. Good thing you live pretty close." I look down the street. I'm honestly not even sure where we are. I just know we're not far from campus, which means we're not too far from my house.

"Do you live with your family?" Gravlin asks as we step into the line.

"No, it's just me."

"You said you're not in Oxford, so what dorm are you in?" Oswald inches forward.

"I'm not in a dorm. I live just off campus." I see the girl in front of us half turn around, clearly listening to our conversation, and that makes me more uncomfortable than telling them where I live. I lower my eyes and pretend I didn't just see her checking out both guys.

Gravlin shifts until his back is to the group in front of us. It can't really stop them from listening to us, but the gesture is nice. When the line moves again, we hang back just a little so we're not so close. The ugly feeling of envy I was experiencing fades with the slight space.

"Memphis has his own place too. I stay with him most of the time. I hate the dorms," Oswald confesses.

"Try *all* of the time. What building do you live in?" Gravlin asks, his eyes slightly squinted.

"Um…"

"I'm not going to show up at your door," he says when I hesitate.

I shake my head quickly. "No, I didn't think… I mean, you could come over if you wanted." I catch myself as I continue to ramble and take a deep breath. "It's just, I don't live in a building. I have a house," I admit the last part softly. I'm not ashamed, I just don't want them to think I'm bragging either.

Both guys look at each other for a long second. "You live by yourself?" Gravlin asks skeptically.

"Yeah," I admit, wondering what they are going to say next.

"You shouldn't be telling people that," comes Gravlin's quick response.

"Do other people know that? Does that guy from the other day know you live alone? How well do you know him?" Oswald fires off.

"No. No, he doesn't, and I just met him," I answer.

Memphis

Every time she opens her mouth, I have more questions. When she said she lived alone, I was curious. I thought maybe she had a shitty little apartment like me in an old building or even rented a room, but she said she has a house. I almost don't want to believe her, but I don't think she could lie to me if she wanted to.

Then it dawns on me how valuable that information is, how easily she shared it with us, two near strangers, and how easy it was to get her in my truck, and my mind goes to a completely different place.

Oz's head works the same way mine does, and he starts asking her questions about a guy I haven't heard anything about.

"Who are you talking about?" I ask my brother.

"Who is he?" Oz lifts his chin in Waylynn's direction. It's clear he's demanding an answer to our question.

"Um..." She squints her eyes and wrinkles her nose. Her lips slip down into a pretty little pout, and she admits, "I can't remember his name. He's in my math class." I thought she was just stalling, but again, I believe her.

"The south quad isn't near the math building, and that's where you guys were." Oz crosses his arms over his chest.

"We had lunch there." She takes a few steps forward, bringing us closer to the building. Why does it bother me that she went out to lunch with someone I don't even know?

"Does he live in my building?" Oz asks like he owns the whole place, even though he barely even stays there.

"No, he told me his dorm name, but I forgot that too."

"What's my name and phone number?"

"Oswald Gravlin, 734-344-2100," she replies without missing a beat.

"So you don't have a memory issue, he just wasn't worth remembering." Oz smiles at her, and she looks down, then tucks a piece of dark hair behind her ear when it falls in her face. She's shy and sweet as fuck. My dick twitches just like it did when she called me Mr. Gravlin. Oh hell.

Waylynn

My leg starts to bounce under the table. It feels like we've been here a while, and I need to get back to school. I don't want to be late for class, which makes me think about the guy from math. I can't believe I don't remember his name.

"What's wrong?" Gravlin touches my arm to get my attention. His voice is so familiar, it makes me feel like we've had this conversation before, but we haven't.

"I'm trying to decide how crazy that guy is going to think I am when I can't remember his name and how to tell him I'm full and don't want to grab food after class." I probably should have kept that to myself and just told him I was thinking about class, but it's too late now.

Gravlin's brows rise. "You're that convinced he's going to ask?"

A spike of embarrassment makes my stomach tighten, like he thinks I'm being conceded. "He asked me Monday if I wanted to get food after class again." I ball up my napkin and push back from the table. "I need to get back to school."

I notice when Oswald shoots his brother a *what the hell* face, but I turn away and pretend I didn't. "I can meet you after class, and you can tell him we made plans." He catches up to me at the trash bin.

"It's fine. I've got it," I reply dismissively. The guy might have already forgotten by now anyway.

Gravlin meets us near the sidewalk, and we make our way back to their truck silently. I wish there was a way for me to sit in the backseat without seeming like a pouting brat, but there isn't, so I'm going to have to suck it up and sit between them. I am going to fasten my own seatbelt though.

I adjust the belt strap before I even get in to make sure I can reach it on my own and buckle up without a fuss. I have my knees locked together so tightly, I can feel the muscles burn on my inner thighs.

Gravlin's movements are a little jerky when he puts on his own seatbelt and shifts the truck into drive. The tension in the cab is making me feel jittery, so I run my palms over my legs. I can't wait to get out of here. All I can think about is how I shouldn't have stormed away from the table. I shouldn't have let him see that the question bothered me. Now we're in an awkward stalemate because I got offended over a question.

When Gravlin turns into the parking lot, I click my seatbelt off, and by the time he parks, I'm already turned so I can get out of the car as soon as Oswald does. His fingers curl around the handle, but he stalls. "Do you have lunch tomorrow around the same time?"

"A little earlier. I should get going," I remind him.

"Yeah, okay." Oswald hops down and extends his hand to me again. When our palms connect, I get a flash of anger, then a wave of fuzzy calmness dampens it for the briefest of moments before I tug my hand away.

I know it's rude, but I don't thank either of them or say goodbye, I just hustle down the walkway. I realize about thirty seconds later I don't have my bag, but I can't bring myself to stop. I feel like the biggest idiot.

The stomp of running feet can be heard before he calls my name. "Waylynn." When I turn, Oswald is rushing forward with my bag strap over his shoulder. "I think you'll need this."

His lips are holding a mock grin as he lets my bag slip down his arm and deftly catches it before it can hit the ground.

"Sorry, thank you." I take the weight of the bag, not sure if I should say anything else, like sorry I'm a bundle of nerves, feel free to ignore me from now on and forget this ever happened.

"I've got to run, but I'll see you soon." He starts to back away.

"Bye, Oswald," I say softly. I'm not even sure he hears me, but he sends me a quick wave and takes off, sprinting back where we came from.

I'm so wrapped up in my head, I end up taking the long way to the math building, which nearly makes me late. I'm searching the filled rows for an empty seat from the back of the room when the TA steps up to the podium. She glances over at me once, and I think about just leaning against the back wall instead of trying to get into one of the few empty seats remaining in the middle of the rows, but I think that will put more attention on me.

Biting the bullet, I slip into the closest row and shimmy past desks and laptops, hoping my butt isn't going to knock off someone's computer. When I drop into a seat, I could cry in relief, but I get busy sliding my desk in place and getting my own computer open. When Emily, the TA, starts speaking, I tug out my phone to record the class. I already know I'm going to be torturing myself with how I acted for the next few hours, so I probably won't remember the lecture later. There's a text on the screen from an unfamiliar number.

Unknown: Call when you get home.

I swallow and struggle to find the voice recorder. Once I hit record, I set the phone down, but I can't stop thinking about the text. There's only one person it could be from. I just don't know what he wants or why Oswald gave him my number.

I'm exhausted at the end of class. My mind has been working overtime, and it wasn't on math equations. "Hey, I saved you a seat. I didn't think you made it to class." As soon as I see his face, I remember his name—Liam.

"Oh yeah, I was running late, but thank you. It's been a crazy day." I start to walk up the aisle with him at my side.

"You still up for food?" he asks hopefully.

I'm on the verge of saying yes and pretending to eat because I feel bad, when I see people abruptly dodging to the left of the hall. Oswald's dark hair flops as he jogs through the crowd and stops right in front of me. He's breathing hard enough that his chest is rising and falling in sharp jerks. There's a sheen of sweat on his forehead and across his cheeks, but damn he looks good. My stomach does that flippy thing.

"Sorry…I'm late," he pants.

I open my mouth to tell him he isn't late, since I didn't expect him to come, but I roll my lips in instead.

"Hey again." Oswald eyes Liam, but this time, it's different. I don't know what has changed, just that something has.

Now I feel even worse about telling Liam I don't want to go with him. He would know I was blowing him off.

"You're cool if I tag along, right? She mentioned you guys might grab something to eat." Oswald directs his question to Liam.

"Yeah, sure, man," Liam agrees, but the lightness that was in their conversation yesterday is absent. Everything feels a little forced now. My shoulders hunch as we walk toward the exit.

"So where are we going?" Oswald asks, interrupting the silence between us.

"You guys can decide. I'm not really that hungry," I admit.

"Still full from lunch? It was good though, right?" Oswald supplies, and it feels intentional, as if he wanted Liam to know we ate together earlier, yet I'm the one who opened the door for him to say it.

"You guys already ate?" Liam asks, and his steps slow.

"Yeah, at Barney's," Oswald replies.

"Oh, well if you're not hungry…" Liam looks at me with a clear question in his eyes.

"I can still sit with you," I offer. This is so damn awkward. I don't know if I'll have the nerve to agree to go to lunch with anyone again.

"Nah, it's all right, maybe another time." Liam stops fully.

A quick but abrasive sense of inadequacy brushes against me, but it's gone in a flash.

"All right, man, see you around." Oswald reaches for my bag and hauls it right off my shoulder, then continues walking. I glance over at Liam, but he's already turned away to head in the other direction.

I take a few quick steps and catch up with Oswald. "You didn't have to come. I could have just sat with him so he didn't have to eat alone."

He looks down at me with furrowed brows. "You're worried about him eating alone?"

I shrug. "It sucks to eat alone in a new place. Are you late for class or something?"

"No, why?"

"You're walking fast, and where are we going?"

Oswald stops, and a few students have to swerve to get around us. "Maybe you're slow." He turns to face me, his grin sweet and teasing.

"Maybe you have an unfair advantage because your legs are longer," I counter.

He steps a little closer, but his smile stays in place. "Maybe I do, but I like your legs just fine." I'm not sure how to respond to that or the way he's looking at me, so I don't. "Where are *you* going?" he asks softly.

"Home, I guess."

"Can I come?"

"Um…" Why is my first reaction to say yes?

"I don't get many afternoons off from practice, but they went light on us this week because classes just started. I just want to hang out while we can, no pressure."

"Okay." A bubble of happiness makes my chest feel light after I answer. "My car is over by the English building." Which is in the complete opposite direction.

When we start walking again, Oswald works to slow his pace, and I feel like I can breathe without panting, which is a nice change.

We walk in relative silence to the lot where I parked. Thankfully, I don't see any tickets on my car, and it's still where I parked it. "Hey, I can take that." I reach for my bag when we get near the trunk of my car. Oswald allows me to take it from his shoulder, and I can feel the tightness of his bicep when it skips down his arm.

When he starts to follow me toward the driver's side, I say, "This is me."

He looks down at the sleek black car, then up at me again with a heavy frown. Instead of monitoring his reaction, I get behind the wheel. Normally, I would toss my bag on the passenger seat, but I slip it into the back instead.

Oswald knocks on the window, and I think he's about to tell me he changed his mind about coming over, but when I roll the window down, he asks, "How do I open the door?"

I tap the button on the touchscreen and then hear the handle release. "Sorry. I haven't had any passengers," I explain once he sits down.

Oswald looks around the interior, and I start the car. I can barely tell it's running, it's so quiet, but I'm used to it now, so I feel the slight hum. "Seatbelt," I remind him after clicking my own. He reaches over his shoulder and clicks it into place, but he's still not saying anything. I feel weird.

I'm not dumb, I know my Tesla is expensive, but I've seen G-Wagons and BMWs all over, so I didn't think it would stick out too much.

"I'm a little intimidated, Waylynn," Oswald finally says as I start to back up.

I can't just ignore his words. I have to ask, "Why?"

"This car, for starters. It's nice as hell. You've seen our truck." He catches my eye from the side as I look to the left to make a turn out of the lot.

"I don't have a problem with your truck. It got us to the restaurant just fine." I give him my true feelings. I've been judged way too much to do that to someone else, especially about a vehicle or money. "The hinges could use some oil though."

Oswald barks out a laugh. "Calling me out on my doors?" He continues to chuckle but pulls his phone out of his pocket. "Pick up some WD-40," he says slowly as he types. "I told Memphis."

"Don't tell him I said it." I gasp, appalled.

"Why not? It's funny as hell."

"Just don't, please." I don't want to admit I'm afraid it will make him think poorly of me out loud—well, more than he might already. I shouldn't have said anything.

Oswald's phone buzzes, and he looks down. "He said he would pick some up. He wants to know where I am." Oswald looks over at me with his thumbs poised to type.

"Are you not supposed to be with me or something?" I question, wondering why he would tell me that.

"No, I'm just usually at his place when I'm not at practice or school…or eating," he adds as an afterthought.

"Oh, did you want to invite him?" I feel weird offering, so then I add, "Or I can drop you at his place."

"You don't mind?" Oswald is watching me.

"No, it's fine. Where does he live?"

"I mean, you don't mind if he comes over too? It would be nice to get him out of the house. All he does is work."

"Sure, that's fine." I tell him my address then instruct, "The driveway is off Granger, around the side of the house." I can't believe I'm doing this. What am I going to do with them at my house?

"Shit." Oswald lets his hands fall to his lap as I'm turning onto Granger. "I didn't tell him I was with you, I just sent the address and Bates is with him."

"Bates?" I turn into my driveway and hit the button to open the detached garage.

Oswald looks right and left, taking in the house and garden. "Yeah, Bates, a friend." He sounds distracted.

"Um…"

85

"He's not... He's a good guy, I promise. I'll text him back and tell them not to come though." he says quickly, already holding his phone.

"No, it's okay." I pull into the garage and park, then hit the button to turn off the car.

"No, I get it. You don't know us, and I just invited them over. That's... There's only one of you and you're a girl," he continues, saying all the things I should be thinking, but I'm really not. "I swear I didn't plan this. I'm not a creep," he defends.

"I don't think you planned it." I open my car door. "And it's fine. They can stay if they want, but fair warning, I'm not a good host."

"A good host?" He climbs out of the car and grabs both of our bags, pulling them between the seats.

"I might have some popcorn and cereal, but not much else." I unlock the backdoor and turn off the alarm. Oswald makes a point of spinning around so he can't see what I'm doing. Hopefully, that means my trust in him isn't misplaced. Still, I plan on keeping my phone in my pocket just in case. I'm learning to live a little, not trying to get killed.

"Holy shit." Oswald spins around, taking in my kitchen. I love the white tile mixed with black cabinets and commercial appliances. I hope he likes it too. "This is really your house?" His eyes scan me up and down, but it's as if he's looking for something he didn't see before. It's the first time he's ever made me uncomfortable, like he's trying to see how he didn't notice I had a lot of money before now.

My arms tighten to my body and my back stiffens. I can just imagine what he's thinking of me, I've heard it all before—trust fund baby, rich bitch—and that was from kids who came from families nearly as wealthy as my own. Maybe I shouldn't have invited him after all.

"It is." I nod my head, waiting to hear what he has to say.

Memphis

"I thought Oz would be here." Bates is bent over with his head in my small fridge.

"So did I. He doesn't have practice today. He's probably eating. Wait, he's texting me now."

Oz: We need WD-40.

What the hell?

Me: I'll pick some up later. Where are you?

"Tell him to bring me some food." Bates slams the fridge shut, but it's not intentional.

Oz: 9122 Cambridge, meet up?

"He's out and asking us to meet him," I tell Bates.

He looks down at his jeans and T-shirt, which has the name of the electrical company he works for on the pocket, then up to me. "Whatever, I'm not showering."

"You don't need to look pretty for me." I grab my keys and phone from my desk.

About seven minutes later, we're turning down Cambridge. "Is he at a fucking frat house?" Bates ducks his head a little to see all the fancy ass houses we're passing.

"He better not be, unless he just wanted a ride home, lazy fucker. Did he say anything else?" I hand my phone over to Bates for him to check while I'm driving, and he keys in my passcode.

"He said the driveway is off Granger. It is a house, man. What the hell?" Bates tosses my phone on the seat between us, clearly disgusted.

"That's not a frat house." I look out the passenger window, seeing a really nice white house with green shutters and a big ass front yard.

"Go around the corner. He better be waiting. I'm not fighting some girl's dad he just got done hooking up with."

I snort, remembering a time or two when I called him to help me get out of a sticky situation when I fucked around a bunch in high school.

I pull into the driveway but keep the bed of my truck near the road so I can back out quickly if I need to. When I don't see him anywhere, I send him a text.

Me: Here.

His reply comes swiftly.

Oz: Come in.

"Fuck that!" Bates reads his message over my arm. "Just tell him to come out."

Me: I'm going to leave your ass here.

I look into the rearview mirror and notice a nature park behind me. It triggers a memory of Oz telling me that Waylynn lived by a park near Hill Street. "Shit." I look around at the manicured hedges and the house.

"What?" Bates looks around, following my gaze.

Oz: Whatever.

"We're going in," I announce, putting the truck in drive and pulling closer to the garage at a slow crawl.

"Why? All he said was whatever." Bates opens his door, and it squeals like a motherfucker in this quiet neighborhood. Damn, why haven't I ever noticed that before?

Like he was waiting for us to knock, Oz opens the door and leans against the frame with a grin so wide, you'd think he just discovered pussy for the first time. He steps back and casts his arm out to the side, allowing us to enter the house.

Bates curses, and I know the problem when he looks down at his boots. The white tile is clean enough to eat off of, and his work boots have seen better days.

With a defiant step, he stomps into the house, dirty boots and all, then shuts the door behind him. The rattle is hard enough that I hear it echo through some of the glass cabinet doors in the kitchen.

"Damn it, Bates, quit slamming shit," Oz chastises.

"It's okay," comes her soft voice. I spot Waylynn standing

near a huge marble island. Bates' head leans to the side, and I watch his eyes scan her. Damn, I wonder if I was that obvious when I got my first real look at her.

Her cheeks are a little flushed, and it makes her hazel eyes look greener, but it's her full lips turned in a slight frown that gets to me. "What are you doing here, and why did you invite us over?" I pose the question to Oz, but I don't miss when Waylynn tucks her arm over her waist and takes a step back.

"We were going to watch a movie or something, and I thought you might like getting out of the house, but you can go if you're going to be a dick," Oz snaps at me.

Damn it, I did sound like an asshole. "You shouldn't be inviting people to your house," I tell Waylynn.

"Okay," she agrees in a small voice.

"Somebody want to fill me in?" Bates says, and Waylynn's eyes go wide, and her mouth falls open. I know she couldn't have just noticed him. He's a big guy, so what's with the reaction?

THREE'S THE CHARM OR CURSE?

Waylynn

I FEEL WOOZY AGAIN. Just when I think I've come to terms with Oswald's and Gravlin's voices being so similar to the ones I've heard in my head since I was a kid, it happens again. When the guy Oswald called Bates speaks, my brain threatens to short-circuit, because for the third time in my life, the shit I thought was only in my head is somehow invading my real life.

I lean my palm on the cool counter to ground myself, hoping no one notices. When did it become so hard to act normal? Thankfully, Oswald starts speaking, and it gives me a few precious moments to regain my equilibrium.

"Damn, Memphis, you're not her dad."

"I know I'm not her dad," Gravlin grits out between his teeth, "but if she invites you over, who else is she going to invite here?"

Even as distracted as I am, I feel the insult in those words. He thinks I'm dumb or too trusting.

"Jesus Christ, Memphis, do you have any idea how that sounds?" Oswald pulls his head back as if his brother's words surprised him.

Bates drops his hand on Gravlin's shoulder in what seems like a show of support. "He's just trying to protect you, man. You know what cleat chasers are like."

"Cleat chasers," I whisper the word to myself as the meaning dawns on me.

"No, no, that's not what—" Gravlin starts.

"I would like you to leave now, please." My voice is soft when I interrupt. Why do I feel like crying?

"Waylynn." Oswald turns to look at me with wide eyes, and he's shaking his head back and forth slowly.

"I would like you *all* to leave now, please." My voice is firmer but still not as forceful as I would like. I pull my phone out of my pocket and grip the thing like a lifeline. Gravlin's eyes dip to my hand as if he understands why I have it clutched in my palm without me saying it.

"Oswald, let's go."

"He didn't mean that, he just doesn't know you," Oswald implores.

"*You* don't know me," I accuse. "Leave, please."

"We need to go." Gravlin places his hand on his brother's shoulder much like Bates did to him, only Oswald shrugs off his touch when he jerks his arm away.

"I'm sorry, Waylynn. None of that... I'll go. I'm sorry." He looks at me for two seconds longer, then pivots and damn near bowls his brother over to push him toward the exit.

Bates' eyes bounce around, but he moves pretty quickly himself and hauls the door open, making himself the first one out. I rush over to the door once it's closed and flip the deadbolt. I can hear the muffled sounds of angry words being exchanged, but fragments of sounds are piercing my mind too, warring with what's real and what isn't.

I back away from the door and haul ass up to my room, where I turn on the television and increase the volume to drown out the words I can't deny I heard in my head and the ones that were coming from outside.

Oswald, Gravlin, and their friend are not healthy for me to be around, no matter how much I wish that weren't true.

BATES

MEMPHIS MUST REALLY NOT like this chick. I don't think I've ever heard him talk to a woman the way he did her, which is too bad because she's...stunning. That's not a word I usually use to describe someone. Usually it's hot, fuckable, cute, or hell, even beautiful, but not stunning.

Why the hell would Oz call us over here if he knew how Memphis felt about her? But he seems pretty surprised by his brother's attitude too. "Somebody want to fill me in?"

The girl lists to the side like she might fall over, but she slaps her palm on the counter and recovers. Oswald doesn't seem to notice, he's too busy chewing Memphis out.

"He's just trying to protect you, man. You know what cleat chasers are like." I watch her mouth move, the tip of her tongue peeking out and touching the middle of her top lip, but I can't hear what she says. When her lips seal again, it's only for a breath because she asks us to leave, even adding a please.

Why is my gut twisting, and why do I wish I would have kept my mouth shut?

Oswald's trying to explain something, but his words get tangled, and the girl...the girl looks devastated and embarrassed, not like she got caught out, but really humiliated. The next thing I know, Oswald is pushing up against Memphis and we're leaving in a huff.

Once we get outside, I hear the click of the lock, and I actually grunt. Damn, I don't know that girl, but I sure as shit don't like that I'm part of the reason she looked like she did before we left.

Oz shoves Memphis in the chest, and he stumbles backward but doesn't fall. I put myself between them as fast as I can and separate them. Oz is yelling at Memphis, and this isn't some *you ate my food* bullshit. He's pissed.

Memphis is either too shocked to respond or…or I don't know what, because he's acting like his brain isn't working, and he's a smart motherfucker, so that's worrying me.

"Knock it off before she calls the cops, you dummies," I snarl between my teeth. Oz looks over his shoulder as if he's just now realizing she could be watching this, or at the very least hearing it.

"I'll fucking walk," Oz spits out and takes a few steps back. "Get the fuck out of here. I'm not leaving until you two do." He includes me in his venomous glare.

"Stay away from her," Memphis says in a tone I've never heard him talk to Oswald in.

"Kiss my ass," he retorts with no intention of listening.

I grab Memphis by the arm when he moves like he might try to get back in Oz's face. "You need to cool off, you both do," I say, reminding them this isn't the time or place for this. He jerks his arm away from me and stomps over to his truck. When he starts the damn thing up, he revs the engine like he's preparing for a race. I throw myself into the passenger seat, and he slaps the gear shift down, reversing out of the driveway like he just robbed the place.

I grab the door and brace myself on the dash so I don't go slipping around as he spins the wheel to turn. "What the fuck, Memphis?"

"You called her a cleat chaser!" He spares me a glance, and it isn't pretty.

"You were the one acting like she was trying to pin a baby on Oz," I defend.

"No, I wasn't," he spits. "I was telling her she needs to be more careful. She's... She's... What if she let some guy over who wasn't like Oswald?"

"Man, that was you being worried about her?" My doubt is clear in my tone.

"Just shut up for a minute." He slams the heel of his palm on top of the steering wheel.

I sit back in my seat. I don't even know what the fuck just happened, but it feels big. Memphis and Oswald never fight—well, they never fight like that—and as much as it bothers me, seeing her face after I called her a cleat chaser is even worse.

When Memphis parks his truck, I hop out of the cab and shut the door. As badly as I want them to fill me in on how we got to that point this evening, I don't think I would get many answers, so I fist the keys to my work van and leave Memphis stewing behind the wheel.

Waylynn

I WENT to class on Thursday, only because I knew I wouldn't run into Oswald or Gravlin, and then I spent the weekend holed up in my house like a freaking hermit, regretting my choices about trusting my gut.

I blocked Oswald's and the unknown numbers from my phone Wednesday night and even drafted a notice that I was going to drop Hilbrand's class, but I haven't had the nerve to send it yet. With Gravlin being the TA, he will more than likely see it, so I may just stop going altogether so I can avoid him completely. I don't care if I have to pay for the class again. It would be worth it so I don't have to be around them. I just hate losing the credits, because it means I'll have to make them up later with a heavier class load.

On Sunday, I finally get the nerve to leave the house. I feel foolish now for thinking they would even try to see me or speak to me again. There are several coffee shops on and near campus, but I avoid them and drive to the one four miles away. It's in front of a strip mall with a grocery store, which reminds me I need to get food. Grubhub is getting old, even with the endless choices.

Instead of grabbing my drink and heading back home, I park near the store. I could order it online and have it delivered, but I'm in that weird space again where I'm feeling lonely even though I don't really want to deal with people.

It's not until my shopping basket is half full with a bunch of mismatched stuff that I realize I should have had a better plan than this. I'm feeling slightly overwhelmed and thinking about abandoning my cart altogether, but I don't want to make more work for the employees by making them put everything away. Plus, what if they remember me the next time I come here?

Forging on, I make my way past the freezer aisle and snag a carton of ice cream and some chocolate syrup that is hanging off the door, then head to the checkout. Half this stuff will be shoved in the freezer and forgotten, but I'm past caring, I'm just ready to get out of here.

The person in front of me has an overflowing cart and two kids. One is strapped to her chest in some sort of sling, she keeps bracing the little thing's head when she bends over, and the other is sitting in the top seat, happily chirping away. The rush I was feeling to get out of the store slowly ebbs as I watch the three of them.

The little girl in the cart makes a high-pitched squeal that brings an instant smile to my face, but the mom leans over and shushes her with a kiss to the side of her head. When I look up again, I see a familiar face through the large store windows.

Gravlin walks like he has a purpose as he crosses the parking lot. He's looking straight ahead, so I'm free to inspect his profile without him catching me. He's as handsome as the first day I saw him, maybe even more so because I know what he looks like close up, and he's just as closed off. I wonder what made him so abrasive, or maybe it's just me he doesn't like. Once he passes the window, I push my cart forward the few inches I gained. The lady in front of me almost has all of her stuff unloaded, and the cashier is already ringing her up, so hopefully, I can get out of here soon.

A little of the urgency I was feeling earlier pecks at me again. I'm not sure if he is coming into this store or not, but I would rather get out of here just in case.

As hard as it is not to look for him, I keep my face forward, which limits my view. I haven't seen him return the way he came, so he must still be around.

Even when it's time to pay, I try to keep my back to the rest of the store, but as luck would have it, as soon as I grab my receipt and push my cart past the end of the counter, Gravlin is standing right there with two small bags in his fist, watching me.

"Pardon me," I mumble when he continues to block my path.

He nearly hops to the side to get out of the way. I avert my eyes and trudge forward. Even though I can't see him, I can feel his presence looming behind me. I fluff out the back of my shirt, trying to seem casual, and debate leaving the full cart and just getting into my car to flee, but that's questionable behavior, and I don't need more people thinking I'm crazy.

You've got this. He's not even talking to you, I tell myself and unzip my purse for my keys. My pill bottle is on the top, so I shove it deeper into my bag with shaking hands and try to find the fob for my car.

Once the slick thing is in my grip, I have a complete mind blank. I can't remember where to tap to get the trunk open. I tap the middle to unlock the car, then mash my thumb from the bottom to the top, and my car chirps. After taking a deep breath and focusing, I touch the bottom of the fob twice, and the sound of the trunk releasing has me letting out an audible groan.

"Waylynn."

I jump when he says my name. "Sorry," I mutter, even though I don't have a reason to.

I'm glad it's bright out and I have a reason to shade my eyes with my hand when I turn to look at him. It helps so I'm not able to see his entire face, but it doesn't stop me from seeing him lick his lips before he says, "Sorry about the other night. I… I just wanted… I… It came out wrong."

I'm a little surprised. First, for the apology, and second, by the stammering. Memphis Gravlin does not seem like one to stumble over his words.

"Thank you for your apology." I slowly lower my hand, thinking he's going to walk away, but he doesn't.

Memphis

She lowers her hand, and the bright sun allows me to see the tiny freckles along the tops of her cheeks and across her nose. She's probably wondering why I'm just staring at her, but hell, I don't know what to say, and I don't want her to leave yet. I tried texting when I got home after the shitshow, but none of my messages showed up as delivered, so I'm pretty sure she blocked me. Oz confirmed my suspicion when he told me he tried to call her and got an unavailable message and the line disconnected before he could leave a message.

I bet he would have showed up at her house if he didn't have an away game this weekend. I just got back to town myself and needed something to put in the microwave for dinner.

"Bates didn't mean it either." I feel the need to defend my oldest friend, since he was feeding off me.

"Apology accepted, Mr. Gravlin. You were right—I was being naïve." I hate how she just addressed me even more formally than the first time she did it. Not only do I have a visceral reaction to it, like I want to put my hand around her throat and dare her to say it again while I run my tongue over her lips, but it also feels like she's trying to put distance between us and remind me I'm her teacher, which I don't like at all.

"My name is Memphis to you unless…unless we're in class." I manage not to say *unless I'm inside you*, which was what I really wanted to tell her.

"I should probably load up." She sways her hand to the side, gesturing to the open trunk and cart full of groceries.

"Here, I'll help since I held you up." I set my bags on the ground and grab several of hers to place in the spotless trunk.

"Are you having a party?" I ask, just trying to make conversation. This is a lot of food for one person.

"No, sir," she answers hurriedly, as if she thinks admitting it would get her in trouble. God damn, her words land right beneath my belt buckle. What the hell is that about? Still leaning over her trunk, I look up, and she's right there, close enough that I can smell the soap she uses or whatever perfume she's wearing. Her face is turned down, focusing on the bag she's placing in the trunk, allowing her long, dark hair to obscure my view.

Without thinking, I reach over and tuck it behind her ear. She stills for a breath, then straightens before glancing at me. Her brows are slightly furrowed, making me think she's confused, not that I blame her. She's probably wondering what the hell I'm doing touching her.

"Do you have plans today?" I ask instead of explaining myself.

"I actually came to get a coffee." She looks over at the back of another building. "But now I'm going to have to get home and find a place to put all this." She pretends I didn't make things awkward and continues putting the bags in the trunk. There are only a few left, and I still don't want her to leave.

"Do you need a hand?" I offer.

"Um…" She averts her eyes from mine. I don't take back my proposal because I want her to be the one to tell me no if she's going to, but really, I'm hoping she will agree to let me go home with her.

"Aren't you busy? I wouldn't want to keep you. And what about your stuff?" She motions to my bags of microwave dinners sitting on the pavement.

"I don't have anything going on."

"Didn't you tell me I shouldn't invite people over?" she questions with genuine curiosity, but the moment I look into her eyes, she averts her gaze.

I touch my finger to her chin and lift it. "You shouldn't invite anyone *else* over."

"Only you?" she asks while staring right into my eyes. Her attention is feeding whatever she stoked inside me, and damn, I like the way she makes me feel.

"I can't keep you all to myself, Oz would probably kill me," I tell her honestly. Things between my brother and me have been tense for days, and it's my fault. I'm the one who let how protective and possessive I feel about her make me into an idiot.

She pulls back just enough so my finger is no longer touching her and lowers her eyes again. I see the shift in her posture as her shoulders roll in a little and know she's about to tell me no, so I don't give her a chance. "I'll follow you."

"Okay," she says softly after a short pause. I close the trunk of her car, then grab her cart so I can return it. "I guess I'll see you." She looks like she doesn't know what to do for a second, then dashes toward her car door.

The moment I have the cart returned, I jog to my truck and toss the bags on the seat while simultaneously putting the key in the ignition and trying to call Oz.

"Where are you?" I ask as soon as he answers.

"Why?" I can hear his pissy tone, even in the single word.

"I ran into her at the grocery store. I'm following her back to her house."

"Bro, you're stalking her?"

"No, she knows I'm behind her," I defend.

"Is that why she's not answering the door?"

"Who's the stalker now?" I knew he was going to show up at her house. I just didn't expect it to be so soon. He must have gone as soon as he got off the bus.

"I needed to apologize, and she wouldn't answer my calls." He's defensive now.

"She'll be there in a few minutes. She's a little more stand-offish than before."

"Your fault," Oz snaps, telling the truth.

"I know, but I'm trying to fix that, and I called you," I remind him, so he knows I'm not trying to steal her from him.

"Why are you calling me anyway? I can tell you like her."

"You do too," I explain.

"Yeah," he admits easily. "Not that I'm opposed to banging her, but I..."

"Oz," I warn.

"Can you let me finish?"

"Make it quick, we're almost there," I urge, hurrying him along.

"I want to get to know her. I've got to go, she's pulling in," Oz says in a rush. The line goes dead just as Waylynn makes the tight turn into her driveway.

"I want to do a lot more than get to know her," I mumble under my breath after ditching the phone on the seat.

SHAKY GROUND

WAYLYNN

"Oh crap!" I holler and slam on the brakes when Oswald steps into my driveway. He hops back and waves me forward. My heart is beating so fast, I'm hesitant to hit the gas, but I inch forward enough so my trunk is near the path to the kitchen door.

"What are you doing? I could have hit you," I say as soon as I'm out of the car.

"You had miles," he replies dismissively.

"You scared the heck out of me." I turn to the left and watch his brother coast into the driveway and park behind me. "He was at the grocery store," I explain.

"He called me," Oswald answers.

"Oh." That catches me off guard. Gravlin, Memphis, exits his truck, and the door doesn't squeal. A small smile graces my lips, and I don't even really know why. Seeing the two bags in his hands reminds me to open the trunk. Thankfully, I don't fumble like I did in the parking lot.

"Jesus, are you expecting company?" Oswald reaches in and grabs a few bags.

"I was hungry, and I just kept adding stuff to the cart. Before I knew it…this," I confess, waving at the full trunk.

"Don't you know that you can't go shopping for food when you're hungry?" Oswald tells me.

"We've got this." Gravlin nudges me out of the way using his body. "You open the door." I listen without hesitation, and they are fast on my heels. Within minutes, the kitchen island is covered in plastic bags all overflowing with food.

"Are you using any of this today or tomorrow, or do you want all the meat in the freezer?" Gravlin starts digging through the bags.

"I'll keep the chicken out."

"Which one?" Oswald chuckles, holding up three packages of chicken breasts.

"What are you going to make?" Gravlin starts sorting the rest of the meat and taking a pile to the freezer.

A bubble of laughter escapes me. "Not sure yet."

"Memphis makes this amazing sticky chicken stuff," Oswald offers.

I look over at Memphis. It's going to be hard not to slip up and call him Gravlin since that's what he's been in my head for a few days now. "I can teach you," he offers as he lines up a few jars and cans. "We would need some honey though."

"I have honey. I like it on my toast. What else?" I'm very intrigued by the idea of him cooking, and his offer to teach me makes it impossible to deny, even when I know I shouldn't have even let them in my house after what happened the other day.

"Soy sauce, cornstarch, and rice. Sesame seeds are good but not required."

"I don't have cornstarch." I pick up my phone and pull up the store we just left. It would probably be faster to go back myself, but I don't want to.

"I can go grab it," Oswald offers.

"No, it's okay, I'll order it." I type cornstarch into the search bar and hit enter. The end of my phone tips away when Oswald pushes it down.

"I'll run back, it will be faster and cheaper."

"Okay, are you sure there isn't anything else we need?" I look over at Gravlin. I kind of hope he goes with Oswald, because having both of them here is easier to deal with than just one, though I don't know why.

"How much rice do you have? He's carb loading." He doesn't even look in Oswald's direction, he just continues to put all my groceries away.

I put my phone down and get busy helping so I can show him exactly what I have.

Before Oswald leaves, alone, he has a list. Apparently, I didn't have enough honey or rice, and we added some vegetables to serve with the chicken since he had to go to the store anyway.

Once the door closes, the silence feels heavy. "Thanks for doing all that." I motion to the kitchen.

"You're welcome." He looks around. "How long have you lived here?"

"A little over a week." I close the pantry door.

"Wow, I never would have guessed, everything is…settled. Like you've been here a long time."

I don't tell him the movers and stagers did all the work. I just picked a bunch of stuff out. Instead, I offer, "Did you want to look around?"

"Sure, what's your favorite room?" He catches me off guard with his question.

"Um…the sunroom, my bedroom." I shrug, telling the truth.

"Is this the sunroom?" He motions to the open entryway off the kitchen.

"Yeah." I duck past him and enter the room. It's not a traditional sunroom, there's far too much wood paneling for that. It's almost like a study with lots of windows, but I call it a sunroom anyway.

The windows start a few inches off the floor and are a lovely lead glass with transom windows above that, which open with antique brass hardware that hangs down the side for easy access. A few of the narrow windows have been made into doors that allow you to exit right into the back garden, but they are very well concealed, so it's hard to tell unless you're looking for the door latch.

Instead of studying the room or the garden, Memphis picks up the book I have sitting on the table between two of the overstuffed chairs. The title alone is enough to have me blushing, *Dark Lover*, but when he spins the book to read the back, I want to pull it right from his hand.

"Ready to see the rest of the house?" My voice is high, but I pretend it's completely normal as I go stand near the entryway. Hell, I'll show him my room to get him out of here now.

"Is this any good?" He lifts his eyes to mine, still clutching the book. "It looks well worn." It's clear he's asking how many times I've read it, which is more than I can count.

He has to know I'm uncomfortable. "It's an older book, but I enjoy it," I defend weakly.

"Have you finished it?" He continues to watch me.

"I have. You're welcome to borrow it." I pivot and head toward the kitchen. That should end that conversation, I hope. I can't imagine him actually reading the book, he's just trying to mess with me. Why does he get under my skin so much? I could probably laugh it off if it were Oswald who asked me.

Memphis places the book on the island as if he has every intention of borrowing the damn thing. That'll teach me to put stuff away. Now I'm wondering if I left anything else out I should be worried about.

I thought showing him around would help pass the time until Oswald got back, but maybe I should have just asked if he wanted a drink or a snack or something.

"Where's your room?" His eyes scan the other doorways out of the kitchen.

"Upstairs," I chirp.

"Good. Show it to me?" He's pretending it's a question, but I have my doubts.

My stomach does that flippy floppy thing, and I agree. "Okay."

The moment my hand touches the rail to the stairs, I have second thoughts, not because I care if he sees my room, but because he's going to be behind me on the stairs and my butt is going to be in his face. Gah, I'm so weird. Do other people think about stuff like this?

I almost trip up the stairs, I hustle up them so fast. I'm breathing a little heavily when I reach the top, but I think it's mostly from nerves. I've had friends in my room before, but there was always someone home, and we're alone. This feels different.

My bedroom is in the back corner overlooking the garden, so when we pass the spare rooms, I point them out. "Bedroom, bedroom, bathroom, bathroom." When we reach my door, I just push it open for him, expecting him to look inside, but he waltzes right past me, walks over to the balcony, and tries the door, finding it locked.

I lean against the wall and watch him move to the

windows next, checking them. "I have an alarm," I tell him, a little crestfallen. I'm not sad he's worried about my safety, I'm sad that's all he seems concerned with, but I think it's helping me understand him a little more. He's a caregiver. It makes me wonder if he raised Oswald, or what happened to make him worry about things like this.

When I know him a little better and it won't be too intrusive, I'll ask. The thought strikes me as funny since he's roaming around my bedroom. When he passes the television, he taps the button on the side, and the screen blips on to show a still image of *John Wick*, asking me if I would like to resume the movie.

Memphis' brow rises, and he looks over at me. "Vampires and violence," he says as if he's just summarized my entire being because he found one of my favorite books and movies.

"You're nosy," I blurt out, then cover my lips with my fingers. One side of Memphis' lips curl up in a slight smile, but he doesn't respond to my rude remark beyond that.

"What's through there?" He points to a door.

"My bathroom, nothing fancy, and a closet." I gesture to the other door.

"Why do you live here alone?" he questions while standing near my bed.

"Because I thought I would like it. Do you live alone?"

"Technically yes, but Oz is always there, so it doesn't seem like it."

"I bet that's nice," I say genuinely.

"It can be. Do you have any siblings?"

"Not anymore."

"What does that mean?" His brows drop suddenly.

"I had an older brother, but he died when I was little. I don't remember him." This isn't something I usually share. It makes people feel sorry for me, and I don't like that.

"Damn, I'm sorry. I don't know what I would do without Oz." Memphis takes a few steps, as if he's about to leave my room, so I move to the side, but just before he reaches me, he turns back around and checks the door to the balcony again. It's still locked.

"You can open it if you want," I offer, since he seems so curious.

He flips the deadbolt and pulls the door open. Once he steps out, I enter the room so I can continue to watch him. There's a single chair and a table that I haven't really used yet. There's not much room for anything else on the small balcony, plus it overlooks the neighbor's backyard, but he seems more interested in the side of the house and the drop down as he leans over to look into the garden.

"Make sure you keep this locked," he says when he turns around to face me.

"Hello! Hello up there!" a thin voice calls.

"Oh crap." I inch backward, even though I know there's no way she could have seen me.

"Young man, hello."

Memphis looks at me, and I freeze. I should wave him in

and tell him to ignore her, but I don't, so he spins back around and acknowledges the nosy old lady from next door. They should get along quite well actually. "Hello." His voice is a little gruff.

"I'm Eddy. Your sister is a gem."

"She's not my sister."

Dang it. I don't want him telling her I live alone, so I step out onto the balcony before things can go more sideways.

"Um, hello, Eddy." I try not to stand too close to Memphis, but he's a fairly big guy, so I don't have much of a choice unless I'm going to hop on the little table.

"Waylynn, have you told your parents I stopped by?" She's glancing between me and Memphis, scrutinizing each of us in turn.

"I did." I can feel Memphis looking at the side of my face. I tap the side of his leg with the backs of my fingers, hoping he's not going to rat me out.

"Oh, I haven't seen them around, dear." Now she sounds concerned. This is going to get really awkward.

"Eddy, my parents don't live with me," I confess, then dart my gaze over to Memphis with a wide-eyed stare. I hope he goes along with this. "This is one of my roommates," I tell her in a bid to keep her from telling everyone I live alone.

"Oh, well." Her thin brows furrow deeply. "The Morleys sold to a buyer, not a broker, and there's no multiunit homes on this street." Damn it, I thought I would alleviate her concern and get her to stop asking about my parents, but now she sounds like she's about to call the mayor and try to have me evicted.

Memphis is still staring at the side of my face. He's probably trying to figure out what the hell is going on. "Oh no, I own the house, I'm not renting from a broker," I tell her. I should have just kept my mouth shut.

Memphis lifts his arm and wraps it around my waist. "We're not really roommates," he says, and while it is the truth, it also implies that we're more than roommates when he tucks me into his side. I can feel heat rising to my cheeks, not to mention I like the way his hand feels wrapped around my hip and the line of his body next to mine.

A heavy breath leaves my parted lips, and I relax against him. Heavens, he smells really good up close, and why does the heat of his body feel so amazing? You'd think I'd be pushing him away, not ready to bury my nose in the collar of his shirt.

Eddy surprises me when her lips curl and she smiles wide. "Oh, me and my Harold lived together before we got married too. It was a big deal back then. I thought we nearly killed my poor mother." She waves her hand dismissively. "I'm glad to know you won't be alone over there."

Just as she says that, Oswald turns his truck into the drive. I see Eddy go up on her toes to try to see over the hedge, but she can't see into my yard. "That's my brother, Oswald. He'll be around to keep an eye on Waylynn too," Memphis tells my neighbor while he flexes his fingers on my hip.

"Oh, how lovely! Having a close family is so important," Eddy coos up at us.

I use his arrival as an escape. "Well, we should go help with the groceries."

"I'm always around, so let me know if you need anything," she says while I try to back away, but Memphis doesn't release me so much as take me by the hips and guide me back into my bedroom.

Now I'm going to have to explain what the hell just happened. Once we're inside and I have enough space to pull away from him, I do. I don't meet his eyes as I close the door and lock it.

When I pivot to face him again, it's with an apology on my lips. "I'm so sorry. I didn't want her telling the entire neighborhood I lived alone, so I let her think my parents lived with me, but she kept asking, and then when she saw you and made the assumption, I just... I just..."

"Waylynn." Memphis takes a step closer to me and tips my chin up. "Eyes on me," he tells me and pauses for a few seconds as if to make sure I'm not going to look away.

I start rambling again. "I thought she might forget about me if—"

"She's not going to forget about you. You live next door," he interrupts with a slight smile.

"Memphis? Waylynn?" Oswald calls from downstairs.

"I didn't mean to put you on the spot like that. I'm sorry," I whisper.

"Stop telling me you're sorry." I have the urge to look away again, but he still has his finger under my chin, so I don't. "I'm happy you told her I'll be here, but she needs to mind her own business."

"Where are you guys?" Oswald calls again, but his voice is a little louder.

Memphis leans to the left to say, "Just a minute," then returns his focus to me. It's so much easier to look at him when he's not staring back at me. His eyes are blue, but a darker shade than Oswald's. I shouldn't be comparing them, and I certainly shouldn't be thinking about both of them the way I am. Why do I even like both of them when they are so vastly different?

"Let me know if she or anyone else gives you a problem," he tells me.

"Okay," I reply instead of asking what I should do when she asks why he's never around. I take a quick step back when I hear Oswald on the stairs. I don't want to have to explain what's going on between his brother and me, and I don't want to rehash the stuff with the neighbor.

"What are you guys doing?" From the corner of my eye, I can see Oswald looking between the two of us.

"She was showing me around. This is her room," Memphis tells his brother without an ounce of hesitance. "She also has a meerkat living next door."

"Really? You can't even tell she has neighbors." Oswald walks over and pulls back my curtain to see my back garden

SEEING SOUND

and part of Eddy's yard. I don't know if she's even still out there. "Wow, it looks cool from up here. It's so symmetrical." He lets the curtain fall closed and looks around my room.

I follow his gaze, wondering what he thinks. "Her room is bigger than your apartment, bro. You could fit like three beds in here." Well, that answers my question. He was guesstimating square footage. I suppose that's better than him checking all my locks. I should probably worry about Memphis, since he seems to be so concerned about my safety.

"Do you have stuff we need to unload?" I walk toward my door, expecting them to follow.

"Nah, it was just a few bags. I left them on the counter," Oswald replies with his head still swiveling. "Were you watching that or…"

"It's a good movie," I defend.

"It is." Oswald puts his hands in front of his chest, warding me off. "Just not what I would expect you to be chilling with on a Sunday afternoon."

"I watched it last night." And many nights before, but I don't tell him that.

"Just you?" Memphis slowly starts to walk toward me and the door to leave my room, thankfully.

"Yes, other than my parents, you guys and your friend are the only people I've had over since I moved in."

"No one else," Memphis says as he passes me. It serves as a reminder of our talk in the parking lot when he told me he and Oswald are the only people I should allow over.

"Memphis, you're making it seem like you don't believe her," Oswald says to his brother's back as he follows him out of my room.

"No, she knows what I meant." Those words have Oswald bouncing down the stairs after Memphis, looking for clarification about the statement, but Memphis mostly ignores the prodding *what do you mean* questions.

I trail after them, much more subdued, but I still enjoy having them here, even if they are bossy and nosy like I would imagine older brothers would be. Too bad that's not how I felt when I was cuddled up next to Memphis or when I look at Oswald.

By the time I join them in the kitchen, Memphis has most of the groceries stowed in the fridge, and Oswald is walking out of the pantry empty-handed. Dang it, I'm hungry, I was hoping we'd eat soon. I glance at the clock and realize it is much too early for dinner, but I can't wait hours to eat.

"Should I cook the chicken now?" I offer, not wanting to assume they are going to stick around all day.

"Are you trying to get rid of us, Waylynn?" Oswald hops onto one of the chairs pushed up against the island.

"No," I say too quickly. "I just don't want you to feel like you have to stay here all day, and…I'm hungry," I admit.

"We can make the chicken later. What do you want now?" Memphis asks, and it feels like he's going to try to make it for me.

"Do you guys want a sandwich or something?" I look between them on my way over to the fridge.

"I'm always down to eat," Oswald says, and his tone implies I should already know this.

"Gravlin." I think about calling him Memphis, but I can't bring myself to say it out loud, it feels too informal. "Would you like anything?"

His eyes narrow just the tiniest bit, and I pretend it's really important to look into the fridge. It takes me a second to find the lunchmeat and cheese, but I set it out on the counter with the lettuce and mayo.

When I look up, I realize Memphis is gone, and my heart falls for just a second before I see him walking out of the pantry with a loaf of bread. Oswald is smirking when I glance over at him. Crap, he caught me looking for his brother. I spin back around and grab the pickles out of the fridge and look for anything else we could use.

"Why are you just sitting there? Get some plates," Memphis instructs. I can't tell if I like how he just takes over everything, or if I'm just too intimidated to do anything about it. He's so sure of himself and confident.

"Where are the plates, Waylynn?" Oswald asks, already rounding the island.

"Right there. I would have grabbed them," I tell him, pointing to the cabinet next to the sink.

"Do you have paper so we don't make a mess?" He looks over his arm at me after opening the door, and I get stuck looking at the ropes of muscle along the back of his bicep for a second too long.

I drop my eyes to the sink and turn on the water to wash my hands. "No, but I have a dishwasher, so no worries."

Memphis nudges me to the side with his body and reaches past me to get to the soap. It smells like strawberry poundcake, and there's something amusing about knowing he's going to smell like my soap.

"Oh." I hit Memphis' shoulder when Oswald comes up from the other side and shoves his hands into the water, sandwiching me between them. I pull back after the suds are gone and stand there with my hands dripping instead of reaching for the hand towel on the bar in the tiny space left between them.

As soon as Memphis turns around, he looks at my dripping fingers and steps forward with the towel. I reach for the fabric, but he just wraps it over my hands and gently massages my fingers, drying them for me. It's strangely intimate. Hell, even sharing the sink with them felt like a big deal.

"Thanks," I mutter when I don't have an excuse to let him continue.

"Got any mustard?" Oswald asks, and it gives me a reason to step away from Memphis. Damn, he's distracting and so forward, and I'm a little worried about how much I like it.

"I'm sorry, I don't," I answer with a small wince.

"It's okay, we can get some next time." He shrugs and untwists the tie on the bread to open it. The *next time* part gives me little butterflies in my stomach.

MIND GAMES

*S*andwiches made, I lead the guys into the television room. I haven't hung out in here much, since I spend a lot of time in my room. I think I'm still getting used to having the whole house to roam, either that or I can forget I'm alone when I'm in my room.

I walk to the curve of the sectional and take a seat. It's not until my legs are folded under me that I realize I've taken the center of the couch. It's probably weird that I've put myself between them. When I lean forward to get up, Oswald stops me by asking, "Where are you going?" He falls back on the sofa, keeping his plate level and secure as he drops down right next to me.

"I just wanted to make sure there was room," I say, pretending I was just getting comfy.

Memphis walks past our legs and takes a seat on the other

side of me. He's not as close as Oswald, but he's still near enough that I can smell his cologne and reach out and touch him if I wanted.

"The remote's right there. You can turn on whatever you want." I pull a piece of bread off the corner of my sandwich and place it in my mouth.

Oswald is the one to snag the remote from the table in front of us. "What have you been watching down here?" he questions with a smirk right before hitting the power button.

"Nothing, I haven't even turned it on."

"What?" He snaps his head to the side and looks at me like I'm crazy. I shrug, not really having an explanation for him. "I would kill to have this much space to stretch out and watch the game and not have to see KJ's hairy ass."

I'm really hoping KJ is his roommate, a male roommate, or that would be unfortunate for so many reasons. "You're welcome to hang out anytime," I offer and take my first real bite of food. I'm so hungry, I'm kind of past it, and the turkey doesn't taste nearly as good as I'd hoped.

"Now you've done it," Memphis says on a sigh. "He's going to be here every day. You'll never get him to leave."

"I don't mind the company," I reply, telling the truth.

"Well, Memphis, you know where to find me." Oswald sprawls back on the sofa, placing his arm behind me on the top of the couch while keeping the other hand on the sofa with the remote.

"Yeah, well, she already told the meerkat next door I was her roommate, so I'll be right here with you."

"Do what?" Oswald sits forward so fast, his empty plate tips to the side on his lap, spilling tiny breadcrumbs on the floor and couch. "Shit, sorry."

"It's okay, I'll get it." I take both his plate and mine, hoping to escape the room so Memphis can explain while I'm gone. I'd really like to avoid that conversation.

"You are not cleaning up his mess," Memphis states and looks past me to Oswald, who is already getting up and scooping the crumbs on the couch into his palm.

"Where's your vacuum?" Oswald asks, standing from a crouched position.

"It's not a big deal," I tell him dismissively and try to move past him so I can get to the kitchen.

"For my sake, tell me where it is so I don't have to listen to him later." Oswald gives me sweet puppy dog eyes, and I fold.

"Come on." I try to shimmy past him with the plates, and he turns at the same time so my butt ends up brushing against his front while I'm navigating the space between him, the couch, and the table. I feel like apologizing, since I'm always bumping into them, but I pretend it didn't happen instead.

After putting the plates in the sink, I open the laundry room door on the other side of the kitchen. Thankfully, I don't have a mess of clothes on the floor. As I reach for the handle of my stick vacuum, Oswald lays his hand over mine. Awareness tingles up my arm, and I look over my shoulder.

He's almost close enough to kiss. My eyes drop to his lips, and in my head, I hear, *She must be loaded.* I jerk my arm back and watch his face as a curious frown slips over his features. "Everything okay?"

"Yeah, fine." I try to sound unaffected, but I don't do a great job. Here I was, thinking about kissing him, and I hear his voice in my head wondering about how much money I have. Not my finest moment.

The splash of water hitting the sink pulls me out of my head, and I remember I'm not supposed to just be staring at him. That's something a crazy person would do.

"Please let me get that." I reach toward the vacuum, but I don't get close enough to touch him.

"No way, just tell me how to turn this thing on." He tucks my Dyson closer to his chest.

"Pull the trigger right there by your finger." I point.

The machine whirrs to life for just a moment, and his eyes go wide before he releases the trigger and the sound dies just as quickly.

Oswald

Waylynn scoots back from me as I start to leave her utility room as if she's afraid I'm going to try to snatch her up. I don't know what the hell just happened, but I wish I could rewind time.

Two minutes ago, she was looking at my lips like she wondered what they tasted like, but then she jerked away as if my skin was on fire. I want to ask what happened, but she actually looks kind of freaked out.

Memphis is loading the dishwasher like he fucking lives here when I walk out of the room. I've never once seen him so comfortable in someone else's house, and we've stayed at a few. He leans back against the counter and crosses his arms, watching me as I push the weird ass vacuum back to the living room. I tip my head back toward Waylynn and give him a look, letting him know there's something up.

His eyes skip behind me, and I know he's watching her emerge from the room I just did. "You didn't need to do that," she tells him dolefully.

"Roommates are supposed to clean up after themselves."

I pretend to keep walking, but really, I just go to the other side of the doorway, where they won't be able to see me listening to their conversation. I'm familiar with that teasing tone from Memphis, and I want to know why he is so comfortable with her, plus I really want to know what this roommate business is about.

"You told her yourself, you're not really my roommate, and guests don't need to clean up after themselves," Waylynn counters.

"The idea is growing on me," Memphis tells her as if being her roommate is really an option. What the hell? Did she ask him to be her roommate? Why not me? Plus, we can't afford a place like this anyway. The only way we could afford a place like this is if I go pro, and that's not happening for a few years, if ever.

"Sure it is." Her tone is dismissive and patronizing, which is kind of weird. What am I missing? "I'm going to see if Oswald needs any help."

Oh damn. I pick up the vacuum and haul ass to the living room, hoping I can get there before she catches me eavesdropping.

Memphis

I'm tempted to stop Waylynn when she leaves the kitchen, but I let her go. I don't know what happened in the few minutes she was alone with Oz, but something did. I would have known even if he didn't tell me something was up.

I can see it in the set of her shoulders and the way her full lips are curled down at the corners, but she must not be too upset with him, because she's going to find him now, or maybe she just wants to get away from me that badly. Did I push her too much with the roommate thing? I really hope not, because there was truth to my words. I can see us here with her.

The minute she told the old lady next door I was going to be living with her, it felt fucking right, like we'd stepped into a future I didn't know I wanted so badly until it was dangled right in front of my face.

I make my way back to the living room and watch as Oz finishes cleaning the floor near the sofa. Waylynn is standing a few feet back, looking in his direction, but I know she's not seeing him. Her eyes are unfocused, and she's too busy rubbing her thumb nail along her lip.

Just as the vacuum shuts off, a phone vibrates. I tap my pocket out of habit, but it's not mine. Waylynn looks around as if she's been pulled into the present but doesn't know why. The phone buzzes again, and she eyes me and Oswald.

"It's you." I point toward her back pocket, and she slaps her hand on her ass and grabs her phone.

"I need to take this. Make yourselves comfortable," she tells us distractedly while looking at the phone and rushing from the room.

Oswald makes his way over to me while eyeing the archway she left through and whispers, "Roommate?"

At the same time, I ask, "What the hell happened?"

"I have no clue. One second, we were in the utility room and she was looking at me like she wanted me to kiss her, and the next, she jerked away from me. Maybe we're coming on too strong. Tell me about the roommate thing," he urges in a hushed whisper.

"She didn't want the lady next door knowing she lived

alone. She told her I was her roommate so she would stop asking where her parents are."

"Don't you think it's strange she lives here alone? How rich do you think she is?" He lowers his voice even more.

"I wouldn't like her living alone anywhere. I'm fucking glad she has a nice house and an alarm."

"How much do you think a house like this costs?" He scans the living room.

"I don't know," I tell him. It's not that I don't recognize that Waylynn must come from money, it's just that I don't care.

"Do you think we could ever afford a place like this?" Why is he so hung up on her house?

"Did you say something to her about it? Like ask her shit like that?" I snap in a harsh tone.

"No," he scoffs. "It's just… Why would she want us if she already has all this?" He lifts the vacuum in the air when he widens his arms, showing me the room.

Damn it, this is probably my fault. I've been telling him to watch out for people trying to take advantage of him since middle school. "I'm pretty sure any hope she might have had at us being secret heirs to a fortune were doused when she saw the truck," I deadpan.

"How come you act like you know her so well? You weren't as comfortable at Uncle Steve's as you are here, and we lived there for two years."

I dart my eyes away from his and look for Waylynn. "I

don't know. It's like I know she needs me or something. Don't ask me to explain it, because I can't do a better job than that."

Oswald nods his head. I have a feeling he gets what I'm saying, and I'm glad. Thinking about the whys of shit doesn't get you anywhere anyway. "I'm going to put this away. Who do you think was on the phone?" Oswald jiggles the vacuum.

"I don't know. Think we should go find out?" I arch one eyebrow, and Oz grins.

Waylynn

I HOLD off answering the call until the fourth ring. I didn't want to answer it in front of Oswald and Memphis. Who knows if they would have stayed quiet if I asked them to, and I don't want them to hear my one-sided conversation with my mom, where she asks me how I'm doing twenty different ways.

I'm a little breathless when I reach the top of the stairs. "Hello."

"Hey, Waylynn, is everything okay?" I don't know if she's reacting to the way I answered the phone or if this is just her first inquiry into my well-being.

"Yep, just running up the stairs. I left my phone in my room."

"Oh, okay, so how's your weekend been? Are you ready

for your classes next week?" I'm sure she assumes I spent my weekend studying. That's how I usually spent them.

"I went grocery shopping today," I offer.

"Oh, that reminds me, Beth made lasagna. I should send you some."

"That's okay." I chuckle, thinking about my mom figuring out how to ship something and keep it frozen.

"Are you still liking it there?" she asks airily. I'm starting to think she was planning on me hating it here and running back to California.

"Yeah, I like it. I like my classes. I've even made a few friends." I plop down on my bed and look out the window. Friends might be a slight exaggeration, but I feel like Oswald is pretty close. I don't know about Memphis though. He's confusing.

"You have?" she chirps. "Tell me about them."

"Well, his name—"

"His?" she interrupts.

"Yes, *his*. His name is Oswald." If she's wondering why I said his name so quietly, she doesn't ask, which I'm thankful for because I don't have any plans to tell her he's here right now. "He's in my English class, his brother is actually the TA. We've had lunch."

"Oh, that's lovely. Just the two of you?" I can practically hear how excited she is. I never really mentioned guys to her. Oh great, I thought telling her I made a friend would make her happy, but I didn't think it through. She's probably already wondering when she can meet him.

"No, his brother was there too." I hope that tamps down her expectations a little.

"Oh, the teaching assistant, he must be smart," she coos. "What are his plans for the future?"

"I don't know." I sigh dramatically.

"Well, that will give you something else to talk about. You know how much men like talking about themselves."

"Yeah, how's James?" I'm hoping she will let me change the subject when I ask about my dad by name to rib her.

"He's off with your grandfather this week, I may go out to see them. Have you talked with Dr. Tobin or Maxwell?" She's derailed, just not the way I would have hoped.

"No, my appointment isn't until Wednesday afternoon. Every two weeks," I remind her.

"Is your medicine okay? Do you need a refill?"

"Yes, it's fine, and no. I'll take it to a local pharmacy when I do." There's no way I'm going to tell her I've heard the voices again a few times, like just a few minutes ago.

"Are you sure? I can have it shipped right to you." When she offers things like this, it makes me think she's embarrassed that I'm on medication, but I know she thinks she's helping.

"No, it's okay. I'd rather take care of it myself."

"Okay… I miss you. I even miss seeing your shoes." She tinkles out a laugh filled with so much emotion.

"I miss you too. I'll come back soon," I promise, but it feels like a lie, even though it's not my intention.

"Thanksgiving? Unless you're going to host, then we can come to you and meet some of your friends!" she replies enthusiastically.

That is the last thing I want to happen. "Maybe," I hedge, giving her the smidgen of hope she wants.

"Well, I won't keep you. I just wanted to let you know I was thinking about you and see how you were."

"Thanks for calling me."

"I love you, Waylynn. Call me if you need anything."

"Love you too, bye."

I hit the end button, and the sadness that was weighing me down lightens as I disconnect from her. I toss my phone on the bed and just breathe for a few seconds until I feel more like myself.

I glance toward the door, hating that I know I should put distance between myself, Oswald, and Memphis because something about them triggers the voices. The association is too clear to ignore after what just happened in the laundry room. Why do the voices have to sound so much like theirs?

A creak from the stairs has me grabbing my phone and hopping up from the bed. I might as well enjoy the little time I have with them today. It's not like I'm going to go down there and kick them out.

VACANT

Memphis

When Waylynn comes downstairs, she's distant, even more so than before the call. Oz and I stick around, watch TV, and eventually make dinner. She goes through the motions, smiling when she should and engaging in small talk, but everything is only on the surface.

After dinner is cleaned up, she starts to get fidgety. I can tell she wants us to go, but I'm hesitant to leave her. Hell, I'm reluctant.

Oswald is picking up on the same cues I am. We both know when we're not wanted, but the difference here is I don't think that's really what's going on. Something certainly spooked Waylynn, and I have every intention of finding out what that was, but then my brother says, "We should get going."

I let him see my aggravation, but he still rises from the chair and lays a hand on my shoulder. "Thank you for letting us crash at your place all day. We'll let you get some rest."

I huff under my breath and push up to stand, dislodging his hand. "I'll see you in class tomorrow." It ends up coming out like a threat, but only because I'm pissed at Oz.

"Yes, Mr. Gravlin." Waylynn bobs her head twice, reacting to my tone.

The way Oswald jerks his head around to look at her draws my attention. Damn it, that's mine. I grunt and grab his arm to haul him toward the door, suddenly in a rush when I wasn't before.

"See you tomorrow," he calls as I shove him out. Once we're in the truck, he murmurs, "That was hot as fuck."

"Shut up," I mumble dejectedly. I don't need him to tell me. I get a fucking hard-on every time she says shit like that.

"Do you think she went to a Catholic school with all girls and little skirts?" He's looking at the door wistfully. "Or a boarding school where—"

"Stop," I tell him, but the thoughts are already in my head, and I'm having a hard time not picturing sweet Waylynn in white thigh highs and not much else. "Who do you think was on the phone?"

"I don't know, someone from back home. You think it was a boyfriend?"

"I don't know. She said she missed them and told them she loved them." I almost feel bad for listening to her call, almost.

"She seemed kind of sad after too," Oz agrees. "It could have been her family. I hear my teammates say shit like that sometimes to theirs."

Damn, it's been so long since I thought of anyone else besides Oswald when it comes to family, that didn't even cross my mind, or maybe it's just because it involves her and I can't seem to think straight where she's concerned. "You're right—it was probably her family." That makes me feel better.

"Do you think we should have asked her what was wrong? I mean, it felt like we were already barging into her life as it was. I didn't want to push her," Oz muses.

"I didn't ask because I knew she wouldn't tell us. I was going to see if she would soften up if we stayed longer."

"How much longer? We've been there most of the day." He snorts.

"Are you sure you don't know what happened? You didn't say something?"

"Unless she thinks I'm a dumbass because I didn't know how to work the vacuum, I've got nothing."

"Am I taking you to the dorm?" I question as we leave her quiet neighborhood for sorority row.

"I don't have my shit," he says in lieu of answering.

"So that means you want me to wait for you while you go in and get your shit."

"If you don't want to, I can get up early and grab my stuff in the morning." He avoids answering again.

"It's fine, just be quick. I don't want to be waiting out here forever." I sigh.

"You can come in and say hi to some of your old friends," he offers jokingly. I never made a ton of friends. I hung out and partied with a few people, but not friends. I only have two of those—Bates and Oz.

"I'm good. Bates called me earlier, and I didn't pick up," I tell him so he knows I have something to do.

"Oh shit, we probably should have invited him to Waylynn's. We always do Sunday dinner if he doesn't have a show." Oswald is looking at me instead of getting out of the car.

"He knew there was a possibility we wouldn't make it back with the game being out of town."

"Why didn't he come?"

"He had to work Saturday. It was overtime. Go, I want to get home," I urge.

Oz slams the truck door and jogs down the long path to the south quad, and I shoot a text off to Bates.

Me: Headed home.

A text bubble pops up just a few seconds later.

Bates: Food tomorrow? Does the knucklehead have practice?

Me: Yes, probably since they lost. Oz was pissed he didn't get any field time. South quad for dinner? I'll sneak your broke ass in like old times.

Bates: Free food? I'm there, and I make more than you, asshole.

I chuckle at the last part. He sure does. He spent the last four years apprenticing to become an electrician. He's scheduled to take his test next month to become a journeyman. When he passes, he'll be making really good money.

Me: Text me when you get off.

Bates: You really want to know that shit?

I groan at the bad joke.

Me: No, we both know you'd be texting me ten times a day. Text me when you get off work!

I drop my phone to the seat when Oz climbs back in. He doesn't even have his bag, just a wad of clothes. I bet he didn't unpack when he got home—not that I'm much better, my shit is still in the backseat.

He mutters, "Ready," when he pulls the door closed.

"Bates is going to meet us at your dorm to eat after work. What time do you think you'll be done with practice?"

Oz slams his head back against the headrest. "Hell if I know. Tomorrow is going to suck balls."

"I know, that's why I thought it would be good to meet there. You can just come down after your shower or whatever."

"I almost don't want to go to lifting in the morning

because I know they are going to push us at afternoon practice."

"That might piss them off more," I warn. He's been working with the coaches all summer, so he knows what he can and can't get away with.

He grunts and knocks his head back again. "I hate Mondays after a loss."

"You hate any day after a loss. Just show them what a mistake they made by not putting you in."

"Fucking Bevins, he was a wreck, but they still put him out there play after play."

I'm surprised by how little he talked about football at Waylynn's. I wonder if it was on purpose or if it just didn't dominate his thoughts like it usually does. "They'll start to trust you more, just give it time," I tell him as I pull into the small parking lot of my apartment. When I kill the truck, I look up at the building. It's just a square box made of brick with windows that needed to be replaced ten years ago and iffy AC, but it's mine—well, mine and Oswald's, since we end up sharing everything.

"I wish it was Saturday night instead of Sunday," Oz says when he pushes the door open with his leg.

"Another day would be nice," I agree.

"I know what I would do. I would be right back at Waylynn's house, but I'd ask what the hell was wrong this time," he mumbles.

"I couldn't believe it when I saw her at the store. It's fucking strange how often she turns up."

"I feel like I'm always hunting her down." He moves to the side as I unlock the door to the apartment and use my foot to push it open.

"You have revealed some stalkerish tendencies," I tease.

"Fuck you," he retorts with no heat to his words. "You're the one that gets all *'let me tuck you in my pocket and growl at anyone that looks at you'* with her."

He's not wrong. Waylynn brings something out in me I didn't know existed—the capability to care for someone other than Oz and Bates. "Someone needs to take care of her."

"Does she really need someone though? I mean, it sure seems like she has her shit together," Oz counters as he tosses his bag on the futon.

"How many times have I told you money doesn't buy happiness?"

"About as many times as you reminded me that I need to do something with my life so you wouldn't have to support me forever," he fires back.

"I just meant not to expect shit to be handed to you. If you want something, go after it, but I do think she needs someone—"

Oswald clears his throat, interrupting me.

"Possibly more than one someone in her life," I amend.

"She seems chill, but also kind of sweet and innocent," he says, and I know where his thoughts have gone. He's wondering what she will think when she finds out we both want her.

Oz is the only real family I have left, and we decided years ago that whoever came into our lives would need to accept us both. At the time, I was thinking I didn't want to lose my brother to a girl, but as the years passed, the idea changed into maybe just having one girl we could both be with. I'm not exactly sure how it happened, maybe it started as a joke, but the idea stuck and here we are, which works for me. I don't know if I'm even capable of loving someone the way they should be loved, and Oz can, so as long as he's happy, I can be too.

"What's not to like? Everyone loves a two for one special." I make light of the situation because I don't want him to worry. I think we can make her see the benefits of being with both of us, plus I'm not sure she really has another option. I'm not giving up.

Waylynn

ONCE THE GUYS LEAVE, I lock the door and set the alarm. It's not as if I'm worried they are going to return, but the house feels so empty now that I'm alone—another reason I shouldn't have let them come over.

When I pull the covers up to my chin after climbing into

bed, loneliness threatens to engulf me. I've already tried all my usual tricks, like a comfort movie and the radio while I was in the shower, but I still can't get used to how empty the house feels now. Maybe it's knowing I don't plan on having them back that has me feeling this way.

Instead of dwelling on what isn't, I revert back to my old counting technique and hope I can fall asleep quickly.

~

BUTTERFLIES EXPLODE in my stomach the moment I walk into English and see Memphis standing at the front of the room. It wasn't my intention to look for him. The plan was to keep my head down and sit on the opposite side of the room and hope neither he nor Oswald noticed me, but that's all blown to hell in the first three seconds.

His eyes track me as I navigate the back of the room, taking me as far from him as possible. I don't mean to keep peering up at him, but I can't help it. When he leans his head back and crosses his arms over his chest, I almost lose my nerve to sit down where I want, but I hastily drop my bag on the ground and slip into the farthest outside seat. The scowl I see from the corner of my eye leads me to believe I've disappointed him.

The seats near me slowly start to fill in, and before I know it, there's low chattering all around the room. It makes me feel brave enough to lift my head up, and a tiny sense of relief has me letting out a sigh when I don't find Memphis watching me. It's short-lived, however, because I feel fingers touch my shoulder, and I instinctively look up. His dark blue eyes are only a few inches away when he says, "Eyes on me," so quietly, I can barely hear him. Then he's walking down to the stage, leaving me to wonder if he really said it out loud or if my mind is playing tricks on me again.

"You're in my seat." Oswald's voice comes before I even have time to recover from his brother's.

The guy next to me looks over at Oswald, who's standing on the other side of me with a furrowed brow, and his mouth drops open to say, "Huh?"

I shrink down in my seat.

"There's an open seat right there." Oswald points a few rows down to the center of a pretty full row instead of repeating himself.

"You could have told me you were saving the seat." The guy directs his ire toward me as he snatches up his stuff and begins to rise.

"Sorry," I mumble. This is not going to plan, and I don't know how to get it back on track.

"Don't apologize. I'm the one who told him to move, and he didn't say shit to me." Oswald barely moves, so the guy has to work to get around him, and he stares him down the entire time. If I could melt into a puddle, I would. I feel like everyone around us is watching and whispering.

If I really want to avoid these two, I'm going to have to

drop the class. I can see that now. Oswald drops into the recently vacated seat and lets out an *oof*. I glance over at him to see sweat dotting his temples. He must have had to run. Maybe he overslept. He still looks tired, actually.

"Do you need a drink?" I offer. The embarrassment I was feeling begins to fade as concern for him takes over. Did he get any sleep last night?

"As long as it's not coffee. I just drank about a gallon of water, and I'll probably piss myself before class is over if I have a diuretic."

I pull my water jug from my bag and hand it over to him. "It's just water, and I haven't had any, so it's clean," I inform him.

Oswald squints at me and takes the purple jug one-handed. As I'm pulling my arm back, he darts forward and swipes his tongue across my lips. I'm so surprised, I jerk back, but my first instinct is to lick my lips. His blue eyes track the path of my tongue, and he says, "Your lips and hands can touch anything you like."

My stomach does this hollowing out thing, and I feel a tingle between my legs. Holy crap, that was... I don't know how to put it into words other than *hot*. I look away from him because I don't know what to say, and he can probably see how stunned I am, yet he's acting like it's no big deal.

I flip open my laptop and enter the password to give myself something to focus on other than Oswald. Thankfully, the clock tells me class should start any minute, so now I just have to sit next to him for ninety minutes and act normal, which is fairly challenging for a girl who everyone thinks is slightly off her rocker.

"If I could have your attention." Memphis' voice rings through the room. I don't want to look up from my computer, but I know I need to. Keeping my head lowered, I peer beyond my screen, noting only Memphis near the lectern.

Great, he must be teaching the entire class. Why the heck does he have to make boring light brown slacks and a white button-up so distracting? Even worse, what if he saw what Oswald did? I can't meet his eyes. I doubt I'm going to be able to concentrate on what he's saying.

Memphis starts the lecture, and I find myself watching his every move. While Hilbrand seems to favor standing at the podium, he's much more animated. He uses the entire floor space to pace and gesture while speaking. I'm surprised how engaging he is with the class, allowing for more discussion and interaction among the students. Not only is it a different style than Hilbrand's, it's also surprising to see him being so open in this environment. He seemed much more standoffish the previous times he spoke, or maybe that was because he was being accosted.

I find myself taking notes as he speaks, fully engaged in what he's saying and captivated by his passion for the subject, or at least the ability to make it seem that way.

Several times through the class, I feel like he looks directly at me. Once, I even see his chin lower as if he's nodding in approval that I'm paying attention, but I could just be seeing something that's not there.

When he walks past the lectern and closes the book he never really went to for information, I glance at the clock in the corner of my computer, shocked to see it's nearly eleven-thirty.

Memphis reminds us what papers are due and what reading materials we're responsible for. As soon as he's done speaking, I see the slight change in his features, his eyes shrinking to a shrewder gaze. It seems like he's shuttering up, and even his posture shifts, becoming more intimidating and unapproachable, yet it doesn't stop someone from asking, "Will you be teaching the remainder of the classes?"

"Not all," he replies, and I swear even his voice has changed. He's no longer welcoming questions or dialogue. Thankfully, no one yells out anything inappropriate as the students start to leave. It would really diminish what just happened in this room and prove they didn't respect him.

I feel Oswald's gaze on the side of my face and remember I'm supposed to be packing up myself. When I close the top of my laptop a little too forcefully, it makes a loud snapping noise which draws more attention than I want, so I pretend not to notice as I start cramming things in my bag.

"Want some help?" Oswald offers. His bag is already looped over his chest, and he's standing.

"I've got it, thanks," I reply, although my fumbling hands would have me think otherwise.

"Lunch, you pick today," he says as if it's a foregone conclusion that we're already going out together.

"Um…" I need to be resolute, but words are failing me. I don't want to disappoint him.

"Okay, I'll pick." Oswald pulls the strap of my bag from my fingers the moment I try to hoist it over my shoulder.

"I don't think I have time today. I have to study for math." My excuse sounds lame, even to me.

"I'll help you," Memphis says over my shoulder. When I look up, he's staring at his brother, but I know his words were meant for me.

"No, I don't want to take up your time, you guys should go."

"Meet me at the truck," he instructs, still only looking at Oswald, but I get the feeling he's talking to me.

"Let's go before he hauls you over his shoulder and gets himself in trouble," Oswald says quietly while urging me forward with his body. I scoot past Memphis, who steps to the side, and then he peers down at me as if to say, *I'd do it too.*

Once we're out of the room, I open my mouth to tell Oswald I can't go, but he drops his arm over my shoulders and hauls me close to his side, and I lose my train of thought. He smells good, not the same as Memphis, more like fresh soap, and I find myself inhaling to catch another whiff.

"Luckily for us, Memphis is a whiz at math, so he'll have you straightened out in no time."

"Oh no, that's okay. I signed up for the study group. I just don't want to get behind."

"We won't let you. You won't even need the study group." Oswald keeps shooting down all my denials.

"Really, it's okay. I'm sure he has enough to do." I try to sound steadfast.

He ignores my last statement and changes the subject. "What do you feel like eating?"

"I..." I think about working up another denial, but it seems pretty pointless at this rate. "Anything is fine."

"Oh, no, no. That will not do at all, Wavy baby."

I stop dead in my tracks, causing Oswald to look down at me when my movement dislodges his arm from around my shoulders. "Wavy baby?" I question.

Oswald has the nerve to look pleased with himself. "It rhymes," he says like I somehow missed that fact, "and flows, Wavy baby."

I'm still staring at him at a total loss for what to say. That has to be the silliest term of endearment ever.

"Come on, he's going to beat us to the truck." I allow him to tug me along when he grabs for my hand this time. Even with his bag and mine, he still walks faster than me.

"How come you were so tired this morning?" If I'm here, I might as well make conversation, plus I selfishly want to know what he was doing last night.

"Lifting." He groans as if he hates even thinking about it.

"Lifting what?" We're at the truck now, and he opens the

door and urges me to get in with a little pressure on the small of my back.

Oswald tosses our bags in the rear seat, climbs in next to me, and slams the door before answering. "Weights."

"Oh, at the gym," I surmise in a short breath. It's hot as heck in the truck.

"It's conditioning for football," he says softly.

"Do you play here?" I remember the guy from math saying something about sports to Oswald that first day and him mentioning practice, but we've never talked about it.

"Someday," he answers as Memphis gets into the truck.

"Someday what? Where are we going?" He slides the key into the ignition.

Oswald skips over the first part of the question. "It's Waylynn's turn to pick."

"Please just pick. I have no idea where to go." I make the mistake of turning my head to plead with Memphis, and he's so close, I can see the flecks of gold in his blue irises.

I drop my gaze and face the front again. My god, they are both so attractive. I know why I've been thinking about them too much, and how good-looking they are is only a very small part of it. It might actually be easier to be around them if they weren't so damn gorgeous. I've been so busy wondering why their voices are so familiar that I haven't actually given thought to why they give me the time of day. Why do they hover over me like two older brothers?

"How come you guys invite me to lunch and to hang out?"

"What?" I can tell Oswald is gawking at me, even though I'm not looking at him.

I shrug, feeling uncomfortable, but I need to know the answer now that the question is in my head. It's completely illogical to think they know anything about my past or feel sorry for me because of it, but my brain is telling me that must be the reason they are making an effort to be my friend.

Oswald looks over my head at his brother. Gosh, I wish I would have just kept my mouth shut.

"You act like we're the only people who have talked to you," Oswald replies.

"No, but you are the only ones who do stuff like this."

"Like what?" Memphis asks.

He's going to make me say it, ugh. "Make me go to lunch and actually seek me out."

"Yeah, and why would that be?" Memphis coaxes like he thinks I already have an answer.

"I don't know, that's why I asked." I know I'm not the picture of a dream girl. My jean size is in the double digits, and while I know slim thick is a thing, my stomach isn't flat enough for that body type.

It's not like I think I'm a troll, my mother blessed me with her pretty features, but I have my dad's round face, so while I'm pretty, I'm not beautiful. I'm the friend, the safe girl to bring your boyfriend around, and I've always been okay with that. I've never really wanted to be too close to anyone or have a boyfriend because I come with a lot of baggage.

How do you explain to your boyfriend you won't be around for several weeks because your parents think it's best you go back to in-person treatment because your medicine isn't working to diminish the voices in your head? There are only so many times you can pretend to be on vacation before people close to you start asking questions.

"Why do you think we want to spend time with you?" Memphis goads again.

"I just told you I don't know." I can honestly say I don't think it has anything to do with my money. They couldn't have known I come from a very wealthy family the first time they invited me to lunch.

Memphis pulls into a parking lot and turns off the truck. I expect one of them to open the door, but they just sit there. The silence stretches until it becomes as oppressive as the heat in the cab of the truck.

Finally, Oswald says, "You might think I'm crazy if I tell you."

I jerk my head to the right and gawk at him. I want to ask him why he would use that particular word, but my tongue is glued to the roof of my mouth. I don't want to say anything that will make him think I'm the one that's insane, like *do you hear voices when it's really quiet too?* When I'm confident I'm not going to blurt the wrong thing out, I tell him, "I won't think you're crazy, I promise."

Oswald's features soften, and I realize his words were just a turn of phrase, not something deeper like I imagined, but something in my tone or words must have reflected how serious I was. "There's just something about you, I like being around you," he admits, and I feel like his confession is more authentic than he originally planned before I responded like I did.

"We both do," comes from behind me.

A wide smile crosses Oswald's features, and he reaches for the door handle of the truck. "Let's eat. I'm starving."

"You're always starving," Memphis grumbles indulgently, and just like that, the serious moment is gone.

As we walk toward a restaurant, I realize two things—one, I would probably let them take me anywhere, and two, I'm not going to be able to give them up, despite how unhealthy it is, no matter what I keep telling myself. They make me feel something, something other than crazy, which is the exact opposite of how I should feel, considering I think they make my symptoms worse.

RISKY

Memphis

Waylynn follows Oz out of the truck, and I'm right behind them, but I can't stop thinking about the way she sounded when she promised not to think Oswald was crazy when he was teasing her. It was a vow if I've ever heard one.

Oz pulls open the door to the dumpy diner we've been going to for years. It's farther from school, but not nearly as busy as all the restaurants around campus, so it's an even trade off.

"Have a seat. Someone will be right with you," a woman calls as she passes us with a stained coffee pot. Waylynn hangs back, ensuring that we pick the table. There's a big part of me that likes that she does little things like that, because it makes me feel like she trusts us.

I place my hand on the small of her back to guide her to a booth in the back corner. When I stop, she naturally slides in and scoots toward the wall. I hesitate for a moment. I want to sit next to her and feel the heat of her leg pressed against mine, but I really shouldn't. I'm already crossing lines I shouldn't with her being my student. Oz happily sits down next to her when I sit on the opposite side of the table.

Just like I did when we were in class, I can pretend I'm here with my brother, who I received permission to teach when Hilbrand's original TA left for a different position two weeks before the class started, since he was already enrolled in the course. Not that I think anyone here would notice who we are, but I can't get too comfortable.

I hand Waylynn a menu, and Oz reaches for one himself. I watch her eyes scan the plastic up and down before they lift and land on me. I don't look away when she catches me watching her.

She tucks a piece of hair behind her ear and moves her gaze from mine. "What are you getting?"

A hard-on, I think, but I answer, "Country fried steak." Waylynn's eyes go really wide, and she dips her head a little more. I have no idea why the tops of her cheeks are slightly pink, but it looks good on her.

"Hot turkey sandwich," Oswald says and pushes his menu away.

"What do you want?" I demand. Hell, that did not sound like I was asking about food.

"Um..."

I've noticed she stammers a little when she's flustered.

"Anything sound good?" Oz leans closer to her, pretending to look at the menu.

"I like lasagna." She makes it sound like a question. I scan the menu, noting the lack of Italian options, and decide to take her somewhere that will have it tomorrow. Shit, I probably won't see her tomorrow. I don't like that.

"You should have said that when I asked what you wanted earlier." Oz bumps her shoulder playfully. "That'll teach you to speak up."

"Next time." I level her with my stare. I'm already trying to figure out how to make sure next time is tomorrow.

The waitress makes her way over to us, setting the dishes she just cleared on the table behind us and grabbing a notepad from her apron. "Afternoon, what can I get ya?" Her question comes out perfunctory before she even looks up. I reach for the menus to hand her ours, prepared to tell her we need a few more minutes so Waylynn can decide, but the waitress says, "Gravlin," softly, like she knows me, but I have no clue who she is. Oswald looks over and his eyes narrow. It's not me she knows, it's him.

"Hey," he says really slowly. There's not a lot of recognition going on. I hope this isn't some chick he hooked up with. This could go bad quickly.

The girl licks her bottom lip, and her eyes dart to Waylynn briefly before she focuses back on my brother. "Hey, Oz, I haven't seen you in a while." Her voice is noticeably softer.

Oswald tilts his head to the side right before his eyes widen just a little. "Wait, you're Jackson's sister, right? How is he?"

The girl's shoulders fall, as does the curl of her lips. "Right, Mickey. He's doing okay. Going to Central." Her voice is a little flat, but there's still a gleam of hope in her eyes.

Waylynn keeps her eyes on the menu, shielding her face a little and seeming like she wants to disappear altogether, especially when she sinks lower in the seat.

"Have you decided yet?" I brush the tip of my finger along hers, which is curled around the menu, to get her attention.

She pushes the plastic to the side and meets my eyes. "I'll have what you're having, please." Her voice is soft, but not in the same way the waitress' was. She's not trying to sound breathy and sweet, she's just trying to be quiet.

I take her menu from her hand so she can't keep hiding behind it and hold it up to the girl, who's trying to work up the courage to be more obvious while flirting with my brother, even though he has a girl sitting right next to him. The waitress fumbles for just a second, then takes the menu, seeming to remember there's a reason she's here. "Let me grab your drink orders."

"We're ready to order," I tell her so she can't slip away before we finish.

"Oh, okay." She rearranges the menus again as she tries to get her pen from her apron, her face turning red as she finally just sets the plastic-coated paper on the table behind us.

"For you?" She blinks several times while looking at me.

"We'll both have the country fried steak, with hash browns and wheat toast. What would you like to drink?" I direct my question to Waylynn.

"Water with lemon, please." She makes eye contact with the waitress as she speaks.

"I'll have the same. Oswald?"

"I'll have a water, no lemon, and the hot turkey sandwich, double the meat and gravy."

The waitress finishes writing our orders down, then smiles at Oz. "I'll get this right in and be back with your drinks."

"I played ball with her brother," Oz tells us the moment she walks away from the table, explaining what is already obvious.

"A lot of people know you from football, but you haven't mentioned it much." Waylynn's shoulders come up high near her ears, as if she's pushing against the bench seat with her hands.

"I guess." Oz shrugs. "But that's all they really know about me."

"Water, no lemon." The waitress places Oswald's drink down in front of him first. "Two with lemon." Waylynn's glass gets left in the center of the table, so Oz moves it closer to her while the waitress passes out the straws in the same order. "It shouldn't be too long, we're not very busy."

"Great, thanks." Oz gives her a placating smile, then turns his attention back toward the table. She stands there for just a second longer than she should before striding away. I watch her walk over to another waitress near the front of the restaurant and say something before looking back in our direction. She's still all smiles for now, and I want to keep it that way while she has access to our food.

"You do that too?" Oz wrinkles up his nose while Waylynn squeezes her lemon into her water, then drops the tiny sliver into her glass.

"It's good, and good for you," she tells him while taking a sip.

I can't help but say, "Told you."

"Now he's gloating." Oz waves his hand toward me, which makes Waylynn look in my direction at the exact moment she licks the water from her lips. I know it's not meant to be seductive, but that doesn't mean it isn't.

If I want her this badly when I haven't even touched her, then how bad is it going to be when I have? She's going to consume me.

There's a significant pause, like she can feel the tension between us just as much as I can, and her eyes lower to the table. "Eyes up, Waylynn." She hesitates for just a second, then peers up at me from under her lashes. The words *good girl* form in my mind, and I just manage to keep the thoughts from slipping past my lips. I have no idea what her reaction would be, but I know I'm not prepared for it—not here, not now.

Oz throws his arm over her shoulders and pulls her back against his chest a little. "Don't be afraid to tell him he's being too bossy," he says softly near her ear.

Her eyes stay trained on mine, but she settles deeper into his embrace. The stiffness of her shoulders relaxes as the tension in her body wanes. "I like to know I have your attention," I confess.

"You do," Waylynn replies, and I'll be damned if the simple response, spoken with conviction, doesn't give me an ego boost.

The waitress returns to the table with a platter of cheese sticks surrounding a large side of ranch. When she sets them on the table, we all look at her. "We didn't order any appetizers," Oz tells her with his arm still curled around Waylynn.

"Oh, I know. I just remember you used to really like them." She wrings her hands in her apron.

"Thanks?" Oswald says, then looks over at me like I'm going to be of some help.

"Yeah, it's no big deal at all. Your food should be up soon." She backs away slowly as if she's waiting for something else.

Oz leans over the table, pulling Waylynn with him, and whispers, "Do you think these are safe to eat?"

"I don't think she roofied the cheese sticks," I deadpan, then grab one off the plate to eat it. Oz looks over at Waylynn, who's still tucked into his side, and gives a lazy shrug before grabbing one himself and dunking it in the ranch.

"Want a bite?" He offers it to Waylynn first, but she just shakes her head, so he eats half of it in one go.

When our lunch arrives, Waylynn stares at the massive amount of food on her plate for a solid ten seconds, then looks up at me. "What's country fried steak?"

I start to chuckle, but she looks completely serious. I can't blame her for asking if she's never had it. There's a mess of gravy dripping off the side of the dish, making the meat indiscernible, and the hash browns are smothered too. "It's beef, fried like chicken, covered in gravy."

Waylynn looks down again and swallows. The waitress rushes back to the table and sets two more plates down with buttered wheat toast. "Does everything look okay?" she asks with her hands on her hips.

"We're good," I tell her dismissively.

"I'll check on you in a few," she adds, but I'm already ignoring her.

"You don't have to eat it if you don't like it," I tell Waylynn as she takes a deep breath and unravels her napkin wrapped silverware and places the napkin under the table, probably over her lap.

. . .

Waylynn

"It's so good." Oswald elongates the word and cuts a hunk of turkey with his fork before shoving it in his mouth.

I can feel Memphis watching me as I cut a sliver of meat from the steak and bring it to my lips.

"Well, do you want something else?" he urges after I chew a few times.

I bring my napkin up and dab my lips. If I would have known this was so messy, I would have definitely picked something else, but I was too busy wondering how well Oswald knew the waitress to think about food. "No, no," I reply when I don't have food in my mouth. I wouldn't order anything else even if I hated this, and I don't. I like the pepperiness of the gravy. I just wish the meat wasn't so chewy and dense. "It's good," I finish.

Memphis narrows his eyes on me and accuses, "You don't lie well."

"I like the gravy," I say instead, and he nods his head once as if he believes me now.

"Do you want some of mine?" Oswald kindly offers with a bite already on his fork.

"No, eat your lunch. I'm good." I reach for a triangle of toast and dip the corner into the gravy.

"Just try it," he coaxes while moving the fork closer.

"Fine." I can't remember a time when anyone has ever fed

me, but I might as well get it over with, since neither Oswald nor Memphis give up when they want something.

Mickey, the waitress, appears at the side of the table as soon as I open my mouth. This entire time, she's been staring at Oswald, but now she's looking at me. Perfect timing.

I close my mouth around the fork and pull back quickly. "It's good, right?" Oswald says, seemingly unaware that the girl with the obvious crush is back. Not that I blame her, Oswald is more than crush worthy.

"It's good," I agree, even though I can't even recall what it tasted like. I just wanted to get it out of my mouth as soon as possible.

"How is everything?" she asks with a plastic smile.

"We'll let you know if we need anything," Memphis tells her in the no-nonsense voice I've heard him use in class.

"Great," she mumbles and leaves the table hurriedly. I don't know if I should feel sorry for her or relieved that Memphis dismissed her.

"Tell me about your math class. What are you having trouble with?" Memphis says between bites.

"I'm not," I tell him. "I just don't want to get behind."

"Standard level?" he asks.

"Yes." Although, anything with the name calculus in the title does not seem standard to me.

"If you need me, all you have to do is call, but first you'll have to unblock my number." Memphis' brows rise in a clear challenge.

I want to pretend I don't know what he's talking about, but that would be a lie. I could try to act like I didn't know the number belonged to him, but again, I think the effort would be wasted.

"Mine too," Oswald adds, proving he knew I blocked him as well. This is embarrassing.

"Okay, but I signed up for the study group. I think I'll be fine," I tell them again while grazing over the whole blocked numbers thing.

"The offer stands, but I still need you to unblock our numbers," Memphis says and continues eating. I poke around my meat a little more but end up only really eating the toast and gravy with a few bites of hash browns.

When the waitress comes back, things get a little more awkward. "How was everything?" She directs her question to both guys and ignores me.

"Good, I think my girl needs a box." Oswald wraps his arm over my shoulders and pulls me close to his side again.

She inhales heavily and sighs. "Oh, okay." I know what he's doing, I did the same thing to Memphis with Eddy, but my heart is still beating really fast, and it doesn't diminish how much I like the feeling of him calling me his girl.

"One bill then?" She glances at Memphis for a second.

I open my mouth to say no, but that would ruin the illusion Oswald just created. "Yeah," Oswald answers for the group.

"I'll be right back with that box and the bill." Mickey turns to leave, and her smile slips.

"I should have let her know what was up the second she got all googly," Oswald mutters under his breath.

I reach for my purse and pull out my wallet, making sure my pill bottle isn't visible, then I place a twenty on the table before she can come back. "We invited you, plus you fed us yesterday." Memphis pushes the money back toward me with the tip of his finger.

"You cooked and showed me how to make it for myself," I argue and push the money back.

"Waylynn." Memphis lowers his voice and leans over the table. "Put that money back in your purse. We are buying." One brow tips up, and the edge in his tone is similar to the voice he uses at school—intimidating.

"Yes, sir," I say and drop my eyes while retrieving the money to tuck it back in my bag.

I'm so close to Oswald, I can feel him shaking his head, but I pretend not to notice whatever secret conversation they seem to be having while I'm occupied.

"No rush, I can take this up whenever you're ready," Mickey says, sliding the bill, face down, to the center of the table. Memphis lays a card over top of the receipt without even looking at the bill.

It's ironic, really. Pretty much anyone I used to hang around came from families just like mine, and most of them were the last to offer to pay a bill, yet I know that's not the case for Memphis and Oswald, and they are buying me lunch.

"Thank you, my treat next time."

"Is that your way of inviting us to dinner tonight?" Oswald rubs my arm while looking down at me.

"If—"

"We can't tonight," Memphis interrupts before I can finish.

I swallow the invite I was going to extend as the waitress returns with Memphis' card, a pen, and a box. "I have class this afternoon, I'm not going to be able to take this with me." I feel guilty for wasting the food, especially since they paid for it.

"I'll take it." Oswald grabs the box from the waitress. "Will you put it in the fridge for me until later?" he asks Memphis.

"Do you honestly think it's going to make it back to school?" he deadpans as Oswald forks a bite into his mouth.

"If we had more time, it wouldn't, but Wavy has class."

I internally cringe a little at the nickname, but at least he left out the baby part. I peer up at Memphis to see what his reaction is going to be. It doesn't disappoint. His brows are raised high on his forehead. "Wavy?" he questions while pulling the receipt over to sign.

"Got a problem with that?" Oswald takes his arm from my shoulders and lifts the plate so he can slide the food into the box.

"No, I just prefer her name." Memphis pushes the signed bill toward the edge of the table and puts his card back into a slim wallet.

"Well, I like Wavy baby." Oswald's tongue pokes out the

side of his lips as he concentrates to get the leftover gravy on top of the meat.

"It rhymes." Memphis sounds affronted for me.

"I know, it rolls right off my tongue. Wavy baby." Oswald sighs softly. I have to admit, it does sound sweet the way he says it, and I like the baby part more than Wavy.

"Come here." Memphis slips from the booth and motions for me to come nearer to him as Oswald rises from the seat. When I get close, he leans in so his mouth is near my ear. I fight to suppress a shiver as his warm breath fans over my neck and he mumbles, "Let's make him walk back."

When I look up, Mickey is staring at me and Memphis with her head tilted to the side. She's probably wondering why the brother of the guy that just called me his girl is whispering into my ear and I'm looking like I'm about to faint.

Even though Oswald isn't really my boyfriend, I feel ashamed of my reaction, and it gets worse when Oswald reaches for my hand as we walk past the waitress. She probably thinks I'm cheating on him. *Great.*

DISTRACTIONS

Oz

WAYLYNN IS JITTERY AFTER LUNCH. It's like she can't wait to get out of the truck. The moment we make it back to school, she's angled toward me, ready to go as fast as possible.

"Waylynn." Her body stiffens when Memphis curls his hand over her thigh just above the knee. "Unblock our numbers before you go."

She lets out a heavy breath as if she was expecting him to say something else, then leans to the side to pull her phone from her back pocket. Her thumbs move over the keyboard too fast for me to register her password. Once she pulls up the contacts in her phone, she freezes, then looks up. "How do I do that? I've never unblocked a number."

"I can do it for you." I extend my hand, and she pulls her phone closer to her chest. "I'm not going to go through your messages or anything," I tell her, but I have to admit, I'm more curious now than I was before.

"I could do it. I just don't know how." She sluggishly brings her phone down and places it on my palm. The contacts are already open, so I scroll through slowly, noting a few guys' names and several doctors.

Once I reach my name, I tap the icon and get to work unblocking my number. "I didn't see Memphis," I say, expecting her to tell me what she put him under.

"Um..."

"Give me that." My brother keeps his right hand clutched over Waylynn's leg and reaches for the phone with his left hand. "You didn't even put my name in?" he mumbles under his breath.

"I wasn't positive it was you." She runs her hands over the tops of her thighs, and I swear her fingers knead and linger where his were before he started thumbing through her phone. He better not have hurt her by squeezing too hard.

Memphis stops what he was doing and slowly turns his head to look at her. He doesn't even have to say anything else, and she cracks under the pressure of his stare. "I figured it was probably you," she admits, and her voice is soft, sweet.

Memphis turns his attention back to her phone, and when he hands it back, I get a second to glimpse the screen. His name isn't shown under the contact, Sir is. I'm going to give him shit for that as soon as she gets out of the car. My brother has always had a controlling streak, but there is something about Waylynn that tips it over the edge into something more.

"Thank you for lunch. I should get to class," she mumbles, and I decide we've steamrolled her enough for now and let her out of the truck. I watch her ass bounce when her feet hit the ground. I don't even try to hide the fact I was checking her out when she turns to grab her bag. At least she's not running from us today.

The urge to lean down, pull her against me so I can feel her curves under my hands, and kiss her is strong, but I'm not sure our girl is ready for that yet.

"I'll talk to you later," she mumbles and dashes off.

"I'll text you tonight," I holler after her loudly enough that several people notice, which was my intent. I may not be able to kiss her yet, but there are other ways to show people she belongs to me. She looks over her shoulder, and I can just make out her little smile.

"Sir?" I question when Memphis meets me in front of the truck.

"She is my student. She shouldn't even have my number unless I make it available to everyone."

"But Sir?" I dig again. I have to give him shit, since no one else is brave enough to.

"Shut up. Wavy baby is the dumbest shit I've ever heard." He's being defensive, so I know I hit my mark.

I chuckle and start walking backwards. "I'll text you when practice is over so we can eat."

Memphis doesn't respond, but I know he hears me.

I hit the sidewalk at a slow jog. My calves are tight for the first hundred yards from this morning's workout, but it fades into a comfortable burn after a few seconds, allowing me to pick up my pace so I won't be late to my next class.

Bates

Walking right past the girl standing at the check-in counter is easy. She's all sexy smiles when Memphis swipes his card. I think the fact that he's made himself off-limits makes him even more desirable than he already was to the female population, and that's saying something.

We both grab a tray, and she gives me a once-over as well while licking her bottom lip. I'm still in my work clothes—a gray T-shirt that's damn near threadbare, a pair of jeans, and work boots. I get my own fair share of attention, and when I have my cello between my legs, I can rival my best friend.

Memphis heads over to one of the smaller rooms situated off to the side of the main dining hall and places his tray on a table against the wall. "Oz should be here soon."

"How was the game?" I drop into the seat. My feet are killing me. I've been up since five-thirty this morning.

"Bullshit. They didn't put him in at all," Memphis gripes and lowers himself to the seat across from me.

"You two are getting along better though?" I haven't really talked to them much since last week when they were at each other's throats.

"Yeah." He looks around to see if anyone might be listening. "Do you remember me telling you someone ran into me when I was looking for Oz at orientation?"

"Yeah, you mentioned someone smacked your ass and you thought it was Oz."

"Well, it wasn't. It was her, Waylynn, the girl from the house."

"Bold." I shrug, wondering if that was what made Memphis not like her.

"It was an accident. She ran into me and hid before I could yell at her for it."

"Is that why you don't like her?" That seems a bit harsh if he believes it was an accident.

"No, I do like her. That's part of the problem." Memphis finally looks at me, and that's all it takes for me to see right through his *I'm always in control* front he shows everyone.

"Oh." It takes me a second to think about what to say next. I know whatever I decide, it will go one of two ways. Memphis will spill his guts, or he will shut down, but I'm thinking it's going to be the former since he's the one who brought her up, and he already admitted he likes her. "So why were you so pissed? Don't tell me it's because your brother was with her?" Memphis and Oz have been toying with the idea of sharing a woman for a while.

"No." Memphis takes a slow breath and scoots his chair closer to the table. When he speaks again, his voice is lower. "She lives alone. I got pissed thinking about her inviting someone else over. They could take advantage."

"Take advantage… You mean try to get in her pants before you could?" I joke.

Memphis glares at me. "Nobody is going to touch her, but yes, she's too trusting."

"Shit, no wonder she kicked us out when I called her a cleat chaser." I snort.

"Yeah, well, that was my fault. She makes me crazy," he admits, and it's different than when he says the same thing about Oz making him nuts. "She blocked both of us after we left."

"Can't really blame her, can you?" I question.

"No, but I can't get her out of my head."

"So go talk to her. I mean, you were a dick, but it's not unsalvageable." Selfishly, I'm already thinking about how much she's going to hate me. She probably won't want me around after what I said. I could lose my best friends over this.

"I did. She forgave us way too fucking easily, but I didn't really give her a choice."

"I'm going to leave the last half of that statement alone

and try to figure out why you seem bothered she forgave you. Isn't that what you wanted? I'm really fucking confused."

"Yes, I wanted her to forgive me, but not some other asshole." Memphis tugs his phone from his pocket and tosses it up on the table.

Damn, she really is in his head. I hope she doesn't know what kind of power she has over him right now. I knew someday, someone would come along and knock the immovable Memphis Gravlin on his ass, I just wasn't expecting it to be so soon or for it to shake my own foundation.

"Well, hopefully that means she will forgive me."

"She will, she's too fucking sweet for her own good." I watch him peer down at his phone as if he's expecting a text or call. I want to push him for more details, but I don't know if it's a good idea because he seems a little raw.

"Is Oz on his way down?" I ask to fill the uncomfortable tension I'm feeling.

"Should be. He showered at the facility."

I look up toward the entrance just in time to see a group of about nine people scanning the line. I do a double take of the dark-haired girl toward the back and the guy standing next to her. It's definitely not Oz, but the girl is familiar and the topic of our conversation, even though I don't know her name.

She's clinging to the straps of her backpack near her shoulders, making her arms frame her tits perfectly, and I'm not the only one to notice. The guy next to her is looking down at her chest. I almost say something to Memphis and ask him if it really is her, but something stops me.

Maybe I'll wait to see what she has going on with the guy next to her. He seems interested, but she's not giving off the same vibes. She actually looks uncomfortable. Just as I'm about to open my mouth to tell him he's not going to believe who just walked in, someone walks into my line of sight, breaking my view of her and sitting in the chair right next to Memphis.

"Hey there, boys," Makayla coos. She's trying to be cute, but it bugs the hell out of me when she acts like this. "Did you have a good summer?" She leans a little closer to Memphis. He doesn't back away from her, but I can see the tic in his jaw.

I know she's not really asking how his summer was, she's asking if he missed her. Memphis has never and will never miss her. They had an arrangement that he broke off the second she started trying to elevate herself to more than a hookup.

"Summer was good, quiet," he says and turns his head so he's actually looking at her. I don't know what she sees, but it's clearly something different than what I do, because it's obvious to me he doesn't want to participate in the conversation at all.

"Mine too, I wish you would have come out to see me." She lifts her hand as if she might try to touch him, but she stops herself and curls her fingers in.

"What are you doing here?" Oswald drops heavily into the

seat next to me. I didn't even notice him come in. I glance around, looking for the group their girl was with, but I don't see them. Damn it, I got distracted.

"Hello, Oz," Makayla says flatly. I wonder how she would act if she knew how important Memphis' brother is to him. Would she have treated him as something other than the burden she seems to think he is? I don't think she ever stood a real chance with Memphis. Hell, until today, I didn't think anyone really did, but she ruined any chance she might have had when she acted like Oz was a third wheel.

"Why are you here?" Oswald says again, but he speaks slower, like Makayla was too dumb to understand his question the first time. I try not to smile, but I don't put much effort into it.

Instead of replying to Oz, Makayla turns her head to look at Memphis, who's kind of smiling now too, and she says, "I called you a few times."

"Let's eat." Oz hits my arm with the back of his hand to get my attention. "Maybe I'll get lucky, and she will be gone when we get back." He pushes his chair back, not waiting for a reply from me, but I join him all the same.

"You'd think she'd get tired of being shut down," he mutters as he makes his way to the food court.

"I warned him about repeat offending." I grab a tray from the pasta station behind Oz. He doesn't do much more than point and grunt at the people serving the food. He's either tired, or seeing Makayla really put him in a bad mood.

"Hit it and quit it," Oz agrees loudly.

"Classy." A female smacks her lips. "I like it."

"That's how we do," Oswald teases and spins around. There's a blonde with her hip cocked out and a wide smile on her lips, but the face that draws my attention is the one just behind her.

I know the moment Oz notices her too, because he inhales sharply and exhales. "Wavy." Her name clicks in my head —*Waylynn*. I don't know how I could have forgotten that.

"I guess you haven't found a diesel yet. Once is never enough with us, that's just a warmup," the blonde says, and Waylynn suddenly finds the ground much more interesting than this conversation. "Why do you look so familiar?" The blonde squints her eyes and tilts her head to the side.

"He's Gravlin's little brother, plays football," someone else chimes in.

"Now I see it." She snaps her fingers and points. "I bet you know exactly what I'm talking about, little Gravlin." She looks Oswald up and down.

Normally, I would be all about the banter, but I know this would piss Memphis off. He likes to keep his private life private, and this is about as personal as it gets, not to mention he likes Waylynn, and this might hurt his chances with her. He's been too good of a friend to me to let this explode.

I accept the blame. "That was a bad joke on me."

"No need to backtrack, handsome, we're all adults." The

girl looks around her small group. I notice Waylynn inching backward. She's trying to escape, and I don't blame her.

"Waylynn." Oz leans to the left to see her through the others.

"Oh, you two know each other?" the blonde nearly singsongs.

"Um," comes her less than articulate reply.

"Yeah," Oswald answers with more conviction while sizing up the guy that seems to be sticking close to Waylynn's side.

"Grabbing dinner after class?" Oz says, but it comes out more like an accusation.

"Study group," the guy replies and shifts his weight to the other foot, so it looks like he's even closer to Waylynn.

"Don't let us hold you up." Oz plasters a fake ass smile on his lips as he waves his hand to the ladies in the front of the group and steps back from the counter so they can go ahead of him. I follow his lead.

I don't know if everyone can feel the tension in the air, but I can. I've also known Oz and Memphis for a long time and know when shit is about to go down. The guy tries to usher Waylynn in front of him, but she's slipped even farther back, so she's the last of the group, and it looks like he would have to push her to get her moving, which would get him in trouble with more than just Oz.

"Waylynn." Oswald steps right into her space, and she lifts only her eyes to peer up at him when he says her name. "I told you we have you covered for math, anything you need." His voice is soft, cajoling.

"I know, but you guys are busy. I don't want to use up all your time." If I hadn't moved closer, I wouldn't have been able to hear her.

"We want you to," he tells her, and she gives a soft little "Okay" that I'm not even sure is audible.

"Are you done here? Come eat with us," he tells her before she can even answer his first question.

Her eyes dart over to me, and she looks frightened, like a little mouse. I want to ask her if she's okay, but I don't know her well enough yet.

"You remember Bates, right?" Oz steps to the side a little.

"Yes." She tugs her backpack straps closer together, squeezing her tits so the fabric of her shirt gets pinched in her cleavage and tightens over her chest. Damn, I shouldn't be noticing shit like that.

"Sorry I was a dick," I blurt.

"It's okay," she says swiftly. "Mist…Gr…explained it was a misunderstanding."

"Let's get food." Oz wraps his arm around her shoulders and starts to haul her along to a different kitchen with his tray from the pasta station still in hand.

"Hit it and quit it." One of the girl's cackles as they walk past. Oz pretends not to hear them, but I see the way Waylynn's spine snaps straight under the weight of his arm.

It's a reminder of why I never did the college thing. I hate this kind of shit.

I catch up to Waylynn. Oz is standing on her other side. I don't know if it's Memphis' words influencing me or not, but she does seem too soft and sweet to be left alone.

Memphis

The chair makes a squelching sound as Makayla tries to scoot even closer to me. I thought my disinterest would be enough to get her to leave me alone, but it's clear that's not going to work when she's still talking to me five minutes after Oz and Bates left to get food.

"Did you do anything over the summer?"

"Worked." I don't go into details, and she doesn't ask for any.

"I miss hanging out with you," she tells me just as I see Oz, Waylynn, and Bates walking toward the table. She looks exactly like she did this afternoon, wearing fitted jeans and a T-shirt that slides off her shoulder every once in a while, exposing her pink bra strap. Her fingers are curled tightly around a dining tray.

I forget all about who's next to me until I see her eyes drift to the left. I get to my feet as Oswald places his heaping tray on the table. "Look who I found." He takes Waylynn's tray from her hands and places it next to his.

Bates grabs the top of a chair from another table and spins it around so it's sitting at the end, near Waylynn. The table only seats four, so there's barely any room for his tray, but he makes it work.

The moment Waylynn lowers herself into the chair Oz pulled out for her, Makayla does a weird finger wave. "Hey, I'm Makayla."

"I'm going to get something to eat," I announce before Waylynn can respond. Everyone at the table looks at me like I'm a dick, or maybe I just feel like one, besides Waylynn, who keeps her eyes on the table.

The urge to tell her to look at me is strong, but I clench my jaw. "Hurry up so we're not done before you even get your food," Oz tells me.

Makayla pushes up from the table, but instead of walking away like I hoped she would, she follows me.

"Your brother has a girlfriend?" She lingers near the salad counter.

"Does it matter?"

"I didn't know the Gravlin men committed, and she's not what I expected." Her reply is flippant.

"Expected how?" I turn to face her. It might be the first time I've actually looked at her today.

"I don't know." She lifts a shoulder. "Have they been together long? You never mentioned her."

"I don't recall us talking much about anything," I retort. It wasn't meant to be a compliment, but it seems like that's the way she takes it when she pushes her chest closer to me and peers up at me through her lashes. It does absolutely nothing for me. My pulse doesn't quicken the way it does when Waylynn looks at me like this, and my fingers don't ache to grab her. If anything, I just want her to move the hell away from me.

"That's because we were always busy doing other things." Her voice is pitched low in an attempt to be alluring.

I take a step back from her, creating space. "And now we're not doing either."

"We could be," she offers while still gazing up at me.

She's not getting it. I'm going to have to tell her—again. "I need to focus." She knew what our arrangement was from the beginning. She already admitted that when she said she didn't know a Gravlin would commit.

"I can help you with that," she says while sliding her foot forward, coming closer again.

"I'm not interested, Makayla."

She freezes mid-movement but doesn't retreat. Her chest rises sharply, but her face remains utterly calm. "I knew I was making a mistake falling for you. I told myself a hundred times what it was and what it wasn't, but you're a really good guy, Memphis." I feel like she's blaming me for not being a complete dick to her, which is fucking strange. "I always would have wondered if I didn't try." She steps back, and her eyes roam over my face as if she's trying to see something that isn't there or commit what is to memory. "I might already be gone when you realize what you lost," she murmurs sadly, then turns to walk away.

The only thing I feel is relief. I glance in the direction of our table, grateful I can't see it, which means Waylynn didn't see what just happened.

INTERRUPTIONS

Waylynn

I CAN FEEL my backpack slipping down my shoulders. Between the weight of my laptop and purse, it isn't sitting comfortably, and add in the tray of food Oswald kept heaping food on, and I feel like I'm going to drop something any second.

I'm really trying to watch where I'm walking, so I don't see Memphis and the pretty girl sitting right next to him until we round a corner. My heart slips into my stomach before I have the time to remind myself I have no right to be jealous.

I feel dumb standing next to the table that clearly doesn't have enough room for me, but Oswald takes my tray and places it on the table across from Memphis. I place my bag on the floor near my feet, unable to force myself to look up, even when the girl introduces herself.

Memphis speaks right after her so I wouldn't have been able to respond if I wanted to. "I'm going to get something to eat." His voice is tight, but not as harsh as I've heard it before. I wonder if he's mad Oswald invited me to eat with them.

He strolls away with Makayla in tow. Maybe I can make an excuse to leave before they come back. How do I keep allowing myself to get in these uncomfortable situations? I didn't even want to come when the study group invited me to eat, but I didn't want to be rude, so here I am.

"I'm starving. I haven't eaten since lunch." Oswald stabs a hunk of fish with his fork.

"How's the team?" Bates asks, and I'm grateful I don't need to carry on a conversation. There's too much stuff in my head, like the fact that someone from the study group said *hit it and quit it*, referring to Oswald and me. I don't know if I should feel flattered or insulted. Then there's how I felt seeing Makayla with Memphis. I never really thought about him having a girlfriend. Their names even sound good together.

"It's a new team," Oswald answers between bites. "We're adjusting."

"Do you think you'll get any time on the field this weekend?" Bates' question pulls me from my own musings and into their conversation.

"I fucking hope so."

I'm confused. When I asked Oswald if he played for the

school, he said someday. "You already made the team?" I assumed he was trying out or something.

Oswald wipes his mouth with a balled up napkin. "Yeah, but I'm a freshman," he says as if that explains something.

"What do you love about football?" The question spills from my lips before I have time to think about how it will sound. He's never even told me he loves it, I can just feel that he does when he talks about it, which isn't all that often.

Oswald's brows furrow, and his nose wrinkles a little. "When I was younger, I liked that I was good at it and everyone told me I was." He has a smile on his lips, but it slips when he looks off in the distance. "I like pushing myself. I like that I don't have to think about anything other than the game when I'm on the field." He blinks a few times and resumes eating.

I feel like he just gave me a tiny glimpse of himself. Oswald always seems so full of everything—life, energy, and witty replies—but there was more to that answer, and I feel like there was even more left unsaid.

"Bates plays the cello," Oswald blurts as if he wants to change the subject.

My eyes drop to Bates' hands. They are stained, much in the same way John the gardener's are no matter how many times he washes them. His nails are perfect though, short and clean. He has beautiful hands. Bates curls his knuckles in and slides his hand under the table. I feel like I got caught doing something I shouldn't have.

The urge to apologize is on the tip of my tongue, but the sound of a tray snapping against the table has me sealing my lips and focusing on my own food. Memphis' tray touches mine as he sits down across from me.

"Damn, I thought she might try to follow you home," Oswald says, and a wave of irritation has me glancing up. Memphis' lips are tight for just a moment, and then he relaxes. The seat next to him is empty, and I realize we're all crowded around my side of the table, but Bates doesn't move or offer to take the other seat.

"You're commenting about a stalker?" Memphis deadpans to Oswald, but I feel like he's talking about me.

Crap, does he think I followed them here?

"Hey, you always told me to go after what I want." Oswald leans back and places his arm on the top of my chair. I can feel his fingers toying with the ends of my hair.

"Why is your tray still full?" Memphis asks, changing the subject. I wait for someone else to answer, and when no one does, I look up. He's looking at me expectantly, one brow arched in question.

"Oswald hasn't taken his stuff yet."

Oswald throws me under the bus. "None of that is mine."

"You put it there," I accuse.

"For you." He looks down at the food, then back at me. I know I'm chunky, but this is way more than I can eat. I don't say that though. I just sit here. "You barely ate at lunch.

Speaking of, you better not have eaten my leftovers." He directs his attention toward his brother.

"You're free to go check the teachers' lounge in the English building," Memphis tells him, not confirming or denying whether he ate it or not.

"Just eat the food you have and stop worrying about it," Bates tells him.

"It's country fried steak from Bricktown," Oswald explains. Bates makes a grunting noise, which makes me think he understands why Oswald wants it.

"Waylynn." My eyes leap up to Memphis'. "How was your class?"

"Fine, and yours?" I ask, being polite out of habit.

"I only questioned why the hell I was doing it twice, so…" I smile, and his lip curls up in a grin in response.

"Not so bad then," I agree.

"She still went to the study group," Oswald tattles like I did something wrong. "That's how I found her here, with them." He makes it seem like I was taking candy from a stranger and about to climb in the back of a white van.

I widen my eyes and peer at Oswald. "They said I only need to bring three friends with me next time to find out about their real mission. Do you have time to learn about your true calling?"

Bates starts to chuckle, while Oswald stares at me for a long second with narrowed eyes. "Not nice, Wavy baby." I hear Memphis sigh, probably from the silly nickname.

"It's a study group, not a cult."

"That guy was certainly doing a lot of studying," Oswald mutters under his breath and jerks my chair closer. I can feel the heat of his body all along the side of mine.

"You weren't even there." I try to sound calm, but I feel like they can hear the sudden shakiness in my tone.

"And I wasn't talking about math." He turns his head to look at me. We're so close, I could count his eyelashes if I tried. "I'm going to have to put my name on you," he says, but I don't even really register the meaning of his words. I'm too busy making sure no one else can hear how hard my heart is beating and trying to act unaffected by his nearness.

"It's our name," Memphis drawls.

"I know, but I don't think you'll have any complaints." Oz resumes eating, and our arms bump a few times once he removes his hand from the back of my chair. I take a sip of water just to give myself something to do other than focus on his pinkie finger touching my thigh under the table.

"Where did you play this weekend?" Oswald seems completely unaffected as he flips back into chatting with Bates.

"A bar in Chelsea."

"Good show?" Memphis chimes in.

"Not bad for a Sunday afternoon. They invited me back Thursday." Bates swirls a hunk of bread around the sauce on his plate and pops the entire thing in his mouth.

"Can you get off work early enough to go?" Memphis

sounds intrigued.

"Yeah, it's not until eight." Bates stands up abruptly and walks away with his tray in hand. When he returns, he drops down into the same seat between Memphis and me.

"Do you have an early class on Friday?"

"Me?" I ask, even though Memphis is looking right at me. "No," I reply before he even answers.

"Send me the info, we'll be there," he tells Bates, and I'm assuming he's talking about me too, but I don't want to ask and look like an idiot.

"I can skip the gym Friday," Oswald offers.

"No, you can't. If you skip practice the day before a game, there's no way they will put you in. We won't stay out too late. You'll be fine in the morning for the gym."

Oswald gives his brother a mock salute. Apparently, I'm not the only one who thinks Memphis is bossy.

The conversation dies down until Oswald finally pushes his tray away and leans back in his chair with his hand over his stomach. "I can't eat anymore."

The amount he consumed was pretty impressive. I bet he's one of the few students the school actually loses money on for the meal plan.

"Are you staying in your own room?" Memphis asks.

"Hell no. The stench of KJ's feet has permeated the entire place. It's all I can smell when I walk through the door. Do I stink?" Oswald tugs the fabric of his shirt toward me. I lean down and take a deep inhale, since he gave me the excuse to.

"No, you smell clean, like soap," I tell him as I lean back.

"Feel free to check anytime. Just bury your face right here." He tips his head back and makes a sloppy circle over his entire neck and torso.

"Are you worried he's rubbing his feet on your things?" I've seen much worse with roommates.

Oswald pulls his head back and gawks at me. "Hell no, I'd smother his ass for doing something like that."

"He just wanted an excuse to have you sniff his neck." Bates shakes his head slowly, but he's kind of smiling too.

"You caught me. Are we getting out of here? I'm starting to stiffen up." Oswald places his palm on the table, readying to stand.

I gather my tray and lean down for my bag, but Oswald is already lifting it, and he makes an exaggerated grunting sound. "Damn, woman, what do you have in here today?"

I reach for my bag, but he evades me like always. "My purse and water bottle."

"I'm surprised you didn't topple over with this thing."

"If it's too heavy for you…" I tease, knowing he won't give it back until he decides to.

"Get out of here before I put you over my shoulder," he mumbles. Bates walks next to me while Memphis and Oswald linger behind us.

"So you're a musician?"

"I work too, but yeah."

"I'd love to be able to play something. I tried the piano, but I was young and gave up quickly."

"It's never too late to learn." Bates lifts his hand and pushes the door open, allowing me to duck under his arm to get outside.

I put my hand out, expecting my bag so we can split up, but instead, Oswald reaches out his own hand and clasps mine. "I need that for class tomorrow, and my keys to get inside the house," I tell him as he tows me along.

"Did you drive to school today?" Memphis asks. I dart my eyes over to the side of Oswald's face for tattling on me, to a teacher no less.

"Yeah, I'm in a lot off of Williams Street." It's only a few blocks away. I'm not supposed to park there, but I'd already circled the block twice this morning, and I was getting desperate.

"Good thing you unblocked our numbers so you'll have someone to call when you get arrested for all those parking tickets," Oswald jokes.

"I think he would leave me there as punishment," I whisper to Oswald, but I'm sure Memphis hears me.

Oswald stops in his tracks and leans his head back to howl with laughter. I watch his neck bob until he lowers his chin, still chuckling. "Oh, I'm certain he would want to punish you, just not by leaving you in lockup."

"Shut up, Oswald," Memphis grumbles and gives his brother a playful shove, so our hands break apart.

Bates lingers near my side as the brothers walk together a few paces ahead of us, throwing fake jabs and small shoves. Oswald is still smiling, but the look on Memphis' face is a little darker. It's not anger, but it's something.

"I hope I didn't offend him. I was only joking," I tell Bates.

"You didn't, but speaking of… I feel like shit for saying that to you the other day. I… We're probably a little too overprotective of Oz."

I lay my hand on his bicep, not expecting it to be so solid or to feel so at ease touching him. "It's really okay. I get it." I pull my hand back and continue walking, hoping the touch didn't make things awkward. "It's nice that you guys look out for each other."

"Who looks out for you?" he questions, and my immediate thought is Maxwell and his team, but that's not what he means.

"Well, Gra… Memphis" —I have such a hard time saying his name out loud, so it comes out just above a whisper— "checked my doors and windows the other day. Does that count?"

"It does seem like they have adopted you," he comments, and something in my chest sinks. Adopted is a familial word. Maybe they really do think of me like a little sister.

There's a breath of silence before Bates asks, "What are you going to school for?"

"Psychology." I don't feel like I'm giving too much away

by sharing that. Psychology happens to be one of the most popular majors for a broad range of things, but that doesn't mean I want to keep talking about me. "What do you do for work?"

"I'm an electrician." His hands make more sense now, as well as his rock-hard bicep. "I came over straight from work." He tugs at his T-shirt near his belt as if he's explaining his clothing. I don't see a problem with his attire at all.

"Oh, that's pretty neat. Do you travel a bunch?"

"Locally, but nothing too far. The company I work for does a lot of commercial and industrial stuff."

"I bet it's exciting doing different things all the time."

"What's going on back here?" Oswald pants lightly as he jogs over and wraps his arm around my neck. "Are you trying to chat up my girl? Good thing I'm okay with sharing," he teases and swipes his tongue up the side of my face.

My heart skips a beat, but I try to cover the fact that it felt kind of good as I let out an, "Ugh," and shove at his chest. He barely budges. "I haven't washed my face since this morning." Now I am a little embarrassed, I didn't even think about that.

Oswald just bounds away, chuckling. I notice my bag isn't on his shoulder anymore, but now Memphis has it slung over his. "How can he run around like that after just eating all that food?" I'm mostly talking to myself, but Bates answers.

"He's always been like that. I wanted to wring his neck before he got serious about football. He made us crazy when he was little."

"You guys have been friends for a long time then?" I glance over at Bates. It's hard to make out the pretty color of his dark eyes with the sun behind us, but I still try.

"It feels like forever most days." He cracks a smile while looking straight ahead, and I follow his gaze to see Memphis holding Oswald in a headlock, giving him a noogie. Bates darts forward and jumps on both of them. I expect them to fall into a heap, but they manage to stay upright.

"Oh my, now that is a sight." I look to the left and see Mia, the girl from orientation, and a few other girls openly watching the guys wrestle and play. I wonder if my face looks entranced and excited like theirs.

I'm tempted to slink away. I don't think she's even noticed me yet, but I need my bag, and there's a tiny little piece of me that wants her to know I'm hanging out with them. As soon as that thought filters through my mind, Oswald lifts his head. "Come on, Wavy baby. Save me."

I can feel every eye from the small group of girls on me. Why did I think it was a good idea that she knew I was with them? When I don't move to come help him, Oswald untangles himself from the other two and jogs over. "I won't let them get too rough, promise." He bends forward, shoves his shoulder into my stomach, and hoists me over his back.

There's too much happening at once for me to process much else besides the air whooshing out of my lungs. *God, now he knows how heavy I really am, my butt is in the air, and the girls are all watching.* When I start to bounce, I grab hold of his sides, and a tiny squeal leaves my lips. A hot crack from a palm lands on my ass, and I gasp. "Oswald." I may sound properly scandalized, but the two halves of my brain are warring because I don't feel scandalized—especially when he kneads the same area all too briefly before tipping back over and setting me on my feet, right in the middle of the three of them.

I feel woozy for a second, and I choose to blame it on the blood draining from my head. At least I have an excuse as to why my face would be bright red.

"What the heck were you doing way back there?" Oswald demands more than asks, but he's still being playful.

"I thought I was at a safe enough distance not to get swept up in your wrestling match."

"I told you we would be gentle."

"Right before you threw me over your shoulder," I retort, keeping my voice down. From the corner of my eye, I can see the group of girls walking closer. Memphis turns his head to follow my gaze and takes several steps back from us, creating the most distance between him and me.

Mia does a double take when she sees my face. "Waverly." She butchers my name, but I have to give her credit for getting kind of close.

"Waylynn," Bates corrects her for me.

"Oh shit, Waverly is a haunted asylum." She taps the side of her head with her pointer finger. My stomach bottoms out. Why would she bring up something like that?

Oswald steps up to my side and wraps his arm around me again. I appreciate his nearness, but the only thing I can think about is what Mia knows about me and what she's going to say next. I watch her eyes scan Memphis.

"Gravlin, right?" She acts like she's unsure, but we both know she's not.

"Yes," he answers.

"You're a TA for Hilbrand, right?"

Memphis

I'm being sloppy and taking risks I shouldn't have. Slipping off campus for lunch is one thing, but I'm carrying Waylynn's fucking backpack for Christ's sake. She's my student.

I despise small talk, but I answer the girl who knows Waylynn in the simplest way I can, hoping it doesn't invite more conversation. "Yes."

"We should get going," Oswald states, speaking directly after me. He knows me well enough to pick up on my mood.

"Get your friend home. We'll meet you at the car," I tell my brother and distance myself from Waylynn even more. "Don't leave this lying around." I hand her bag to my brother without even glancing in her direction, then walk away from them.

Everything about it feels wrong.

FIRSTS

Waylynn

It hurts a little when Memphis acts like I don't exist. I tell myself it probably has more to do with Mia asking if he was a TA than it does me, but I still don't like it.

"Later," Oswald says and pulls me along beside him, heading in the same direction Bates and Memphis went.

"You know that girl?" he asks once we're out of earshot of the group.

"Not really. She was one of the student speakers at orientation."

"She remembers you from orientation?" He sounds doubtful.

"I think it was another reason," I hedge, but I know there's no point, he's going to ask more questions.

"Was it your beautiful face? Man, I've got to keep a closer eye on you," he teases.

"No." I tug on his fingers hanging over my chest. "She witnessed me shoving my nose in your brother's back and wanted to know what he smelled like."

Oswald stops while still clinging to me, so I stop too. "Come again?"

"At orientation, I wasn't watching where I was going, and I ran right into Memphis' back. I thought I broke my nose." I wiggle said nose.

"No, I know that part. He told me you copped a feel too. I'm a little jealous, but we'll get there. She asked you what he smelled like?" His mouth is hanging open in horror. That's what he thinks is the worst part of the story?

"How does one ask that question? Wait, what did you tell her?" He's strangely fascinated.

"The truth, and she just asked." I shrug. "She caught me leaving the south quad after the tour ended, asked if he smelled good, and invited me to eat with her, but then she bailed when her pizza was ready."

"Please tell me you told her he had BO." Oswald tries not to laugh but ends up snickering.

"No," I scoff. "I said he smelled really good, and she told me his name was Gravlin. I thought I was going to die when he was introduced in class as our TA. What are the chances?" I lift my hand, still unable to believe how small the world is, and Oswald grabs my fingers so we're holding hands again. "I was banking on him not having seen me before I hid with the other students, but I must not have been fast enough."

"Then you went and ran into me so I wouldn't feel left out. How did I smell?"

I suck air between my teeth and wince. "It's okay, I know you work out before class now," I say as earnestly as possible, but then I feel guilty when his face drops. "I'm teasing, you smell like you always do—clean and soapy."

"Now your true colors are coming out. Not only are you a rule breaking traffic violator, you're mean!"

"Guilty." I shrug and realize I'm rubbing my thumb along the side of his palm, but I don't stop.

"Good thing we didn't stink, it might have scared you away," Oswald tells me.

"You did scare me away—well, Memphis did. I was so embarrassed when he made that comment about not watching where I was going, I ran away." I don't tell him that I was also having a mini meltdown because he sounded too much like the voice I hear in my head. "He's different…"

Oswald speaks before I can continue. "At school. I know."

"I was going to say when he's not with you. He's intimidating all the time, but you soften his edges."

Oswald stops walking again, and I can feel him peering at the side of my face, so I look up, hoping I didn't offend him and his brother with my observation.

He tugs his fingers from mine and removes his hand from my shoulder. I'm expecting him to step back, but instead, his fingertips trail over my cheek and he leans down to kiss me.

The moment our lips touch, my head spins like I just got done twirling, and thoughts that do not belong to me whisper through my mind. *Fuck, she feels good. I wish we were at home, I want to touch every inch of her.*

The sensory overload only lasts a breath, then the whooshing in my ears fades and I can feel the press of his warm, soft lips against mine. My entire body relaxes, which Oswald takes as a sign to step even closer to me. I feel his chest against mine, and then he opens his mouth and slides his tongue along my bottom lip.

My heart thunders in my chest, quickening my breaths, but I open my mouth, and he slips inside. His kiss is sweet and a little teasing, but it has me lifting up on my toes.

After several long seconds, he slows, giving me a few soft pecks on my top and bottom lip. I know the kiss is about to end, but I return each press of his lips until he finally pulls his mouth away to rest his forehead against mine. He's still holding my cheek, and when I open my eyes, I see him lick his bottom lip and run his teeth over the damp path he just left. My stomach tightens with the most intense sensation of butterflies I've ever had. I want to kiss him again.

A soft groan comes from Oswald's chest before he mutters, "You have to stop looking at me like that, baby."

I blink several times and start to pull away, but he captures my mouth again with a rougher kiss while the tips of his fingers curl just above my ear, holding me tighter. There's no warning or slow pull away, he stops the kiss abruptly by jerking his head back, but his fingers trail down my jaw slowly.

When he turns my shoulder so I'm beside him again instead of facing him, I notice the people walking around. Some are stealing glances at us, but most don't even seem to notice I just had the best kiss of my life.

"Where are you parked again?" Oswald asks, and his voice is deeper.

"Williams," I say, but it comes out more like a croak. Damn, he sounds sexy and I sound like a surprised frog.

"If I know Memphis, he's probably waiting for us." He begins walking again, and I shuffle my feet forward to keep up.

The rest of the walk is quiet. I'm still imagining his lips against mine, and I have a feeling I'm going to be thinking about that a lot, but I have no idea what Oswald is thinking.

Just as he said, Memphis and Bates are waiting for us near the rear of my parked car. I watch his eyes rake over me from head to toe, and I like the way it makes me feel. I just kissed his brother and want to do it again, but I like his attention too. I'm really in trouble.

"What took you so long?" He pushes away from my car and approaches.

"Got held up." Oswald licks his lip, and it feels like we're sharing a secret. I duck my head and move around Oswald, partly to avoid Memphis seeing my red face and partly so I can grab my bag.

Oswald looks over his shoulder as I pull it down his arm. "Hey now." He acts like I'm taking something that doesn't belong to me.

"I need my keys," I tell him and balance the bottom of my bag on my lifted knee as I reach for my purse.

"Your car doesn't even take a key." Oswald snorts.

"I have to have the fob though. It won't sense it through both bags," I explain. "Do you guys want a ride to your car?"

"No," Memphis refuses.

"Can I drive?" Oswald asks at the same time.

I look between the two of them, not sure who to respond to, so I say, "I don't mind."

"Fine," Memphis agrees tightly, indulging his brother.

"You guys decide who else gets the front seat." I open the rear driver's side door and slide in the back.

"It's your car, you should be in the front," Memphis says as soon as he opens the rear passenger door.

I place my purse in the front center console so the car will start. "You guys are all taller than me."

Memphis lowers himself into the seat and glances around before settling his gaze on me. It's unnerving. I fidget with my backpack straps, pretending not to notice. Oswald drops into the driver's seat and the car shakes, making my boobs bounce. If I felt it, Memphis certainly witnessed it.

I lean forward between the seats. "Just press the brake, and it should start."

"Whoa, you can barely tell it's running." Oswald briefly looks over at Bates in the passenger seat. "How do I put it in reverse?"

"Oh, sorry." I scoot over a little so I can point to the screen in the center. "See that dotted line on the left?"

"This?" Oswald points to it.

"Yeah, push in the brake and run your finger down that line."

I watch him do it, and the rear camera comes on, so I know it's in reverse, but we don't move. "Now, you just use the gas like normal."

I let out a little yelp when he punches the pedal too hard and we shoot backwards, then he slams on the brake again, so I end up smashed up against Memphis. "I'm sorry," I tell him, while Oswald mutters, "Oh shit," over and over again. Good thing the lot is almost empty this evening.

"You're good," Memphis says and pulls me back when I try to right myself in my seat.

"He does have a license, right?" I'm mostly joking, but it's a good cover for how breathless I feel pressed up against his side.

"I have a license. How do I put it in drive?"

"Just run your finger up the line, but don't goose the gas," I warn. This car is speedy, and I don't want him to hit a parked car.

"I won't," he mumbles like I'm lecturing him. The acceleration is much smoother, and he glides to the exit and makes a left.

"We're parked the other way," Memphis tells him.

"I know where I'm going."

Bates speaks up for the first time since being in the car. "Well, I need to work tomorrow, so don't get crazy."

"Lame." Oswald takes a few turns, but he never strays far from campus.

Just when I'm starting to get comfortable next to Memphis, Oswald turns into a parking lot, and I spot their truck.

"Touch the P at the top when you're ready to park."

"Will it do it for me?" He glances over his shoulder.

I laugh a little. "It can, but there's a spot right there." I point toward the windshield.

"Fine." He drives slowly into the space and touches the screen to park.

"Most fun you've had all day?" Bates reaches for the door handle.

"Not by a longshot." Oswald catches my eye in the rearview mirror.

"Oh really?" Memphis grumbles, and I realize he caught his brother's look in my direction through the rearview mirror.

I scoot to the left and hop out of the car quickly so he won't ask me for an explanation, but it ends up backfiring because now I'm trapped between the car next to us and

Oswald. I try to shimmy past him, but he doesn't offer an inch of extra space. I end up sliding against his front. "Perfect time to cop that feel," he singsongs. I snort as the tension breaks.

"Are you going straight home?" Memphis levels me with his stare from the front of the car.

His tone alone is enough to have me snapping to attention. "Yes."

I feel Oswald's breath on the side of my neck, and then he whispers, "Yes, what?"

"Yes, I'm going straight home, sir." I feel like I'm back in school and speaking with the principal.

Memphis taps the side of his thigh twice with two fingers, and my eyes are drawn to the movement. "We'll follow you home."

"It's..."

"Not an offer. Get in the car, Waylynn."

"Okay," I agree and get behind the wheel. Oswald is standing in the doorway, so I whisper, "Am I in trouble?"

"No, he just wants to make sure you get home safe, and he likes bossing you around." He grazes his thumb along my jaw. "Tell him if it bothers you, okay?"

"I just don't want him to be mad at me." I'm not sure why it feels so important that he's not upset with me, but I don't like the thought of it at all.

"He's not. I was aggravating him, don't worry."

"Okay," I agree, but I feel like something has been off with him since I sat down at their table for dinner.

"I probably won't see you tomorrow, but I'll text you," Oswald says and steps back so he can close the door. I click my seatbelt and back out of the parking space as soon as he walks away.

Memphis

I could wring Oswald's neck, but I'm standing at the side of Bates' van like a creeper with a semi because he goaded Waylynn into calling me sir.

"Are you planning on tucking her in?" Bates smirks as he climbs into his van.

"No," I bark, and it just makes everything that's going on more obvious.

"I knew you'd get turned inside out someday."

"You think it's funny she makes me irrational?"

Oswald jogs over, and I see Waylynn's car backing out of her spot.

"Didn't you tell her to wait for us?" I accuse.

"You scared the shit out of her, and she thinks she's in trouble." He pushes my shoulder.

"Don't start this shit again." Bates groans.

"We're not, we're leaving. Don't forget to text me the details about the show," I say loud enough for him to hear as I hustle my ass over to the truck. "She said I scared her?" I ask

Oz as I turn too fast from the parking lot so I can try to follow her.

"She asked if she was in trouble and if you were mad at her, but I could tell she was nervous." He adjusts in his seat.

"It's your fault," I accuse weakly. I know that's not the truth. I was wound up before he encouraged her.

"Bullshit," Oz scoffs. "What are you going to do if she calls you sir in class? Bend her over the desk and spank her with a ruler in front of everyone?"

I would use my hand, that way I wouldn't hurt her. "No, I wouldn't let people see her like that."

Oswald goes quiet for a second, then starts to laugh silently. "I'm so glad I'm not in your head right now, but did you see her face when you called her my friend?"

No, because I was doing my damnedest to ignore her, and that would have been impossible if I were looking at her. "I shouldn't be socializing with my students."

"Technically, but you still go to school here too. They can't expect you not to speak to anyone."

My leg starts to bounce when we get stopped by a red light. He might be partially correct, but she's a student and I'm crossing a line I don't want to think about. "I told her we would follow her home, so why didn't she wait?" I mumble.

Oswald doesn't have an answer, but he's rubbernecking just as much as I am when we creep toward her driveway. The lights are on in the kitchen, and I can see her silhouette through one of the windows as she walks past.

I shift into park and pull out my phone.

"What are you doing? She's right there," Oswald points out.

"Making sure her alarm is set. That house is like a glass box with all those windows."

"It's not. Try asking instead of demanding." Oswald is watching her through the window.

I delete what I had and type out a new message.

Me: Please make sure to set your alarm.

"How's that?" I show Oswald.

He nods as he reads the short message. "Good, and you can't even tell we're a couple of stalkers watching her house right now."

"It's not stalking if she knows we're looking out for her."

"You keep telling yourself that." He chuckles.

My phone vibrates, and I look down at the screen. Since I didn't save her info in my contacts, her name doesn't pop up.

Unknown: Thank you for checking, all set.

I know I'm strange, but I like that she uses punctuation and no abbreviations. I think about texting her again but decide against it.

"I hate that she's in there alone," I gripe as I put the truck in drive and ease away from the curb.

"I bet if you called her right now, she would invite us in," Oswald cajoles, and I know it's the truth. I hate thinking about her having met someone else before us and wondering if they would have taken advantage of her.

"That's a bad idea for so many reasons," I caution.

"I can't think of one."

The tone of his voice has me glaring over at him. "What took you two so long to get to the car?"

Oswald closes his eyes, and a smile curls his lips.

"What did you do?"

"Calm down, it was just a kiss." He's still smiling. I kind of want to punch him, because it clearly wasn't a peck.

"She was talking about you, actually," he says cryptically. I glance over at him, waiting for him to say more, but he just sits there. Damn it.

"What did she say?"

"She mentioned being embarrassed that you knew it was her who bumped into you and that you *smelled good*."

Fuck, why does that make me feel good? "She said that?"

"Yeah, she actually said really good. I might have mentioned how much you like your butt touched..." Oswald starts to laugh when I reach over and punch his arm. "I'm joking, but I did tell her you told me about her rubbing your butt and that I was jealous."

"She probably thinks you're crazy." I park in my assigned spot and open the door. It's still relatively early, so there are a few people milling around.

"No, she doesn't, but she does think I soften your rough edges."

I stop. "She said that?" How many times am I going to ask that question?

"Yeah, she said you're different when you're with me. I think you intimidate the shit out of her. You should be nicer." I feel like I'm getting a lecture from my little brother.

"I am nice to her. I'm nicer to her than I am to anyone besides you and Bates."

"I know that, but she doesn't. Plus, I don't think she gets why you like bossing her around so much."

"*I* don't get why I like bossing her around so much," I grumble under my breath and unlock the door to the apartment.

"I bet it has something to do with how sweet and innocent she is, but I'm going to leave that up to you to figure out." Oswald slaps his hand on my shoulder as he walks by. "I'm going to go rub one out while thinking about how her lips felt and imagining they were on my dick."

"Fucking hell, Oz." I toss the keys on the counter, and he slams the bathroom door. "I didn't need to know that."

"You're welcome," he yells, clearly unrepentant.

I start to place my phone on the counter but decide now's a good time to text Waylynn.

Me: So, I smell good?

The message pops up as delivered then read within seconds, but it takes over a minute for the respond bubble to show up. I like knowing she was probably squirming as she thought about how to respond.

Unknown: Yes.

Well, I have to admit I was hoping for more than that, but I'm not above prodding to get it.

Me: Tell me.

Waylynn

I SHOULD HAVE KNOWN Oswald would tattle. I bet he told Memphis everything I said. Did he tell him he kissed me too?

Sir: Tell me.

I drop my phone to the bed so fast, I'm not even sure I read his text right, so I peek at it lying on my bed among my blankets. I was right. Tell him what? How he smelled? That I'm sorry?

Me: I already did.

Hopefully, that answers both questions.

Sir: I want details.

I look around my bedroom, knowing I'm alone but still needing the confirmation because this is thrilling, but it also feels like I'm doing something I shouldn't. I give myself a second to actually think about how he smells. It's easy since I was sitting so close to him in the car.

Me: Like Red Mountain after it rains and pepper. I'm sorry I bumped into you.

Sir: I'm not.

I bite my lip, but that still can't stop my smile. My phone

flashes again, but this time with a call. Oswald's name is on the screen.

"Hello," I answer softly. Does he know I was just texting with his brother?

"Hey." There's a slight echo, but his voice is low too. "I didn't wake you, did I?"

"No, is everything okay?"

"Yeah, I was just thinking about you, about kissing you."

My stomach hollows out. I've been thinking about that too, but I wasn't expecting him to bring it up. I don't know what to say back.

"Have you been thinking about it?" He sounds just like he did after we kissed, sexy.

"Uh-huh," I reply.

"I wish I could see you right now."

"We can FaceTime," I offer.

Oswald does this low, throaty kind of chuckle, and the hair on my arms stands up. "Maybe next time, baby."

"Okay," I whisper.

"Where are you?"

"In my room."

"In bed?" I swear it sounds like he groans the question, but I pretend not to notice.

I don't know where this is going, but I doubt I'm prepared for it. "Yes, where are you?"

"At the apartment." He brushes off my question with a

quick, nondetailed answer. "Do you like being home all alone?"

"No, I thought I would, but it's lonely," I admit.

"That's why I stay with Memphis, we're a package deal," Oswald tells me, and my mind goes to a place it shouldn't. Is he referring to where they live or... "You're okay with that, right, Waylynn?"

"Yes," I answer too fast.

"Good, I'm going to let you go before... Well, I just wanted to hear your voice and say goodnight."

Before what? I'm dying to know, but I swallow the need to uncover what he was about to say and murmur, "Goodnight, Oswald."

Just before the phone disconnects, I hear another groan, and my mind comes up with all kinds of things he could be doing, but I force those thoughts out of my head and scoot down under my covers. My shirt drags across my nipples, and I make a similar needy sound.

I flip onto my side and shove my phone under the pillow next to my head, forcing myself to ignore it, and close my eyes. I can't help that my mind goes to Oswald and his kiss, or the way it felt to be cozied up next to Memphis in the backseat. I'm going to blame it all on hormones and the fact that I spent way more time examining my feelings and what was going on in my head instead of enjoying the things most kids my age have.

When I enter class Wednesday, it feels like a lot more time than a day has passed since I had dinner with Oswald, Memphis, and Bates. I'm not dreading going into class like I have been, but I do have nervous butterflies in my stomach for an entirely different reason.

Someone collides with me the second I clear the door. I feel a warm breath on the side of my neck and smell the scent of fresh soap—Oswald. "There you are." He buries his nose behind my ear. My first instinct is to close my eyes and revel in his touch, but I'm too self-conscious not to look around to see who else is noticing.

We have a few of our classmates' attention, but it's Memphis' gaze that has me transfixed. I expect him to narrow his eyes or express his disapproval in some way, but he just watches me for a long second, then glances around the large room as if he were just looking around.

"I saved you a seat," Oswald says, still speaking into my neck.

"Thank you."

"I don't know if you're going to say that when you find out where we're sitting." He finally moves out from behind me and grabs my hand as he starts to walk down the center aisle. The farther we go, the faster my heart starts to beat.

It's early enough that there are a lot of open seats, especially this close to the front. Oswald guides me into the second row, and we don't stop until we're in the middle. I notice a bag on one of the seats and an open laptop on the other. He snags the bag and places it on the floor. "Sorry, he said he wanted your eyes on him to make sure you were paying attention," he explains.

"I always pay attention," I defend but lower myself into the seat.

"Don't let it bother you, he just wanted to be close to you too," Oswald tells me easily, and I can feel heat crawling up my neck. I don't really know what to do with that information, so I change the subject.

"How was practice yesterday?" We talked on the phone last night for a few minutes, mostly to say hi, and he asked about my classes.

"Fine, I wish they would tell me if I was actually playing this weekend. I hate not knowing."

"Where's the game? Is it here?"

"Yeah, the next three games are at home. You'll come, right?" Oswald is looking at me with wide, hopeful eyes. I would say yes even if I didn't want to, but I really want to see him play.

"I would love to. How do I get tickets?"

Oswald's eyes soften, and he mumbles, "I want to kiss you so badly right now." His eyes even dip to my mouth. "But that's not a good idea, because I won't want to stop." He's silent for a breath then adds, "Don't worry about tickets, you can sit with Memphis and Bates if he can make it."

My thoughts are split between him wanting to kiss me and him inviting me to sit with his brother. "Are you sure they won't mind?" What I'm really asking is if he's sure Memphis won't mind, but I'm not brave enough to say that. I spent way more time than I should have thinking about his behavior at dinner Monday and after.

"I'm positive. I doubt he'd even let you in the stadium without him." Oswald chuckles.

I let that conversation die as the seats around us slowly fill in, even though I have questions about his last statement, but I do glance up at the stage to see Memphis. He's standing next to Hilbrand and peering at something she's pointing at on the lectern.

His hair looks damp, as if he just got out of the shower, the collar of his white shirt is unbuttoned, and his sleeves are rolled up his forearms. It's so much easier to examine him when he's not looking back.

As if he knows I'm studying him, Memphis lifts his eyes, and our gazes connect. I should probably look away, but I don't, not until the chair next to me snaps down when someone takes the seat.

Her floral perfume fills my nose. It's nice but a little strong, like she just applied it. I pull my stuff over to make sure she has enough room, and she twists her head to glance at me. I try for a small smile, but it probably comes off as awkward. She resumes pulling out her laptop without acknowledging me.

"Italian for lunch?" Oswald asks, but it's not really a question.

"Are you already thinking about lunch? Did you eat this morning?"

"Yes and yes." He nods. Even though I'm looking at Oswald, I can still see when the girl next to me leans forward to get a better look at him.

"Do you want a bar?" I haul my backpack up on my lap and pull out one of the snacks I packed because he's always hungry.

"Beautiful and carries munchies in her bag." He snatches the blueberry protein bar from my fingers and smacks a kiss on my lips. "Wait, this wasn't your breakfast, was it?"

"No, you're always starving."

"Aw, Wavy baby, you're killing me." Oswald groans sweetly, and my heart flutters into my throat.

"Let's get started," Memphis announces, calling the class to attention and hopefully distracting Oswald from seeing my goofy grin.

For the next ninety minutes, I allow myself to watch his every breath and move without worrying about who knows how entranced I am by him. He opens the class up to more discussion and shows excitement when the room engages with him.

I swear he looks directly at me a few times, but I bet half the people in the room feel the exact same way. As he makes his way over to the podium, he makes an announcement. "My office hours will be cut short on Thursday by an hour or so. I will be checking emails but most likely not responding until Friday. If you have an urgent concern, get it to me before then. See you next week."

"Ready." Oswald is already on his feet.

I close out my notes app and shut my laptop before sliding it in my bag. When Oswald reaches for it, I intentionally turn so my back is to him. "Nu-uh, you don't always need to carry my stuff."

"Are you trying to distract me with your butt?" He sounds slightly outraged, but when I spin to face him to tell him no, he snatches my bag and smirks down at me. "It worked."

"I was not." I glance around to see if anyone else heard him.

"I know, and that's why it's so adorable. Get moving, Wavy." He uses his body to urge me forward.

"I can't go any faster," I mumble under my breath while tipping my head toward the girl blocking the row. Oswald is so close, I can feel him bump against my body with every movement. My brain must be going a little haywire, because I'm thinking about how much I like it.

"Come on, this way is cleared out," he says and takes my hand to tow me after him. I give one quick glance down toward Memphis when we're about to leave the room, but Oswald catches me looking. "Don't worry, he's coming."

"I wasn't worried." I sound defensive, making it more obvious I was.

Instead of answering me, Oswald backs me up against the wall just outside the classroom and drops his mouth to mine. He nips my bottom lip softly with his teeth, and I make a small, surprised sound. Before I can take a full inhale, his lips seal over mine and he slips his tongue inside my mouth.

My heart is hammering against my chest so hard, I know he must feel it thumping into his. He presses his lower body against mine, and heat swirls low in my belly. I do my best to kiss him back, but mostly, I'm just responding to the swipes of his tongue and press of his lips.

"One guess what they are doing for lunch." A guy snorts.

"Each other," comes the less than witty reply.

Fucking idiots, whispers through my mind just as Oswald says in the same voice, "Ignore them," with his lips still against mine, but he's definitely slowing. I almost wish he wouldn't so everyone has time to leave. I don't want the images of them smirking at me in my mind.

I duck my head when he pulls back completely. I'm nearly panting, and I can't even blame it on the shock of his voice in my head.

"I knew you'd get me in trouble."

I jerk my head back so I'm looking up at him. "Me?"

"Yes, you." He narrows his eyes playfully. "Now come on before you make us late and you really get in trouble with you know who." He grabs my hand and pulls me from the wall, which I'm pretty sure was holding me up.

"You're the one who made us late," I defend.

"It's still your fault. Believe me, he'll sympathize."

"If I get in trouble, I'm going to tell him why we were late," I whisper roughly. I'm not taking the blame.

Oswald makes a grunting sound. "He would understand why I did it, just not where. Maybe we should run." He pretends like he's going to take off but stops the second my arm offers any resistance so he doesn't jerk me forward. "Are you coming?"

"I was not built to run," I state.

Oswald lets out a little laugh. "What?" He's walking backward at this point so he can look at me.

"Trust me, it's not pretty."

He shakes his head and continues to smile at me. "Good thing we're close." When we make it to the sidewalk near the lot Memphis usually parks in, I spot the truck, and it's not empty. "Uh-oh."

"Is he really going to be mad? I won't tell him what happened," I promise quickly, trying not to move my lips too much because I feel like he's already watching us.

"We better go find out." He sounds dead serious.

Memphis

Waylynn is walking slowly toward the truck, like she's dreading climbing inside. I glance at the clock. They typically

SEEING SOUND

beat me here, but I was rushing more than usual today, and it seems they were a bit slower.

Oswald opens the door and tosses their stuff in the back, then crowds Waylynn until she climbs in the truck. Her head is down, and she mumbles, "Sorry we're late." I glance at Oswald over her head, confused.

I wait for Oswald to shut his door before placing my finger under her chin and directing her gaze to mine. "Did something happen? Are you okay?"

"I'm fine," she replies in a slightly husky tone.

"Tell me," I demand. Something upset her, and I need to know what it is.

"I'm sorry we're late."

"You already said that." That's not what I want to hear, and I let her see my disappointment.

"Oswald kissed me," she blurts and blinks several times as if she surprised herself.

"So much for not telling," my brother says, but I can hear the smile in his words.

"Did that bother you?" I ask while she's still staring into my eyes.

"No," she whispers.

"Then why are you upset?" My thumb strokes the side of her jaw, and she leans into my touch just enough that I feel pressure against my fingers.

"He thought you would be mad if we were late."

I'm going to kick his ass. "I'm not mad. He was teasing you."

"Okay." She leans against my fingers a little more.

"We should go," Oswald says with enough urgency that I know to pull my hand back from Waylynn immediately. She rights herself in her seat just as quickly and reaches for her seatbelt.

I pull down the gear shift and scan the people walking around. Hilbrand is nearing my truck, but she's not even looking in our direction. Thank fuck. I make a mental note to thank Oswald later for the cockblock, because I was thinking about kissing Waylynn, and she might not be ready for that. Letting me flirt with her and being receptive is a far cry from where I want this to go. Plus, there's a reason that should be more important, but somehow, it's not. Hilbrand could have seen us.

As soon as we're out of the parking lot, I wrap my fingers over the top of her thigh, down by her knee. She tenses for just a second, then relaxes until I can feel her leg pressed up against mine all the way up to my hip.

"Believe it or not, it was hard to find a restaurant that served lasagna that wasn't a pizza place," I say while taking us farther from the downtown area.

"We can go anywhere," she says quickly.

"No, we can't, I just hope this place lives up to the reviews." I can't stop myself from running my hand up and down her leg a little.

"Where is it? Ypsi?" Oswald looks out the window.

"Close." Thankfully, the parking lot isn't packed. I was hoping to beat the lunch rush if there is one.

Oswald

Memphis places his hand on top of Waylynn's when she reaches for the bill the second the waitress sets the padded folder down. "It's my turn," she says without lifting her head to meet his stare.

I watch my brother's lips thin, but then he releases her hand slowly. "I didn't bring you here for you to pay." His voice is tight, and Waylynn reacts to it by shrinking in on herself as she pulls the folder closer to her chest near the table.

"You've bought me lunch twice," she reminds him.

"You've fed us dinner at your house." He leans closer to her, and I watch her top teeth sink into her full bottom lip. "Give me the bill...please."

She sucks in a shaky inhalation when her hair stirs from his breath on her neck. Without looking up, she slides the folder over to him slowly. "Good girl," he rumbles, and she inhales sharply.

I adjust my dick in my pants, praying the waitress isn't too fast. That last little noise she made put me over the edge. I'm going to have blue balls for my next class.

Memphis stays close to Waylynn as we wait for his card to be returned. He even rests his arm on the back of her chair. It looks casual, but I know it's not. The moment he signs the slip, we all stand.

Memphis walks out the door and holds it open for both of us. When we're in the sun, Waylynn takes a deep breath and says, "I can't go to lunch with you anymore until you promise to let me reciprocate," in a rush, as if she's been holding on to the words for a long time.

"How about dinner tonight?" Memphis says, strolling to the truck. Waylynn seems dumbfounded. Frankly, I am too. He wouldn't let her pay at lunch, but he will tonight at dinner?

"Okay," she drawls.

"We'll be over when he gets done with practice. Do you have anything thawed?" Damn, he's slick. He just secured us an invite to her house and dinner.

Waylynn falters, seeming to understand he just played her, but she can't really deny him since she did pay for all the groceries. "No, but I'll figure it out." She hauls open the truck door before I can and then slips into the middle seat.

NEAR MISS

Waylynn

It's not until I get home and check my phone that I see the reminder for my appointment with Maxwell tonight at five. I panic for a second, knowing he won't let me cancel, and freak out about the guys showing up while I'm in session. I do not want to explain what's going on in my life to any of them.

My fingers shake as I pull up my texts, like Oswald and Memphis might burst through the door any second and somehow know I have to talk to my therapist today. It would be easier to text Oswald, but I know he has practice, so I hit the thread named Sir.

Me: Hello, I'm sorry to bother you. What time does Oswald's practice end?

I hit send before I can chicken out. It was around six when

I got to the dining hall on Monday, and they were there. If that's his norm, it will give me just enough time for my forty minutes with Maxwell before they get here, then I can just order us takeout. Memphis can't insist on paying for food if I already took care of it.

I start to relax a little.

Sir: You're not bothering me. He usually texts me when he's heading to the showers.

"Dang it."

Sir: Why?

Sir: Do you need something?

Sir: Tell me.

He's barely giving me time to think, let alone form a response.

Me: I apologize for the late notice, but something has come up. Can we make it any time after six?

His responding text bubble pops up and disappears several times before my phone rings.

"Hello."

Memphis skips over my greeting. "Are you going to the study group?"

"No," I answer quickly.

"Then what came up?"

"Is six too late?" I counter.

"No, why are you avoiding answering me? Is someone there with you? Where are you?" Memphis presses.

"Because, no, and at home," I rattle off.

"Because?" He repeats my answer slowly in a deep voice, and it's enough for me to give him more of an explanation.

"I have an appointment."

Memphis lets out a long sigh, and I don't know if it's a good thing or a bad thing. "Why didn't you just say that?"

I didn't want you to ask what kind of appointment. "I didn't think it would matter," I offer, but it lacks confidence.

"You'll be home from your appointment at six?"

"Yes." I don't tell him I'm not leaving, it might invite more questions. He always seems concerned about who knows I live alone, and he may think someone is coming over.

"Do you need anything?"

"For tonight, no."

"For tonight, tomorrow, anytime," Memphis clarifies.

"Um, no thank you," I tell him, but my voice goes up high on the end like it's a question.

"I want you to tell me if you do, do you understand?"

"Okay."

"Anything. Now tell me you will."

"I will tell you if I need anything," I repeat softly.

"Good girl. I'll see you at six." My reaction to the words is just as visceral as the first time he said it to me earlier today. My lower stomach tightens, and I want to hear him say it again, which makes little sense to me, other than the desire I have to make him happy.

"Bye." I'm breathy and obvious, so I hang up the phone quickly, hoping he didn't notice. I distract myself by scrolling through my phone and trying to decide what I'm going to order for dinner. I got my fill of red sauce today with lasagna. While it wasn't as good as Beth's, it wasn't bad, but I don't feel like pizza. After fifteen minutes of searching, I opt for an Asian place that has great reviews for their takeout and a huge variety.

As it gets closer to five, I get antsy. I already have my laptop open on my desk with the meeting room pulled up, ready to get this over with. This is only our second appointment since I moved away. So much has changed in such a short amount of time, but I don't know what I want to share with him. I know for a fact he talks to my parents about our sessions, which didn't bother me before, but I don't like the thought of it now.

The loud doorbell ding from the computer alerts me that Maxwell is ready. "Hello, Waylynn." His eyes crinkle at the sides with his smile. He's older, maybe in his fifties, with medium brown hair and dull blue eyes. His tweed blazer is open, revealing a simple white shirt without a tie.

"Hi." I send him an awkward wave.

"How are you this week?" I can't see the pad of paper on his desk, but I know from experience it's there.

"Good," I tell him honestly. "School takes up a lot of my time, and I'm getting to know the area better."

"You're not feeling too overwhelmed with the class load?"

"Not yet, but it's still early."

He looks up from his notes and assesses my face. "How about any student groups or social events?"

I work hard not to seem dodgy when I answer. "I've signed up for the study group in math, and some of us went to the dining hall after."

"That's great. How do you feel about the group? Did it seem helpful?"

"I think so. We've only had one meeting so far. I skipped today so I could be here for this." I don't mention that Oswald and Memphis offered to help me anyway.

"Oh, do we need to adjust your time for next week?"

"Tuesday or Thursday might be better," I agree, knowing I don't see the guys on those days.

"I'll make a note. Cindy will message you with the new time after she checks your class schedule."

It didn't feel intrusive when I sent his office my schedule before, but it feels strange when he mentions it now.

"Any voices?" He gets to the meat of it.

"No." I shake my head in denial too. I usually don't have an issue fibbing, I've had to do it for a long time, but not usually to him, and I'm a little concerned he will know.

"Any symptoms or side effects from the medication?"

"I don't think so."

"No drowsiness, lightheadedness, headaches, or confusion?"

"No," I tell him, even as I'm thinking about the first time the guys spoke to me and I felt all those things and more. Could it just be from my meds?

"How about depression, or are you having a hard time sleeping?"

"No." I feel like a broken record.

"It's okay to tell me if anything is going on," he urges.

"I know."

"I'm really pleased that the Xanax seems to be helping so much, but I don't want you to be discouraged if we have to tweak things. As you get used to the medication and grow older, your system may change."

"Okay," I reply, even though I don't want to make any changes.

"Is there anything you'd like to discuss?"

I know from experience that if I don't bring anything up, he will keep prodding until he finds something to talk about. I settle on the most normal thing I can think of. "I get lonely sometimes."

He nods, and his face softens, and I know I've hit the right cue. "That's totally expected. Being away from home for the first time—"

"Not really the first time," I interrupt.

"We can both agree this is different though, right?" I nod. "Moving to your own place can bring up new feelings and emotions, and it's good to explore those reactions. I'm pleased you're bringing it up and addressing it."

"I think it's just knowing there was someone in the house somewhere, and I'm missing that a little."

We spend the next thirty minutes talking about how I'm feeling and my new house, and he gives me homework to make a few friends.

I look at the clock on the top of the screen more often than I should, and I think he notices, because he brings the meeting to a close about five minutes early. "Cindy will give you a call or text about the new time and day. I'm proud of you, Waylynn. You're doing great. You know I'm available if you need anything, so don't hesitate."

"Thanks, Maxwell," I reply, and it's not lost on me how he said something that sounded similar to Memphis, but the feeling and intensity behind them are so different.

I click back to the delivery website and order way too much food. The wait time is over an hour, but if the guys get here too early, I can always feed Oswald snacks to keep him happy. I add a good tip, hoping the driver will be more inclined to get it here quickly, and give instructions on delivering to the backdoor.

Once I get the text confirmation on my phone, I close my laptop and climb off my bed. When I got home, I changed into joggers, but when I look at the jeans I had on earlier hung over my chair, I can't bring myself to put them back on, or any others. The desire to be comfortable outweighs the need to look put together. It would be different if we were going out.

While I'm waiting for them to get here, I check all the

bathrooms to make sure there's soap and toilet paper, and then make sure I don't have any clothes on the floor in the laundry room. When I'm done, I still have plenty of time to turn on the TV and pretend like I'm not anxious for them to arrive.

By quarter after six, I'm starting to wonder if I should text them, but I decide against it. I do wander into the kitchen so I can watch the driveway. About twenty minutes later, a black car slowly pulls in, and I let my disappointment sink in.

It's nearly seven, and I haven't heard from either of them. I open the door as the guy hops out of the driver's seat. "Hey," he calls and jogs around the car to the passenger backdoor. When he steps back, he has a large cardboard box in his hands with plastic bags billowing out the top. He looks at me then past me, probably noticing there's no one else coming to help. "It's heavy, want me to bring it in?"

"Sure, if you don't mind."

"Not at all." He gives me a smile as I hold open the door for him. "Is here okay?" He's standing near the island.

"Perfect, just one second." I hold up a finger and rush over to my purse to grab a few extra dollars for his trouble.

"Who the hell are you?" Memphis' voice cuts through the room. Oswald steps up right behind him and glares at the delivery man.

"Garrett." I would be a mess if Memphis looked at me the way he glares at the poor guy. "Just dropping off the food." He steps to the side, revealing the large box on the counter.

I fold a twenty and walk past Memphis and Oswald so I can hand it to Garrett. "Sorry about that."

"It's good." He pockets the cash and pivots toward the door Memphis and Oswald are still crowded around.

"I'll move the truck." Oswald backs out the door, and Memphis steps to the side to let Garrett leave, but he continues to glare at him.

Memphis strides over to me and pushes into my space. "Why did you let him in? What if we didn't show up when we did?"

"He offered to bring in the box," I defend, but it's weak.

"Did he know you were here alone?" He's even closer now. I have to lean back so I can see his face.

"No, and I don't think he thought I was eating all that."

Memphis' shoulders relax before he reaches up and curls his fingers around the side of my neck. "You don't even need to open the door. They can leave it on the porch."

"I know. I've done that before," I reply.

"When I pulled up and saw the car with the door wide open..." His tongue sweeps over his bottom lip. "I don't like you being here alone all the time. Anything could happen, and I wouldn't even know."

"You don't have to worry. I have an alarm, and I'm good about locking the doors." My heart is beating fast. He seems genuinely worried, and I hate that it's about me, especially without a real reason.

"I will worry." His grip tightens, and he pulls me a little closer.

The door closes, and I still don't take my eyes off Memphis. "Sorry we're late. They kept us at practice." Oswald fills the room with his presence.

Memphis loosens his hold and trails his fingers softly over my neck and collarbone before stepping back. I miss the heat of his touch immediately. "Next time, I'll come without you and you can walk over."

"It's okay. There's food," I state, not addressing Memphis' warning to his brother.

I start pulling bags from the boxes and opening everything. Once it's all spread out, I realize I went way overboard, even with Oswald eating as much as he does. "Um… It's a lot."

"It's okay, now we have an excuse to come back tomorrow for leftovers." Oswald kisses the side of my head when he walks past me. I glance up at Memphis to see his reaction to the casual touch, but he's already walking toward me to follow his brother.

These two make my head spin, but I wouldn't trade their company for anything, let alone something simple.

∼

"Did Bates forward the info about his show?" Oswald's eyes are only half open when I glance over at him. I wasn't even sure he was awake. He's been quiet for the past thirty minutes of the movie we've been watching.

"Yeah, his set starts at eight-thirty." Memphis tips his head down and asks me, "That's not too late, right?"

"Yeah, I'm looking forward to it. Is anyone else going?" I hope it's not obvious I'm asking if they are bringing anyone else.

"Not with us," comes Memphis' quick reply.

"Just our girl," Oswald adds softly, like he really is half asleep.

"What time are you free tomorrow?" I feel Memphis pick up the ends of my hair.

"My last class lets out around three, so any time after that."

"Are you sure you don't have any appointments?" he questions.

"No, is there a dress code at the bar?" I change the subject, hoping he doesn't ask what kind of appointment it was. I can tell he's fishing.

"No, anything you wear will be fine."

"Have you been there before?" Talking with him is way more interesting than watching the movie.

"Maybe." He lifts his shoulder just enough that I register the movement. "They are all pretty much the same—trendy little bars with cheap booze and bad sound systems."

"How old are you?"

Memphis looks down at me, and for a breath, I think he might not respond, but then he asks, "Why?"

"Just curious."

He leans a little closer and scrutinizes me. "Are you sure you weren't asking if I could get you drinks?"

"No," I scoff. Meds and alcohol don't mix. I tried that once a year or so ago, never again.

"Good, because I won't," he states emphatically, and it makes me wonder if he doesn't believe me.

"That's not why I asked. Sorry I brought it up." I turn to look at the TV, but I can still feel his gaze on the side of my face.

"I'm nearly twenty-four," Memphis tells me in a much softer tone.

I told the truth when I said I was curious. I'm curious about a lot of things when it comes to the Gravlin brothers. "Are you a senior then?"

"Graduate student. I'm mostly still here to help with the tuition his football scholarship didn't pay for. I only have one other class besides assisting for Hilbrand, and it's self-guided with only a few short lectures."

It's clear he and Oswald have a very tight bond, but his answer makes me want to know more, like why he's the one worrying about his brother's tuition, but neither of them have brought up their parents.

"Ask me." Memphis strokes his finger along my jawline. "I can see the questions swirling in your eyes."

"I don't mean to be nosy," I tell him, but I really do. I want to know everything about them.

"Waylynn…" He says my name slowly, as if he's chastising me. "Ask me."

"Why do you take care of him?"

"We take care of each other, we're all we have." There's no inflection in his tone, no anger or hurt. It's just a statement.

"What happened to your parents, your family?"

"They weren't much of a family to begin with, but we lost both our parents."

My heart aches, and I place my hand over his in the small space between us. "I… I don't have any words other than I'm sorry."

He flips his hand over and laces our fingers together. "There's nothing for you to be sorry about."

"I brought it up."

"It was bound to come out some time. I'm glad you talked to me about it, he…" Memphis looks past me. "It's just easier for me to talk about."

"I get that," I confess. "My parents can't talk about my brother." I don't add that I often field the questions in the same way to protect them.

He doesn't have a reply, and I don't need one. Our soft conversation dies, but he's still holding my hand and tracing his thumb along the inside of my wrist. I'm slightly shocked by how good it feels. My skin is super sensitive, or maybe it's just his touch making it that way.

The movie continues to play, but I'm not really paying attention. Oswald's deep, even breaths and Memphis' warm palm are much more interesting.

∽

I TRY to shift my legs and can't, which has me lifting my head up and gasping, ready to shove whatever it is off me—until I see who it is. Oswald has his arm wrapped over my thighs. I can feel the top of his head under my butt, and his face is nestled against the backs of my legs. I try to straighten out so he's not right in my butt, but then I feel the cushion under me shift, and I look down to see I'm lying half on Memphis. His eye slits open, and he gazes up at me.

"I'm sorry, I must have fallen asleep," I whisper, hoping not to wake Oswald. Oh god, this is embarrassing. His face is... I can't even think it. How am I going to get up when he's holding me down?

"Don't apologize to me. It's your house." His voice is thick and gravelly, he must have been sleeping too. I look down and realize my head must have been pretty close to his crotch. "You guys can crash in the spare rooms." I try to sound normal as I pull up my knee to get out from under Oswald, but he's got a tight grip.

Memphis' brows furrow, probably because he can see and feel me jerking around. "What?" He looks past me to his brother.

"He won't let go," I whisper in horror, knowing he can see where Oswald's head is.

"Proof he's not as dumb as he seems," Memphis drones. "Smack his hand."

"No," I exclaim. "Let me just…" I lean down again, bringing my face closer to Memphis' groin, and I'm able to lift my knee enough so he releases his hold a little. I take the tiny advantage and roll off the couch and onto the floor.

Memphis scowls at me. "I would have woken him up myself if I knew you were going to do that."

Once I'm on my butt, I pull my knees up and reach around to rub my tingling toes. We must have been like that for a while since my feet are asleep. "He was cutting off my circulation."

"He's trained to never let go of what's important."

"I'm not a football." I wiggle my feet, but the pins and needles are still there.

"Oswald." I jump at Memphis' commanding tone. "Wake up."

"I'm up," he replies with a sleepy groan. "I was having the best dream. I was eating Waylynn's—"

"Shut up," Memphis snaps and glances over at me.

Oswald picks his head up off the couch and blinks his blurry eyes. "Shit."

"You guys can use the spare rooms, or I can let you out." I bet my face is as red as a fire engine. I know what he was about to say.

"I'd rather get up early than leave now, if you're sure you don't mind," Memphis answers for both of them.

"I don't mind. I'll write down the alarm code so you can leave in the morning," I tell them as I rise. "Let me know if you need anything." I back out of the room a few steps, then turn around to flee up the stairs.

Oh my God, I mouth, feeling like I might need a shower, but also thinking he did say it was a good dream, the best in fact.

The bathroom door closes with a snap as I let my back fall against the door. I lock it just in case, then go pee before washing my hands. When I catch a glimpse of myself in the mirror, I confirm my suspicions. My face is still red.

I don't bother with my full skin care routine, but I do wash my face quickly and apply some lotion before putting on a cute pair of silk sleep shorts and a matching button-up top. I usually just go with a T-shirt, but if there was ever a time for cute pj's, it's now.

Once I'm under the blanket, I turn on the TV and the fan I use for white noise. My head is swimming with so many thoughts, it's hard to focus on one, but one thing I do recognize is the empty feeling in the house is absent, and that makes a huge difference as I snuggle my head back. It's pretty bad I'm already looking forward to hanging out with them tomorrow when they haven't even left yet.

WHAT THE HEART WANTS

Memphis

"Turn on the light, I don't see anything with the alarm code." Oswald flips on the switch, and I squint for a long second before my eyes adjust.

"Maybe she forgot to write it down," he mumbles.

"Damn it, I hate to wake her up so early."

"I'll do it," he offers with a lazy smile.

"I don't trust you to actually wake her up *and* leave her after," I drawl.

Oswald shrugs, as if he can't argue. The stairs are silent as we make our way up. I'm kind of glad he came with me. I don't really trust myself either.

I put my ear near the door, and I hear soft voices. "Maybe

she's awake. I think the TV is on," I murmur and tap the door softly. When there's no reply, I reach for the door handle to see if she locked it.

My heart races when it turns, knowing I could have snuck in here at any time to watch her. Waylynn is curled on her side with her hands tucked under her chin, and her lips are slightly parted as she breathes softly. The blankets are pushed down a little, but it just makes me want to know what's under them even more.

After a long second of committing the sight of her to memory, I approach her bed slowly so as not to startle her. "Waylynn." I murmur her name softly, and she takes a deeper breath but doesn't wake up. "Waylynn," I murmur again, but this time, I run the backs of my fingers along her cheek and jaw.

She flips onto her back, her eyes wide but unfocused, and sucks in a heavy breath. "It's okay, sweetness." I try to sound reassuring.

She blinks several times, her eyes heavy-lidded with sleep. "I'm sorry, did you need something?" Her voice is husky and goes right to my balls.

"The alarm code. I can't find it."

"Shoot." She rubs her fingers over the side of her face. "I'm sorry. I came right to bed and forgot."

"Stop saying sorry."

"Okay," she agrees.

"The code, sweetness," I remind her when she relaxes back into the bed.

Her eyes pop open again, but not with fear. "I almost fell back asleep," she mumbles. "You guys are like Ambien. 2-5-7-4-2-2."

"Anytime you need help sleeping, we're around," Oz offers.

"Is it too soon to offer a key? I think I need roommates." She snuggles back into the bed and pulls the covers up over her shoulder.

I run my hand over her hair. "I like the idea, sweetheart, but not the title. We'll see you later."

"Okay." She sighs softly.

I rise from the side of the bed, and Oswald takes my place, dropping a kiss on her temple. "Dream about me," he tells her, then backs away slowly. I don't really want to leave either.

"I'm going to be late," Oz mutters when we bound down the stairs.

"Your stuff is still in the truck from yesterday. I can take you straight to the gym."

"That's fine. The whole place smells like ass most of the time, so it's not like anyone would notice I didn't shower."

"Speaking of, your face was buried pretty deep in Waylynn last night."

"Fuck, don't remind me." He reaches into the backseat to pull his gym bag into his lap. "I'm lucky I didn't pin her to the couch and dry hump her while I was sleeping."

I snort. "You were holding her legs so tightly, her feet fell asleep."

"Jesus." He chuckles. "I'm not even sorry."

We pull up in front of the field house as close to the door as I can get. "Text me when you're done this afternoon and I'll pick you up."

"I'll try to get out of practice early if I can," he says while climbing out. I nod and wait for him to get inside before I pull away from the curb. It would be nice to go back to Waylynn's. If I had the key she teased at, I would, only I wouldn't be going to the spare room, I would be sneaking back into hers.

Oswald

My legs are killing me when I step out of the shower. I fucking hate elevator squats. "Hey, Gravlin, where have you been?"

"Right here, Miggs. Don't tell me you miss me." I curl my lips into a smile, even though I'd rather he not even speak to me.

"Didn't see you on the field this week," he ribs.

I grind my back teeth. Shit talking is a sport in itself, but that one hits a little hard since I haven't had any real play time during a game. I shrug like it's no big thing. "I'll see if they can serve you popcorn on the bench when you're watching the show."

Several guys make *oh* sounds at the burn.

"I'll believe it when I see it." He snorts and walks away. His comeback is lame, so I let it go, knowing I have every intention to show him as soon as I get the chance.

"You going to be staying at your brother's place all the time, man?" KJ asks from my side as I'm pulling up my socks.

"Why?" I don't have a lot of patience today. I don't even want to go to my classes.

"It would just be nice to know so I could make plans and shit."

"I need to keep my stuff there, but I probably won't sleep there often. No bumping uglies on my bed though," I warn as I rise to my feet.

"So it's your closet?" He snorts with disappointment.

"Don't be too upset, KJ, you'll still see me." My words are teasing, but my tone really isn't. He's pissy because I need to keep some of my shit in *my* room when he should be happy he has it to himself most of the time.

"Maybe you could text me or some shit when you want to come by."

"Are you fucking joking?" Now I'm getting pissed.

"It was just an idea, calm down." He looks around to see who else noticed my response.

"If I were a petty motherfucker, I'd come through in the middle of the night, but you just aren't that important to me.

I'll be in my room when and for how long I fucking feel like it."

"You took it the wrong way, man," he says to my back as I walk away. I make sure he sees my middle finger over my shoulder before I push out of the locker room, otherwise I might do something stupid like punch him in his smelly face.

"Oz," someone calls, and I glare over my shoulder. Higgins joins me as I walk down the hall.

"What's up?" My voice is tight when I speak.

"Want to grab dinner after practice?" He doesn't react to my tone.

"I can't tonight, my buddy has a show I said I'd go to."

"What kind of show? Is he in a band or something?"

"Or something," I say.

"Are you partying on a weeknight right before a game?" Higgins sounds doubtful. We spent most of the summer running drills and preseason practices together, so he knows that's not how I roll.

"Nah, just going to watch him play. I'll be asleep before midnight."

"Where's he playing?" He's a little too interested, and I don't really want any tagalongs this time, not since Waylynn will be there.

"Some small bar in Chelsea. He plays the cello." I say the last part to discourage him.

Higgins sucks air through his teeth, making the incorrect assumption it will be lame. I might have too, but I've been watching and hearing Bates play for years. He's a beast. I feel bad for making it seem like a shitshow now, but I'll make it up to both Higgins and Bates later.

"Another time then." He slows his steps.

"Yeah, for sure," I agree and head to my class. I'm not as pissed as I was, but I'm still irritated with KJ.

Waylynn

Are you fucking joking? The words ring clear in my mind, and I don't question who they came from. Oswald sounded upset, at least in my head. It's silly to think it's really him, but I still pull out my phone and open up the text app.

My thumbs hover over the keyboard for a long second as I debate texting him. I don't know what to say. It's not like I can just ask him directly if he thought the words I just heard in my head.

Me: Morning, sorry about forgetting to leave the code.

I hit send after erasing and retyping the message three times. I watch for a response for several seconds, but when none come, I slip my phone in my back pocket and lock up the house. I don't know what I thought I was going to learn anyway.

I haven't left school early once, and I'm feeling brave, so I leave my car in the garage, walk the few blocks to the corner, and cross over to campus. Students are still hustling to get from place to place, but I don't feel the same sense of urgency I felt last week.

When I enter the room, several of the seats are already taken, but I find a few open spots in the middle of a row near the back. I have to pass several people already seated, but there's nothing I can do but suck in my stomach and butt, then pass them quickly.

After opening my laptop and pulling up my notes from Tuesday, I still have time to check my phone. Oswald still hasn't responded, so I browse my social media, then give into the real reason I opened this app. My thumbs fly over the screen as I type in Oswald's name, but I know the person who comes up isn't him. I delete his name and retype Oz Gravlin, and when an account pops up, I know it's him, even though the picture is old.

I click on his account and look through the posts, most of which are memes and football related stuff, but there are a few with him and Memphis. I check to see if he's tagged in the photos, but nothing comes up.

After looking through his stuff a few times, I eventually go back to the top and click on the people he's following.

Memphis Gravlin is at the top, but when I click on his account, I get notified it's private. I'm not surprised, but that doesn't mean I'm any less curious. I go back to perusing Oswald's page, lingering way longer than I should on the pictures with girls in them, until the professor calls the class to attention.

When class is over, I head home for lunch. I have plenty of time and even more food. I feel my phone buzz when I'm about to cross the street, but I don't check it until I'm on the other side.

Oswald: U r adorable when you sleep.

His text brings a smile to my face.

Oswald: Where ru?

Me: Walking home for lunch. No parking violations today!

Oswald: Yum. Do u have another class? Why don't I have ur schedule?

Me: Yes, I have two classes this afternoon. I don't have yours either.

Oswald: We can trade later. What time do u go back?

Me: One.

Oswald: Dang it, woman, I get out at one.

Me: I promise to save you some food.

Oswald: Food is good, but I would rather see you.

I actually gasp and let out a girly sigh when I read his message, then I rush to type out a response so he doesn't know I was freaking out.

Me: Charmer.

Oswald: Only for u. Now stop distracting me, I'm in class.

There's a grin on my lips the rest of the walk home.

. . .

Memphis

I knock on the door twice before walking over to her small garage and peeking in the window. Her car is inside, but she's not answering the door. It's twenty minutes after three, so she should be home by now. Maybe she's in the bathroom.

Me: Where are you?

Unknown: Trying to get home. Will you call me please? I'm sorry, it will only take a second.

Her phone rings twice before she picks up. "…calling now. I really need to go. See you next week," I hear her telling someone before she says, "Hello," to me.

"Are you okay?" I'm already climbing back behind the wheel of my truck.

"I'm sorry, I'm okay. They just kept talking and talking," Waylynn mumbles into the phone.

"Who? Where are you?"

"Someone from class. I'm headed through the south quad. Where are you?" I can tell she's walking fast by her breathless tone.

"In your driveway. You didn't drive today?"

"Oh, no. I really can't. My friend is waiting for me," she says, but she's not talking to me.

"Are they fucking following you?" I slam the truck in reverse and pull out of her driveway with my phone pressed between my shoulder and ear.

"I have a boyfriend, but thank you," she says loudly, but then in a small voice she makes a soft plea. "Memphis."

"I'm coming, tell me where you are."

"Um... It's okay, just don't hang up, please."

"Waylynn."

"On State Street, near Hutchins Hall. He's going the other way. I'm okay, I'm okay," she whispers through the phone, trying to convince herself just as much as she's trying to convince me.

"Damn it, I hit the light."

"It's okay. He was just...being friendly, but he was... persistent." Her breaths are short and fast.

"I see you. Come get in the truck."

"There are cars behind you." She starts a slow jog while holding her backpack straps near her shoulders, squeezing her tits together with her forearms.

"They can wait." A horn honks, but I still don't move.

"Oh jeez." She throws herself into the truck, and I pull away from the curb as soon as she gets the door closed.

"Seatbelt," I tell her as she leans to the side and tries to pry her backpack off.

"I'm sorry. You didn't need to come." She sighs and lets her head fall back against the headrest for just a moment, then reaches for the shoulder belt.

"Apparently, I did. Why was he following you?"

"I don't think he was really following me like that, I think he just wanted to ask me something, but I left before he could, so he came back over."

"You sounded scared," I remind her.

"It was... I wasn't scared. I just didn't want to be rude. I could tell he was... I don't know, interested?" She looks out the side window so I can't see her face. "Sorry if I made you worry or think it was worse than it was."

I pull the truck into her driveway and put it in park when we're near the backdoor. She plucks two earbuds from her ears and shoves them in one of the pockets of her bag. I didn't even realize she wasn't carrying a phone. Mine is still on the seat next to me, where I dropped it when I saw her coming.

"Stop telling me you're sorry. Whatever it was, clearly, it made you uncomfortable, and you don't need to apologize for that. He should have left you alone."

"Well, thank you for talking to me and the ride." She reaches for the door handle. "Do you want to come in?"

"Yes, but only if you're okay with it." If she tells me to leave, I'll probably sit at the end of her street anyway.

"I'm okay with it. I'd appreciate the company."

She's already out of the cab when I turn off the truck and follow her to the door. She looks over her shoulder toward the street as if she's looking for something—probably the guy who didn't take the hint the first time she tried to blow him off.

When we slip inside, she disarms the alarm, then sets her

backpack on the counter. It's still unzipped from her grabbing her keys, so her purse is almost falling out, but she doesn't seem to notice. "If you'll excuse me for a minute, you can make yourself at home. There are refreshments in the fridge." Her formal word choice is further proof she's not as okay as she would have me believe, but I don't push her on it yet. I'm relieved she reached out to me, even if I was the one to text her first.

I send a message to Oswald. He's at practice, but he will check his phone before he showers.

Me: Some dude was harassing our girl today. I have her now, but I think he's in one of her classes. Might need to make it known she's off-limits.

When Waylynn returns, she seems a little more relaxed, but she's averting her gaze from me, which I don't like.

"Are you hungry? I have all those leftovers. I promised Oswald I'd save him some," she rambles.

"I had lunch, I'm good."

She closes the fridge. "Me too. Want me to turn on the TV?" she offers after spinning around. Instead of answering, I walk past the island, and she backs up until her butt hits the counter behind her, but I still crowd into her space.

"Do you want to watch TV?"

"If you do," she tells me softly.

"What do you usually do when you get home?"

"Hang out in my room and do homework."

"Then let's go." I tip my head to the side, inviting her to

lead the way, but I don't back up, so she has to brush up against me when she steps away from the counter.

My eyes drop to her round ass as she walks ahead of me. Being here alone with her is a bit more challenging than I thought it would be, but only because I was kidding myself when I thought I could be around her and not want to kiss her.

"I forgot my bag downstairs. You can pick the movie." She extends the remote to me and darts out of her room.

I walk around her bed and head right to the side I know she sleeps on. Her phone charger is on the bedside table, along with a few other things like lip shit and lotion. When she returns, she halts in the doorway, and her eyes travel over me. I wonder if she'll tell me I'm in her spot and ask me to move. Hell, I'd be happy if she came over and dropped into my fucking lap.

"Can I get you anything?" she offers and resumes entering the room.

"No." I pat the bed next to me and watch her throat work as she swallows, but she obeys, placing her bag in the middle of the bed before climbing up near the pillows.

To stop myself from telling or showing her how much I like her attentiveness, I try to distract myself. "Have you declared a major?"

"Psychology," she says with conviction.

"I like the confidence. I'd like to see it a little more."

"About what?" she asks softly.

"Everything."

Her lips twitch, and her eyes lower bashfully, but then she peers up at me from under her lashes, and it's something else entirely. Every inch of my body takes notice, with my dick being the first. "I think I need a little more direction than that."

She erases my filter with just a look. "Do you like taking direction?" This is not where I wanted to take this just yet.

Her shoulders curl in. "I think it depends."

"On what?"

"Who it's coming from and why." She leans forward, lifting her ass in the air as she reaches for her bag. She wiggles a bit as she tugs her laptop from the zippered compartment and falls back against the bed. She has no clue how fucking tempting she is. It's probably a good thing she has no idea my mind is in the gutter and my thoughts are solely focused on her.

"Are you sure this isn't too boring?" She flips open her computer and steals a glance at me.

"I promise bored is the last thing I am right now." Unless we're talking as stiff as one.

"I won't blame you if you take a nap. I do sometimes," she admits like it's a sin.

"Are you sleepy now?" I'm thinking about feeling her body curled up against mine.

Waylynn bites the corner of her lip and shakes her head in denial. I have no idea what she is thinking, but a flush burns across her cheeks, and I want to demand she tell me, but I only have so much restraint, and if she were to say anything remotely alluring, I wouldn't be able to stop myself from acting on the invitation.

"If you change your mind, cuddle up any time." I lean back against her pillow before I can see her face, otherwise I might kiss her.

My eyes lift to the top of her headboard, and my mind slips further into a full fantasy of her gripping that rolled iron while she's riding my face. I let my eyes sink closed, but the image comes even stronger. I see my hands curled around her thick hips, tugging and forcing her down until her thighs are quivering next to my ears.

Waylynn

I CAN HEAR his phone vibrating, but he doesn't even move. I let it go the first two times, but when it goes off again, I whisper, "Memphis," hating that I have to wake him up.

Still, he doesn't stir. I look at the time, noting it's after five. He's been out for over an hour. I don't even know what time we need to leave for the show. "Memphis," I say again a little bit louder.

He groans, but that's it. I brush my hand over his arm. He's warm and tight, but in the best way. I'm marveling at how his skin feels under my fingers, and I forget to say his name. When I look up, his eyes are open.

I snatch my hand back so fast, I hit my own stomach. "Your phone is going off," I rush to say in a hushed tone, as if maybe he's not fully awake and won't remember me groping him. His hand slides up from the side, and he tucks it into his front pocket. My eyes are drawn to the movement, and I see a bulge that isn't in the shape of a rectangle.

I've heard the term *morning wood*, but I always thought it was just something that people said. Do guys always wake up with a hard-on? What would it feel like if I were lying next to him? Oh jeez, why am I thinking about this?

"Oz is ready to be picked up," Memphis drawls, and the hair at the back of my neck stands up. I try to hide my shiver when I close my laptop.

"I can pick him up if you want, and you can relax," I offer.

"*We* can go pick him up. I can rub it in his face that I was in your bed first."

"It's a competition?" I tease, preparing to stand.

"Not with you, sweetness, but there's something to be said for firsts. He got the kiss. I get your bed. We'll share the others."

"Oh," is what I say out loud, but in my head, I have questions. Does that mean Memphis wants a kiss from me too? Is Oswald going to sleep in my bed at some point? Why do I get butterflies when he calls me sweetness? It's nearly as evocative as when he calls me a good girl, well, not really, it's not even close, but it does something to me. And what are the other firsts they will share?

I can think of a big one. Does he know I'm a virgin? Can guys tell that sort of thing?

"Should I change before we go, or are we coming back here?" I blurt just so I can stop thinking about the other stuff.

"It's still early, so we don't need to leave yet. If you're okay with us being here, we can come back. Your place is a lot nicer than mine."

"I like having you guys here, but that doesn't matter to me, about your place I mean. I'm sure I will like it if it's yours," I ramble.

"Come on, before he has an aneurysm or I take one of my firsts." He motions for me to follow him as he climbs off the bed.

"*Your* firsts?" I question. Maybe I have this first thing all wrong.

He slows his strides, coming to a full stop at the end of my bed. I watch him slide his left hand into his pocket, and then he beckons me to him with a crook of his right pointer finger. I watch my feet as I make my way over, but once I'm close, I lift my gaze to his.

"A little closer." He's not whispering, but his voice is smooth and low. I take another step, and we're only separated by inches. If I breathe too deeply, my boobs will probably rub against his chest.

"*Our* first, sweetness," he says, then he leans in so slowly, I know what he's going to do, but I can't wrap my head around the fact that it's actually happening. His fingers curl around the back of my neck, and he pulls me forward so I meet his lips instead of him coming all the way to me.

"Open," Memphis says against my mouth, and my lips part. His fingers tighten as he fists the hair at the nape of my neck. He slips the tip of his tongue along the seam of my lips, running from side to side before pushing deeper into my mouth.

I don't even know if I'm breathing. The only thing I know is Memphis Gravlin is kissing me as if I taste like cotton candy and melt like sugar against his tongue. Over my thundering heart, I can hear him breathing and feel the deep drafts of air he's pulling into his lungs.

My tongue slides against his, and a breathy sigh leaves my lips, summing up what I'm feeling better than any words I could muster. He tilts my head and slips deeper into my mouth, and then come the uninvited thoughts. *I can't let anyone know, shouldn't be like this.*

I try to pull back, but Memphis doesn't allow me to retreat. He makes a sound deep in his chest like a warning and nips my lip roughly. My stomach tightens, and I squeeze my thighs. Why did I feel that other places?

Softly and sweetly, he curls his tongue around mine. I'm afraid the thoughts will come again, but that fear only lasts until he sucks on the tip of my tongue with alternating pressure, and then I don't care about the thoughts, or maybe I'm too far gone to even hear them.

I grip his shirt in my fist, but the feeling of something

buzzing against my lower stomach has me jerking back, and this time, Memphis allows it.

"I knew that was a bad idea," he says with his eyes still closed.

My heart sinks, and his words actually hurt something deep in my chest.

When I try to get away from him, he snaps his eyes open. "Eyes on me," he demands roughly, like I'm the one who just said I regret what happened. I look up, even though I don't want to. "Not the kiss. Do you understand?"

I roll my lips in so I don't give him a response, because I don't understand.

"I was talking about how little time we would have, not the kiss," he tells me more emphatically and pushes his chest against mine while keeping a tight grip on my neck and hair. "There is no way you could think anything different. Now tell me."

"Your phone," I say when it vibrates again in his front pocket.

"Can wait," he responds before I'm even finished.

"Okay," I mumble.

"Okay, what?" he prompts. I should have known he wouldn't let me get away with an evasive answer.

"Okay, I understand," I agree. My feelings are slow to catch up, but I do understand that I could have jumped the gun on that.

"It was stupid of me to say it the way I did, but I promise that is not what I meant."

"Okay," I agree again.

When my phone starts to ring, Memphis lets out a sigh that I would call irritated, but I think it goes beyond that. "Let's go."

"Is it okay if I answer?" I ask when he finally releases me to head for the bedroom door.

"It's probably the only way to get him to stop calling." He sulks.

"Hello, we're on the way," I tell Oswald as I bound down the stairs after Memphis.

"You sound out of breath, Wavy. What have ya been doin', baby?"

"Homework," I say too fast.

"Oh yeah, did you have a study partner?" His voice is teasing.

"Um…"

"What subject were you working on?"

"Chemistry."

Oswald bursts out laughing at my response. "Did it have anything to do with attraction?"

"Tell him we'll be there in a minute," Memphis grumbles.

"I heard him. Do me a favor and ask him if he'll be playing the blues all night." Oswald snickers.

"Memphis." He snaps his head over to look at me, and I realize it's the first time I've said his name other than on the phone and when he was sleeping. "Um… He wants to know if you'll be playing the blues."

"Hang up on him." Memphis reaches for my phone, but I hear Oswald chortling before he snatches it away.

"Do you play too? Why was that funny?"

"I'm going to smack him," Memphis mumbles under his breath. "No, I do not *play*, and he's the only one who thinks it's funny. Why don't you ask him what he meant? We'll be there in a minute."

Oswald is freshly showered when he hops into the truck. The scent of his soap is strong in the small cab. "Ask him," Memphis urges.

"Why was Memphis playing the blues funny?"

Oswald's grin slips, and he darts his eyes over to his brother like he betrayed him.

"Yeah, why don't you explain what you meant by that?" Memphis turns out of the lot.

"Wait, really?" he asks me with a frown of confusion.

"Never mind." I decide I really don't need to know.

"You sure you don't want him to explain it?" Memphis prods but looks past me to his brother.

"Yeah, I think I'm less embarrassed not knowing than I would be if you told me," I admit.

"Clever girl," Memphis praises, and I don't feel so bad for not getting the joke.

CONTROL

Oswald

MEMPHIS AND WAYLYNN walk right past the doorman with a small head nod, while I get carded and a black X drawn on the back of my hand. My eyes are on her ass in the tight knee-length skirt as my brother opens the door for her.

When she walked out of the room, I about swallowed my tongue. Memphis must have run his hand over his mouth and chin three times before he could muster up a response. Knowing him, he probably wanted to tell her to go change, but he just told her she looked beautiful and I'm glad. If she changed, it would have been a fucking disservice to her and everyone else who laid eyes on her. She looks amazing.

"No fighting in the club," the doorman tells me after watching my gaze.

I smile. "No worries with us, she keeps us both in line."

"I bet, have a nice night." He chuckles.

Memphis is soaking up the anonymity of being fifteen miles away from home. He has his arm locked around Waylynn's waist as he guides her closer to the stage, where Bates promised he'd save us a table.

The music coming from the speakers is low enough that patrons can feel it through the floorboards, but not loud enough that they have to yell to be heard, which is how I hear a woman say, "He must be her brother. Guys like him only fuck girls that look like her, they don't take them out in public."

My jaw ticks, and I want so badly to say something just as nasty back to her, but Waylynn would inevitably ask what happened when the girl threw a drink in my face, and I'm not repeating her words. We can just show her how wrong she is.

"Hey, baby." I scoot into the booth beside Waylynn.

She's all smiles as she looks around. "These are really good seats."

"The place is tiny. All the seats are good." Bates leans his cello case against the back of the booth.

Waylynn probably picks up on Bates's self-deprecating tone, but it doesn't stop her from saying, "You must be really good, or people wouldn't be here to hear you play."

"They are here for the cheap booze."

"We're not. We're here to see you," she tells him in earnest. I want to smack a kiss on her face, so I do.

Bates is watching her with his head tilted to the side and a soft look in his eyes that he shakes away when Memphis speaks up. "They'll all love you as soon as you start playing. They always do."

"Excuse me." The same woman I overheard talking shit approaches the table with her friends, her eyes locked on Bates.

"Yeah?" Bates responds.

"We just wanted to tell you we watched your show last week and loved it. You're amazing," she gushes, all googly eyed.

"Oh wow, thanks." Bates smiles at them with real gratitude.

"We were wondering if you could sign this?" She's acting all nice now as she hands over a pink paper pamphlet the bar printed out with Bates' name on it and the time of the show, but I know what she's really like.

"Ah, sure." He looks around. "Do you have a pen, darlin'?" He leans over the table to ask Waylynn, who is smiling wide at the other woman.

"Sure." Waylynn reaches for her purse, and the girls' eyes go to the bag, probably knowing a hell of a lot more about the designer label than I do, and then they share a look with each other. If I had the money, I would fork it over right now just so I could tell them I bought it for her. "Here you go, you can keep it." She extends her arm to give Bates the pen and smashes her tits on the table in the process. We all notice, but she's clueless.

"Thanks," Bates says slowly like he forgot why he has the pen in the first place. I would laugh, but I've probably done the same thing before.

"I'm Emma, and this is Harper." The talkative one pushes the papers toward Bates.

"Right." He bends and writes one name on each flyer, then signs his name under that. "Thanks." He passes both papers back, still smiling.

"How exciting," Waylynn says under her breath, looking at both me and Memphis.

"It is for us," the girl says in a nasty tone.

"That's awesome. Now he knows his work is appreciated." She beams.

"I can't tell if she's patronizing me or really happy that she knows you." The woman makes a face like she's confused and trying to be funny at the same time.

Waylynn's sweet expression slips, and she looks down at the table.

"Because it was neither. You can go." It's the nicest thing I can force myself to say.

"Oh, I was just teasing." She tries to act as if I'm the one being an asshole, but I'm not letting her get away with that shit.

"Not likely."

Waylynn lays her hand on my leg under the table and squeezes. "Sorry, overexcited," she apologizes.

I open my mouth to say something, but her fingers tighten over my leg again. I can keep my mouth shut for her, but I fucking hate it.

"Waylynn," Memphis calls so softly, it would be hard for anyone who wasn't seated at the table to hear. She turns her head to look at him with her shoulders high as if she's about to get scolded. "Do not apologize."

"Thanks for coming out again, hope you enjoy the show." Bates turns his back on the two women and closes in on the table, shutting them out.

Waylynn leans a little closer to Memphis, while still holding onto my leg. "I am sorry though. I shouldn't have interrupted his moment. I was just so excited for him. I'm sorry."

"Please don't worry about it," Bates tells me. "She was looking for attention, don't give it to her."

I pat Waylynn's hand on my leg and say, "I'll be right back. Need a hand getting your stuff to the back?" while already rising from the booth. Memphis can talk to her for a minute. I'm too pissed to be any help right now anyway.

"Sure, my stand is right there. I'll grab her." Bates lifts up his cello case. He could easily carry both, but I need a breather.

"That was kind of crazy," Bates says while pushing through a staff only door.

"You should have heard the shit they said when she walked in with Memphis." I loop the strap of his music bag on a chair, getting more pissed.

"What?"

"Some shit about guys fucking girls that look like Waylynn, but not bringing them out in public."

"What?" Bates says again, but I know he heard me. "Are you sure you heard them correctly?"

"Seriously? I heard them fine."

"Because she's not skinny?" Bates whispers.

"I guess, but they are just fucking jealous. She's beautiful."

"Stunning," Bates replies quickly, reaffirming my thoughts.

"It's whatever, don't say anything." I probably should have just kept this shit to myself, but I was pissed and wanted someone to be pissed with me.

"I won't. Waylynn didn't hear what they said though, right?"

"No, she was walking in front of me with Memphis."

"Good, people are assholes."

"I know. Have a good show." I push out the employees' door and head back into the bar. When the table comes into view, I spot Waylynn tucked up under Memphis' arm with rosy cheeks and bright eyes. Whatever he said or did while I was gone seems to have worked.

I scoot unnecessarily close to her other side so I can feel the press of her body next to mine.

"I ordered you pineapple juice," Memphis tells me and lifts an amber bottle to his mouth for a sip. I know it's not beer, but that's not surprising. I can't remember the last time Memphis drank. It's been a few years, at least around me.

Waylynn has a short glass with a few cherries and an orange on a little sword at the top. "What do you have there?"

"A Mai Tai, it has pineapple juice." She offers me the tiny straw when she holds it up.

I glance past her to Memphis, checking to see what he thinks about her ordering a drink and offering it to me, but he doesn't seem bothered. I lean forward and wrap my lips around the straw and take a little pull. It's sweet, like cherries, but the orange juice overpowers it quickly.

"There isn't any alcohol in that," I observe.

Waylynn wrinkles up her nose. "I'm not old enough to order alcohol, but I don't really drink anyway." Memphis' fingers come up and stroke the side of her neck affectionately, possessively. She accepts his touch and encourages him by tilting her head just enough so his fingers trail a little higher up, near her ear.

"I want one of those next time, it's good."

"Not too girly for you?" Waylynn grins.

"Only guys with little... I'm not worried about it." The joke would have easily slipped from my tongue in front of a girl before, but there's something about the sweet way she looks at me that makes me rein it in.

"I'll share," she offers and slides the glass closer to me. Now that I can't ignore.

"Offer accepted," I respond, but I don't pick up the drink because I'm not limiting her suggestion to what's in the glass.

Memphis pulls her closer with his hand on her neck, and his mouth goes to her ear. I can't hear what he's saying, but judging by the way her lips part and her chest rises sharply as she takes a deep breath, I think whatever it is, it's much more direct than I was.

Waylynn

"Waylynn." Memphis' tone is stern, but not flat like it is when he's fending off advances at school. I cling to Oswald's leg but look over at Memphis because I'm helpless not to when he calls my name. "Do not apologize."

"I am sorry though. I shouldn't have interrupted his moment. I was just so excited for him. I'm sorry." I don't know what got into me, or why I felt the need to even say anything.

"Please don't worry about it. She was looking for attention, don't give it to her." Bates shrugs like he's not bothered, but I don't know him well enough to gauge if he's just saying that so I don't feel like crap.

Oswald pats my hand, and I release my death grip on his leg. "I'll be right back. Need a hand getting your stuff to the back?" He slides out of the booth.

Memphis turns my head toward him with just his finger on my chin and a tiny amount of pressure. "Bates was correct—they don't deserve your attention."

"I don't care what they think about me. I won't ever see them again, but he's your friend."

"Sweetness," he murmurs softly and leans forward to give me a soft, chaste, lingering kiss. "Groupies aren't a new phenomenon for Bates. He doesn't care, it's part of the job to be nice to everyone."

"Sorry it took me so long to get over here, can I get you guys anything to drink?" The waitress roams her eyes over both of us, mostly Memphis, and lifts her arm so we can see the back of her hand as she wiggles it around. "I need to see ID or your hands," she says before either of us order.

"A pineapple juice," Memphis tells her, then looks at me to go next, not responding to her request.

"Do you have a non-alcoholic drink menu?"

"We have juice and soda," the waitress answers with a lilt at the end as if she's not even sure of that.

"A Mai Tai?" I'm sure they have orange juice and grenadine to go with the pineapple juice Memphis ordered.

"Virgin, right?"

"Yep," I say quickly. Most of the time, they call them mocktails, but I know what she means.

"I can ask. Anything else?" She looks between us again.

"A Vernors if you have it."

"We have ginger beer," she offers, then plants her hand on her hip.

"That's all," he says, dismissing her.

"Be right back." She spins away, and her shorts are so tiny, I see the bottom of her butt cheeks.

"You don't drink?" Memphis scoots a little closer and puts his hand behind my head along the back of the seat.

"No, I don't really care for how it makes me feel," I tell him truthfully, but I don't admit my meds make the symptoms much worse. "What about you? Pineapple juice and ginger beer?"

"The juice is for Oz, but I don't drink much either. I like to be in control."

A laugh erupts from my lips. I try to cover my mouth with my hand, but I'm too late.

"What's so funny?" His lip is curled up, implying humor, so I answer him honestly.

"Saying you like to be in control is like saying water is wet."

"That obvious, am I? There are different types of control though." His fingers dance over the skin on my neck in a caress before he continues, "Knowing I'll be able to think straight, that I'll have a clear mind if anything comes up, is one thing. But there's also the control that comes with submission when it's freely given, and I'm finding that's quite different."

"Why is it different?" Maybe I can learn something about him and me, like why it feels so natural to yield to him and give into his bossy nature, but most importantly, why I like it so much.

"The first is just perception. We can control very little, even when we pretend we can. The second" —he licks his bottom lip— "is reality. You're being trusted to make decisions, even little ones, for someone else, to take care of them."

"It seems one-sided," I tell him. "What do *you* get out of that?"

Memphis' eyes go wide, and he clears his throat. "Me?" He seems surprised. Were we pretending this was a general conversation? "I thought you were asking what was in it for... the other person."

"No, I think I understand that. They get to let go, and they don't have to worry if what they are doing is right or wrong or if they are making the other person happy, because you show them and tell them what makes you happy. I mean, the person…would show them…how to make…them happy," I amend for sake of not personalizing this strangely personal conversation.

"Here we go. Ginger beer, virgin Mai Tai, and pineapple juice." The waitress sets the drinks down. "Do you want to run a tab? I would need a credit card or driver's license."

"No." Memphis hands over a credit card.

"Be right back." She slips away just as Oswald returns to the table.

"I got you a pineapple juice," Memphis tells him, and I watch his throat move as he tips his head back for a drink.

"What do you have there?" Oswald asks.

"A Mai Tai, it has pineapple juice." I offer him a drink, not worried about using the same straw anymore. He kissed me, so I think we're past that.

"There isn't any alcohol in that," he says after taking a sip.

"I'm not old enough to order alcohol, but I don't really drink anyway," I tell Oswald.

"I want one of those next time, it's good." He points.

"Not too girly for you?" The guys from my high school would never drink something like this.

"Only guys with little… I'm not worried about it." He purses his lips.

"I'll share." I push the glass so it's between us.

"Offer accepted," Oswald replies with a grin that spells trouble.

I feel a tug as Memphis pulls me back and places his lips over my ear to mumble, "He's not talking about the drink, he wants us to share you."

SHARING

Waylynn

I'M NOT GOING to pretend this isn't where my imagination took me with them, but thinking about it and the possibility of it being real are two vastly different things. I feel warm all over, the club is suddenly too loud, and there's a pressure in my head that would make a migraine seem tame.

"Breathe." Memphis exhales against my ear, and I release the air trapped in my lungs. The pressure in my head lessens, but the roaring in my ears takes longer to fade. Memphis makes an approving hum, and my eyes fall slowly closed.

"I get that, right there—acceptance of my instruction without question, your trust that I know what you need."

"I just need a signature on the top copy, you can keep the

other." The waitress puts the small receipt and a pen on the end of the table. I look down, wondering how the mundane normalcy of everyday life is still happening at this very moment.

"You freaked her out," Oswald says as soon as the waitress walks away.

"Could she tell?" I ask, peering up at him.

"Tell what? I was talking about you being freaked out." He seems confused. So am I.

"Oh, I thought you meant the waitress."

"What's going on over there that you thought she would have been freaked out, and why am I not included?" He raises one eyebrow, then dips his head to look under the table.

I pick up my drink and down half of it without using the straw so I can formulate a response that doesn't make me look crazy or like a schoolgirl with her first crush… Is that what this is? It feels like a lot more than a crush.

"Look, Bates will be on soon," Memphis says, drawing the attention away from me and up to the stage.

Another waitress approaches the mic with a wide smile. "You guys are not ready for this." She talks over the house music, but the volume lowers until disappearing altogether. "Some of us were lucky enough to see his show this weekend, and he was so good, we brought him back to hear him again. Please welcome Bates and his cello." She turns to the side and claps while watching Bates haul his instrument over to the chair placed center stage.

SEEING SOUND

The bright lights shine down on his brown hair, making the strands look lighter and his skin a little tanner. "Thank you," he says softly through a mic set up near his mouth. His hands are moving over the strings near the top of the cello as if he's already playing music.

Without another word, he lifts his bow and drags it across the strings, and I'm entranced from the first note. The familiar tune of "A Thousand Years" sings through the club, and everyone takes notice.

Bates moves his upper body with his hands, feeling the music, but he makes it look easy. As soon as the song ends, people erupt in applause, but he transitions into the next, barely seeming to notice.

The next song takes me a little longer to figure out, but when he hits the chorus, I realize it's "Hello." The song has always been sad, but the cello adds so much depth, my heart aches.

The next song is quicker. He bounces the bow over the strings and looks up a few times while playing, but his eyes are unfocused as he bobs his head with the music. "Is this..."

"'WAP'? Yeah. My favorite." Oswald grins.

Bates mesmerizes the crowd with songs I would never have imagined could be played by the cello, let alone sound so beautiful. When he finishes up the cover of "Hold Me While You Wait," he finally rests his bow across his thigh and leans into the mic. He has to wait for the applause to stop, but when it slows, he says, "Thank you. You can follow me at Bates and his Cello for future events." His eyes flow over to our table, and I can see the curl of his lips behind the mic. "This is my last song for the night, and it's for you guys." He points at the table with his bow.

A giddy feeling swirls in my stomach, even though I know I'm just a spectator like everyone else in the club, but when the music starts, I sink into the melody of "Can't Help Falling in Love."

A few couples move onto the dance floor and sway along with the song. I lean to the side so I can see around them and watch Bates. My head ends up almost on Oswald's shoulder.

"I hope you look at me like that when I'm on the field. I'm feeling a little left out."

I snap my mouth closed and dart my eyes up. He's wearing a teasing smile, but something about his soft tone makes me feel like there's a hint of truth to his words and an underlying vulnerability he doesn't show often.

"I won't have any idea what's going on, but I'll be there."

"I'm going to hold you to that." He starts to clap as the song ends, and I do the same. "I bet none of your other boyfriends played football," he says louder to be heard over the applause and whistles.

I shake my head in denial, glad it's too loud to explain that I haven't had other boyfriends.

"We can get going once he comes out," Memphis tells me, draining the last of his drink. I'm only now realizing the waitress never returned to our table during the show.

"Do you mind letting me out?" I look between the two of them. I might as well go to the bathroom before we leave.

Memphis doesn't budge. "Where are you going?" Oswald starts to scoot out before I answer.

"The bathroom."

"I'll go too. Wait for me by the door when you're done if I'm not out," Oswald says, taking my hand as I rise. I haven't even been sitting that long, maybe an hour or two, but my legs are stiff when I get up.

I have to wait in a short line while he walks straight to the door. "You can come with me," he offers with a raised eyebrow.

"I'll come with you, around you, over you, any way you like it," the girl in front of me says. I gawk at the side of her face, seeing her eyes are half closed and her head is swaying from side to side slightly. She's been drinking.

"Sorry, offer's only good for my girl. I'll wait for you to get out."

"Who's his girl?" She blinks as if she's trying to focus.

I lift my hand slowly when her eyes land on me.

"He's gorgeous. Is he...?" She waggles her pinkie finger and lists to the side. "The good-looking ones always have something wrong with them."

I look away from her, pretending not to notice or understand what she means as the line moves forward slowly.

"It's okay, they can't be blessed everywhere." She tries for a whisper, but it comes out more like a smoker's rasp. "Hey, didn't you…" She turns to look at the bathroom door, then faces me again with her eyes squinted and her mouth hanging open.

I jump when I feel a hand on my waist and look up to see Memphis at my side. "Why are you standing here alone? Where's Oz?" He looks down at me, ignoring the clearly confused woman in front of us.

"He went in." I nod to the doors.

Memphis moves with me as I get closer to the bathroom. "He should have waited with you."

"Little ones are okay if you know what to do with them," the woman says as she leans toward us and wiggles her pinkie again. "I'll take a little, itty bitty one over a big, big one any day," she singsongs as she widens her arms at least three feet. "S'okay, she told me. Nobody cares you have a little dick. You're too…hot."

"I didn't…" I start, but Oswald walks up, and the woman points at him, then Memphis, clearly picking up on the resemblance between them and distracting me with incoherent blabber.

"He's not you, and you're not him."

"What the fuck is she talking about?" Oswald questions.

"Ignore her, she's drunk." Memphis sounds bored.

"Let's go. I can hold it." I start to turn away, but Memphis keeps his hand locked on my hip, preventing me from walking away.

"I'm not drunk," she scoffs, pushing air past her lips in a raspberry at least three more times for emphasis.

"Sure, it's your turn." Oswald points to the door as a woman walks out.

"That's what happens when you try to be nice. I'm not drunk." She keeps talking as she pushes into the bathroom.

"Do you attract the crazies or what?" Oswald shakes his head in disbelief.

"It's not me she was interested in." My tone is pissy and defensive from his word choice. As soon as another woman walks out of the bathroom, I pull away from Memphis and slam my hands on the door to push it open.

Oswald

Waylynn's entire body stiffens with my question. I'm not even touching her, and I see the abrupt shift in her posture. "It's not me she was interested in," she snaps and shoves the door open, sealing herself in the bathroom. There's at least six women waiting behind us, but neither Memphis nor I move away from the door.

"Are we in trouble because that drunk lady talked to us?" I ask my brother.

"I don't know, she seemed fine until..."

"Until I joked about her attracting trouble," I finish.

"She did have that guy following her today. Has she said anything else to you about anyone bothering her? Maybe you hit a sore spot."

"No, she hasn't said anything to me. You should tell her she has to talk to us. She listens to you." I push away from the wall when Waylynn exits the restroom. Her hands are still dripping with water as she uses the side of her foot to hold the door open for the next person in line.

Her frown has me worried. "Sorry I got grumpy," she mumbles as she gets close to me. I wasn't expecting her to apologize.

"Are you already ungrumpy?" I wrap my arm around the back of her neck, so she ends up face first in my chest in a half hug.

"I think so. I don't want you to be mad."

I use her shoulder to push her back so I can look at her. "Wavy, I'm not mad. Are you ready to say bye to Bates so we can get out of here?"

She nods, lacking all the excitement she had earlier. I look over her head at Memphis, and we exchange a glance. I don't like the way she's always so worried about our reactions or if she's in trouble.

MEMPHIS

. . .

WAYLYNN'S HEAD is on my shoulder. I can tell she's asleep because it nods with every bump we go over. It's later than I thought it would be. We stayed too long talking with Bates after he signed a few more flyers.

"Think she would mind if we crashed at her place again?" Oswald rolls his head to the left to look at me.

"We'll ask her when we get home."

"To her house, you mean," he corrects me.

"Whatever. When will you find out if you play this weekend?" I change the subject so I don't have to acknowledge my slip of the tongue.

"Tomorrow. I already know they won't start me, but I think they'll put me in. If not, I'm going to bitch to Obermeyer. He promised me field time as a freshman."

"Make sure you request three tickets," I remind him, even though Bates told him he would be there for the game on Saturday too.

"I know." Oz sighs.

"Do you have a jersey or something for her to wear?"

"No, they don't even give us our shirts until the day before the game, and I only get one."

"I'll stop by the Den tomorrow and see if they have anything," I offer.

"M'kay." Oz leans back against the headrest again and shuts his eyes for the rest of the ride, but as soon as we pull into Waylynn's driveway, he opens his eyes as if he wasn't dozing.

"Should have taken her to your place, then we would have had an excuse to all sleep in the same bed," Oz whispers.

It's not a horrible idea, but getting the three of us in my full-sized bed might be challenging. Now her king is a different story.

"Wakey, wakey, Wavy," Oswald whispers into her ear. She sucks in a breath and blinks her eyes sleepily.

"Are we home already?" She looks around.

"Already? It felt like forever when I was listening to you snore," Oswald teases her.

She makes a pouty face, scrunching up her lips and nose. "I was snoring?"

"No," I scoff softly. "Do you have your keys?"

"Oh yeah, sorry." Waylynn unzips the bag she has looped over her body and digs her hand around inside. The slight jingle has me assuming she found them. "I should have left the lights on," she mumbles, looking up at the large house.

"We'll check it out for you," I tell her, opening my door.

"It's okay, I had the alarm set," she replies.

"Do you not want us to check?"

"I just don't want to keep you out any later than it already is," she admits.

Oswald doesn't have any problem welcoming himself to stay. "If you invite us to sleep over again, we can get into bed even faster."

"Of course you can stay," Waylynn says quickly.

"Are you sure you don't mind?" I offer just in case, but it

didn't sound like she was only suggesting it to be nice, which is something I wouldn't doubt she would do.

"No, not at all. I'm always happy with your company." She unlocks the door and sets her bag on the counter after keying the alarm code in.

"Do you need anything? I think I have an extra toothbrush or two. I should have offered those yesterday." She adds the last part as if she's talking to herself.

"I wouldn't turn that down," Oz pipes up. It's a little harder for me to take what she's offering, but only because I'm used to paying my way and I don't like the strings that people attach to things, even when they say it's free.

"If you have enough," I concede. Waylynn hasn't put a cost on anything she's offered, not even any expectations, so I'm willing to take a chance.

"I think I do, but I'll check. The bathrooms should be stocked, but if you need anything, let me know."

"Do you mind if I take a shower? That way I don't have to do it in the morning."

"Of course, whatever you need," Waylynn tells my bold brother. "Let me go grab those toothbrushes, then I'm going to crash if it's okay with you guys."

"You don't have to ask, it's your house," I remind her.

"Just so you know, you can do whatever. Watch TV, have a snack. It won't bother me," she says as she heads for the stairs.

Oswald gives me a little elbow jab. "See? She wanted us to stay. She's not even scared."

"Because we're with her. If she were here alone, I'm sure it would be different."

He shrugs. "I guess it doesn't matter how we get from A to B as long as I get into her cu—" I reach over and shove the back of his head before he can finish that sentence, which makes him chuckle and stumble away from me. "I was just teasing."

"Sorry about the color." Waylynn makes a cute little face when she extends one pink and one purple toothbrush.

"What do you mean? Pink is my favorite color." Oswald proves he's not as tired as he seemed just a little while ago by continuing to clown Waylynn.

"Oh, then this one is perfect." She redirects her hand without missing a beat, making sure he gets the pink one.

"He's just messing with you." I take the presented toothbrush.

"Okay, I'll be in my room if you need anything. Make yourselves at home. Night," she offers and backs toward the stairs again before spinning and darting up.

"She probably heard you," I mutter through clenched teeth.

"No, no. You don't think so, do you?" Oz sounds a little worried. I just shrug. I don't really think she did, but I'm not telling him that so maybe next time he will keep his mouth shut.

MISTAKES

Waylynn

I'M HAVING a tough time falling asleep, and it has everything to do with the two guys just down the hall. Yesterday was fun, but that could be chalked up to friends hanging out, even if things got a little more familiar when Oswald fell asleep, but tonight was different.

I reach up and touch the bottom of my ear, remembering the feeling of Memphis' lips there so vividly, my stomach gets butterflies. I pull my hand away abruptly and force my eyes closed again, but I can still hear him.

He wants us to share you.

I would be more than okay with that. It's not exactly the social norm, but thruples are not unheard of. It would definitely freak my parents out, but I don't really care what they think as long as it doesn't result in them trying to put me into an in-patient treatment center again. I'm not doing that. I'm done being locked in rooms with no way out. They don't even need to know at this point, and it's not like I'm going to invite them both home with me and introduce them as my boyfriends right now.

My emotions circle from excitement to worry as I think about what being with them could be like until I eventually fall asleep.

∼

WHEN I WOKE UP, the guys were already gone, but there's evidence of them being here. I don't even mind tossing the granola wrapper that was left on the counter in the trash, but I know it was Oswald's.

I spend my morning doing laundry and cleaning up a little before showering and heading over to campus. If I'm going to the game tomorrow, I need to show some team support.

The M Den is huge and right near the stadium. The door chimes when I enter, and then I'm in a sea of maize and blue.

"Let me know if I can help you with anything," a girl says as she dashes by. I make several laps around the store, looking at everything from the teddy bears and blankets to the tiny little toddler cheer uniforms. The jerseys are all hung up high on the wall with filled racks beneath them, but I don't see a Gravlin anywhere, so I head over to the counter to ask.

"Excuse me, are these all the jerseys?"

"Is there a certain one you're looking for? If we don't have it, I can check one of the other stores," she continues to fold the sweatshirt she was working on as she looks at me.

"I'm looking for Gravlin, Oswald Gravlin. He's a freshman," I tell her, only now realizing they might not have it yet. He mentioned he hasn't played in a game so far.

"Oh yeah." She winces. "You'll have to see if he has a contract. If he does, you can get one made." She looks around, then leans over the counter to whisper, "It would be much cheaper and faster if you went over to The Sport Hut. They could make you anything you want, especially if he doesn't have a contract to sell merch yet."

"Is it in Ann Arbor?" I question softly so I don't get her in trouble for telling me.

"It's on State, just down the street." She nods.

"Thank you." I smile and peruse the store again to pick up a few things while I'm here. At the last second, I toss an adorable teddy with a varsity jacket in my basket.

The Sport Hut is much smaller and a lot less shiny. They have a big selection, but it's mostly T-shirts and jerseys, not all the novelty stuff from the Den. After a brief conversation with the lady behind the counter, I pick out the jersey I want and tell her the name I want put on the back. "Number?" she questions, and I have to pull out my phone. I almost text Oswald but decide to check to see if I can find the info online.

"Twenty-five, please."

"Okay, I have to finish up this order ahead of you. Do you want to wait, or are you going to pick it up later?"

"Um, does it take a long time?"

"I should have it done in about twenty minutes."

"Oh, I'll wait, thank you." I wasn't expecting it to be that fast. I walk around some more just so she doesn't feel like I'm standing over her shoulder, but the process is pretty neat. The numbers and letters are already ready, all she does is line them up on the shirt then pull down a machine to press them on. Everything gets placed in a brown paper bag with the ticket stapled to the top.

"Thank you," I tell her when I pick up my bag and walk over to the register.

"You're welcome. Have fun at the game." She waves, then pushes down the press again, doing the next order.

MEMPHIS

I'M DISTRACTED and I know it, which means I'm really distracted. There's a small line of students waiting for their fifteen minutes, and I've looked at my watch more times than I care to count, wondering when I can get the hell out of here.

It doesn't help that they could have figured out half the shit I'm explaining on their own if they made the effort. I can't even really blame them. High school is a joke when it comes to preparing students for the independence of college.

"When will we be talking about this in class?" The girl points at her computer screen.

I glance at the info. "We won't. You're expected to read the material and do the assigned work related to it."

"But it doesn't explain how I'm supposed to come up with the answer."

"Have you read the article?"

"Yes." She tucks her hair behind her ears.

"Did you agree or disagree with the representation?" Her shoulders slowly start to come up, but she doesn't answer. "I would say read it again, knowing you need to form an opinion and answer why you feel that way. Did the information sway you in any way? What was it lacking if it didn't?"

She takes a deep breath and reaches for her laptop. "Okay."

The next person moves forward, and I check the time again. I can make it through another hour.

"Hey, Gravlin." I look up at the door and see Bethany leaning her head in. "We're meeting in the Lawyers Club for lunch. TA celebration for making it another week." She points at me expectantly.

"Who's letting you in?"

"Professor Daniels."

I wasn't planning on taking a lunch, but it's hard to pass up the Lawyers Club. "What time?"

"Thirty minutes, baby! I'll walk over with you." She slips away before I can discourage the baby comment. The few students left in the room are watching me with interest, but I just get right back to work.

I check the door to make sure it's locked after I leave the office, then pull my phone from my pocket. My intent is to send a quick text to Waylynn, but Bethany is already waiting for me near the stairs.

"Come on," she urges as if I'm running late.

"It's a two-minute walk," I mutter.

She pushes out the double doors, then spins to face me as I follow. "That's two minutes I could be munching on shrimp pasta and baclava. I'll probably have to eat ramen for years once I get out of this place so I can pay back my loans. Let me enjoy my free food for a little while."

"You didn't have to wait for me."

"Yes I did. Who else besides me would dare to disturb *Mr. Gravlin*?" she teases. The fact that it doesn't affect me at all when she says it is proof Waylynn has a hold on me. I can't explain it, nor do I even care to try. As if thinking about her makes her appear, I notice Waylynn walking up the street with a brown bag in her hands.

Her face lights up when we make eye contact. "Don't look now, but I think you have an admirer coming this way."

Bethany shoves her arm through mine and curls her fingers around my bicep.

Waylynn's smile slips a little, but she covers it well. "Hey," she says softly, unsure.

"My office hours are over for the day. You can leave an email if you need help." My voice is tight because I hate that I'm doing this to her.

"Oh, I wasn't—"

Bethany interrupts. "He's a stickler for the rules. Plus, I wrangled him into a lunch date."

My first instinct is to deny it, but that would just make Bethany ask questions. "I think she's friends with my brother," I blurt out, like admitting that is going to somehow make anything that is happening better, but once it's out, I realize it sounded worse.

"Pardon me. I didn't mean to hold you up. Enjoy your date." Waylynn steps to the side while averting her gaze, then she continues down the sidewalk as if I didn't just treat her like a stranger who *might* know my brother. *Shit.*

"You're welcome," Bethany singsongs and pulls me forward with her arm still locked through mine. The doors to Munger are less than two hundred feet away. If I would have taken the time to text Waylynn instead of allowing Bethany to rush me, we might not have even run into each other.

Once we get inside and meet up with the other TAs from several different departments, I slip to the side and pull my phone out. I don't even know what to say, so I end up just staring at the screen until Bethany calls me again. "Gravlin, let's nom."

Hastily, I type a message.

Me: It's not a date.

Me: I'm sorry.

It's only after I send it that I realize I should have switched the order. I slip the phone into my pocket and spend the entire time I'm eating feeling my pocket for phantom vibrations, waiting for her response that never comes.

I'm the first to leave after a brief thank you to Professor Daniels. Everything tasted like shit, and it was because of my mood, not the food. I don't even wait until I'm back in the office before I'm dialing her number.

When she doesn't answer the first time, I call her right back and leave a voicemail. "Sorry, I should have… It's just, you're a student in my class. Oz is usually with us, and I can…pretend you are with him. It was not a date. It was lunch with several other TAs and a law professor. Call me." I hang up the phone and snarl, "Fuck," under my breath, but the person walking next to me clearly hears it when he turns his head to glance at me.

I ignore him and shut myself in the office behind a locked door. It's bad enough she saw me at dinner the other night with Makayla, but now Bethany told her we were on a date, which might force me to explain that Bethany and I do have a history of hooking up. It hasn't been since last year, and there were never any strings attached, but that might make it worse.

"Fuck!" I repeat and toss my phone on the desk, pissed I allowed this to happen when it would have been a simple conversation to explain to Waylynn that while she's in my class, she's just my brother's girlfriend to me when we're out. Then I wouldn't have freaked out, thinking she was going to say something that would get us both in trouble and this shit could have been avoided.

I look at my computer on the desk, noting the extra emails I didn't get to yesterday because I shortened my hours, and I want to put it all off again, but I can't unless I want to spend the weekend grading papers and answering emails from days earlier.

My replies are professional but even more cross than usual. I glance at my watch, noting I was able to get through three in a matter of minutes and hoping they are all simple, but the next one requires more attention, and it's the beginning of a slippery slope. Before I know it, hours have passed, and I still haven't heard back from Waylynn, nor am I done for the day. I can't even have Oz message her. He has commitments all day, and I don't want to explain what a fuckup I am, though he would probably find it funny that I've been sitting here in knots all day because a girl didn't return my call.

An hour later, I snap the top of my computer shut and reach for my phone in the same movement. I dial her number, and she picks up on the end of the fourth ring, right when I'm about to hang up and drive straight to her house.

"Hello." Her voice is a little raspy, like she hasn't used it in hours.

"You picked up."

"You called." Those two words make me feel a little like an idiot and are well deserved.

"Did you get my messages?"

"Yes."

"You didn't call me back," I tell her, even though that's obvious.

"No, I didn't."

"Can I come talk to you? I just got done with work for the day," I explain, hoping she understands why it took so long.

"Um…"

"Let me at least explain." I bully her into giving me the answer I want before she can deny me. "I won't even come inside." Does that soften the demand? I doubt it.

"There's nothing really to explain. You already told me. I'm your student. I get it," she retorts.

"So why are you upset?"

"I'm not upset," she says quickly.

"Then let me come talk to you," I press.

"What else do you need to say?" Her voice is a little softer, and I know she's closer to giving in.

"I want to see you," I admit. "I hated… I've been thinking about you all day, and I need to see that you're not upset." I know she's mad, even if she's not willing to admit it. I would be worried if she wasn't, and I want to try to make it better. "Just a few minutes."

"It's not necessary, I know why you did it. It's fine."

"I'm not fine with it, Waylynn, and you shouldn't be either." A little irritation seeps into my tone, even though I'm frustrated with myself.

"Okay." She sighs softly. I should feel bad that I harassed her into doing what I want again, not have a hard-on at the thought.

I rush to say goodbye before she changes her mind. "See you in a few minutes."

Waylynn

I'M SITTING in the garden when Memphis pulls into the driveway so fast, his back tires hop the curb. The engine cuts off as soon as the truck stops, and he jumps out. I take a second to examine him while he has no idea I'm watching him.

His hair is a little more tousled than usual, and the back of his shirt isn't tucked all the way in. Was he really thinking about me all day, or was he doing something else that would explain his appearance a little better? Seeing him with the other girl, well, *girls* is messing with my head.

When he starts to plod toward the door, I call out, "Over here." His head snaps around, and he finds me sitting on an iron chair that is more for decoration than comfort. He pauses as if me being outside surprised him, but then he pivots to head toward me.

"Hey." His eyes roam over me, and I pluck at my shirt in discomfort. The woman I saw him with today, the one who was very comfortable cozying up to him, was tiny, just like the one from dinner the other night. I've always been fairly comfortable with my body, but today I felt like a dirty secret, and there's a part of me that wonders if it has something to do with the way I look.

He lowers himself into the chair across from me, and the tension between us thickens. This is why I didn't want him to come over.

Memphis steeples his fingers between his knees and takes in a breath to speak. "I probably should have talked to you about school, but Oz is usually with us, so…"

"I get it," I tell him again. I truly do. The professor made it clear the first day that there was a no fraternization policy, but it's easy to dismiss. One, I don't think Memphis would allow our…friendship to influence how he graded me, and two, I would be willing to drop the class if there was ever an issue, and that's a little scary to admit, even to myself. I'm so wrapped up in him, I'd lose the credits and not even blink. "I should have just kept walking."

"I didn't know what you were going to say." He rubs his hand down the side of his face in what seems like relief.

"I wasn't going to cuddle up close to you and grab your arm, if that's what you were thinking. I was just going to say hello." I feel the need to tell him I'm not stupid, and it allows me to mention exactly what the other girl did that was okay for her, but not for me.

"She's a TA," he explains.

I really don't care at this point. I'm not sure I can handle Memphis, let alone his brother too. I'm in too deep, too fast. I don't give a response to his statement, he already mentioned she was a teaching assistant.

I see the muscle in his jaw tic for a few seconds before he opens his mouth to speak again. "I overreacted."

As soon as he says it, I feel guilty. I've been thinking about what I would or could do like drop the class, but he has a higher cost if he were to get caught. He might lose his position, and it could tarnish his record. "It's fine. I won't speak to you at school. Maybe we shouldn't—"

"Don't say it." He cuts me off, scooting to the edge of his seat as if he's ready to stand up and cover my mouth.

"Have lunch anymore either." It's for the best. The end of the semester isn't that far away, and if he's still interested, I'll still be here.

"I thought you were going to say be around each other at all." He huffs.

"That too. I don't want you getting in trouble." My stomach cramps up, and I know I don't mean the words. I want to take them back before they are even out of my mouth, but I can't, because it's what should happen.

"Not happening, Waylynn. Don't bring it up again." He

eyes me from the other chair, daring me to argue, and when I don't speak, he continues, "I'll talk to Hilbrand on Monday. There are allowances for stuff like this, hence Oswald being in the class I'm running. I'm not allowed to grade any of his work or evaluate his performance. We can do the same for you," he reasons.

"He was your brother before the class, they already made the exception for him."

"It will be fine. I'll tell her you're my brother's girlfriend and I don't feel comfortable grading you. It will be fine," he says with such an air of confidence, it's hard not to believe him. Should I go along with this? Will he hold me responsible if something happens? And what about the other girls? I'm feeling way too much to be able to sort out my own emotions.

"Tomorrow will be fine because you'll be there to watch my brother, just like me and Bates," he says as if he's trying to convince himself.

I don't think it's such a good idea. Now I just need to get the courage to tell him I'll get my own ticket in the student section. "Um…"

"Don't worry, Waylynn, but maybe we shouldn't ride together. Are you okay getting to the game? I could have Bates pick you up," he offers.

"No, I'll be fine on my own, thank you." He just solved my problem for me. I'll send him a text tomorrow saying that I got my own seat.

"Your ticket will be at the will call booth. You'll need your

Mcard to claim it," he reminds me, even though Oswald explained it to me last night after Bates' show ended.

"I'll have it," I assure him, and we fall into an awkward silence that was never a problem before.

"Have you eaten?" he asks in a rush, as if he was struggling to find something to say and that popped into his head.

"I'm not hungry," I reply.

"It wasn't a date," Memphis tells me, and it makes me think he might feel guilty. "She thought she was helping."

"How would that be helpful?" I question, wondering where this will lead.

"By making it seem like I was unavailable."

"Yeah, that was evident. I guess what I was asking was how she knew it would be helpful to you if you seemed unavailable."

Memphis scoots back in the chair, distancing himself from me and the question. "I have a reputation for being an asshole," he admits. "She might have thought she was saving you from me."

Bullshit. Something about his statement doesn't feel true, but I'm not going to keep asking the same question while he evades answering. "Okay." I feel slightly defeated when the words leave me, like I've given up too easily, but the truth is I just don't see this conversation going anywhere productive right now.

I stand up, ready to say goodnight to Memphis. I'm not done feeling sorry for myself just yet. This is the third time he's acted like I was invisible—at dinner in the south quad, after dinner when we ran into Mia and her friends, and again today. While I have an explanation for the behavior, it doesn't make me feel any better about it.

"Where are you going?" He stands too.

"I'm going to call it a night."

"Not yet, you're still mad."

"I'm not mad," I argue.

"Okay, then tell me what you are so I can fix it," he demands.

"I do not need to be fixed." The denial is instant and harsh. His words trigger something inside me that has always felt different, broken, crazy, and too emotional.

"Fuck," he mumbles and briefly looks away. "I don't want to walk away feeling like this. Like I could have done something more to make this better between us." He touches his chest.

His words hit me right in my gooey center, the part where I imagine someone saying all the right things without me having to tell them, so I spill my guts just like I've been trained to do by my therapist. "It's a lot for me right now. The right thing to do is to walk away so I don't risk your future." Memphis takes a step toward me, but he stops when I lift my hand. "But I don't want to do that, and it makes me question if I even deserve to be with you if I don't put your needs above my wants."

"There's no question. I don't want you to do that,

Waylynn. You're lucky this bullshit with school is holding me back the tiniest bit, or I probably would have told you I needed a place to live just so I could see you in the morning before I start my day."

That's not supposed to be sweet, right? Is that a red flag?

"I don't do relationships, never have, but I would lock you down with us in a heartbeat. I'm scared of the things I want from you, but I want them anyway. I can't explain it, and I don't even feel the need to question it because I know it's right."

Lock me down, scared of what he wants from me. I have even more questions now. I look around, realizing we're having this conversation very publicly, and that is the last thing we need to be doing.

"We shouldn't talk about this out here," I whisper, unsure of what else I should say.

"If you don't want me to come in, we can go for a drive or go to my place," he offers.

"We should just go in. Going for a drive or letting someone see me walking into your place isn't a good idea," I remind him.

"We can get out of the city, but I won't argue with going inside." He lifts his hand and gestures for me to go ahead of him. "Did I freak you out?" Memphis asks the second the door is closed and locked behind us.

"No," I reply, but my voice is too high, belying my denial.

"You are a horrible liar."

"Only to you," I retort, and his eyes go a little wide. "I just mean you are the only one who calls me on it, not that I do it all the time and don't get caught."

Now that we're in the house, I don't know how to continue our conversation, or if I really want to delve too deeply into it again. He already said a lot of things that made my heartbeat crazy fast, and I don't know how many more declarations I can handle at the moment. I was already worried about being a little in love with him before he admitted he liked seeing me before he started his day. Can you fall in love this fast without knowing the person inside and out? Because I feel like there's a lot the three of us don't know about each other.

What will they think when I tell them I've heard voices as far back as I can remember? That my parents thought I had an active imagination until I was about nine and started hearing things that scared me? That I heard curse words and angry voices that I thought were real and would come for me, so I would ask to sleep with them the nights it got bad?

The doctors didn't know what to do. Early onset schizophrenia was whispered a lot in the beginning, but I was too young, and my symptoms never quite hit the mark. Doctor after doctor said I would grow out of it, or that it was attention seeking behavior, so I tried to pretend it wasn't happening, that I wasn't hearing strange phrases and words randomly, but all that changed in sixth grade.

Class had just started, and the room was quiet as we wrote in our journals about what we did the weekend before. I hated silence the most, it always made the voices easier to hear, but this would have been heard through a hurricane. A wail so pure and sad ripped through my head and my heart at the same time. I started crying uncontrollably and had to be removed from the class, and that started the rumors about me being unstable.

While the voices had scared me before, I'd never felt like I was experiencing anything from them. This was different. My heart ached with a pain I never could have imagined. I wanted my mom, and I never wanted to hear another word in my head again. Two days later, my mom introduced me to Dr. Tobin, and I've been seeing him and Maxwell ever since.

I wouldn't begin to know how to have that conversation. Maybe I should bring that up at my next therapy session.

"Everything okay?" Memphis questions, and I blink a few times. I wonder how long I was in my own head.

"Yeah, sorry. You said you were hungry. There's food, or I could order something," I offer.

"You're not ordering anything, but I will eat something here if you're sure."

"Whatever you can find." I gesture to the kitchen. Memphis pulls out the Chinese food containers and starts peeking in boxes. "You can't eat that." I move around him, trying to get to the cartons.

"Are you saving it? Here." He holds out the box.

"No, it's too old," I admonish.

"Like hell it is." He pulls the box back.

"That's from *two* days ago," I remind him.

"Yeah, talk to me when it's four, but it won't be here that long because I'm going to eat it."

"If I would have remembered that was in there, I would have thrown it away."

"That would have made Oz cry." He tilts his head to the side and forks a bite of cold noodles into his mouth, then almost spits it out when he starts laughing at my horrified expression.

"You're eating it cold too!"

"Want a bite?" He has to cover his mouth, because he's still chewing.

"No, no." I shiver with the heebie-jeebies.

"Have you ever tried it?" He wiggles the fork, showing me a playful side of himself.

"No. Enjoy that." I wave over my shoulder as I leave him alone in the kitchen with his food.

"I will, and I'm not going to save any for you," he calls loudly, but his voice is still a little muffled with food.

I drop onto the couch, gathering the remote as I do, and turn on the TV. Two hours ago, I was moping in my room, and here I am about to turn on a movie to watch with the guy I was all sulky over. Life is weird.

GAMES

Memphis

"Hello," I answer my phone softly.

"Where are you?" Oz asks, but judging by his shitty tone, I bet he already knows.

"Waylynn's." I run my fingers through the ends of her hair. I'm not worried it will wake her up, since I'm pretty sure it's what put her to sleep.

"You're a dick. What are you guys doing?"

"She's sleeping. I'm watching some movie."

"Come get me," he demands and pleads in the way only family can. "Her beds are made of fairy fucking clouds or some shit."

"It's called good quality."

"It's called I don't wake up with a backache or the smell of anyone else's balls," Oswald retorts with a snort.

"If I come get you, I don't have an excuse to come back. Can't you get a ride from someone?"

"My floor is filled with freshmen, none of which have cars. Fuck it. I'll ride one of those stupid scooters because my legs are killing me."

"Okay, I'll see if I can unlock the door."

"See if you can? You better unlock the door, or I'm going to climb my ass into her bedroom Rapunzel style."

"I already made sure her doors and windows were locked. Good luck with that," I say before hanging up the phone while Oswald yells in the background. I wouldn't be his brother if I didn't give him shit. Hell, he's given me enough for a lifetime.

I allow myself a few more minutes to soak up the feeling of having Waylynn's head in my lap before I try to scoot out from under her without disturbing her sleep.

Her head pops up, and she squints at me. "Sorry I fell asleep." Her voice is just a whisper.

"Don't be. Oswald called. He's on his way over."

"Okay," she murmurs softly and curls up, already closing her eyes again. I head to the kitchen to watch for Oz.

I chuckle when I see the single headlight cruising up the sidewalk and turning into her drive. I open the door to tell him, "Leave it on the sidewalk."

He hops off and plants his feet on the ground. The thing looks tiny, I don't know how it got his big ass here so quickly.

It doesn't help he has his football bag on his back like some turtle.

"Aren't you supposed to stay in the dorm the night before a game?" I ask after he puts down the kickstand and walks toward me.

"They just don't want us out partying or anything," he deflects. "What did you guys do all day? Is there anything to eat?"

"What happened to the team dinner?"

"That was hours ago, before films. Stop avoiding the question." Oz watches me closely. I look back at the slightly open door.

"We got into it a little bit," I confess.

"Into it? What do you mean? You fought? About what?" he questions rapidly.

"I was walking to lunch with another TA—"

"A girl?" he interrupts, sounding disappointed.

"Bethany."

Oz winces. He knows there's history there. I thought he might have been interested in her for a little while, which was okay because I don't dislike her, and I figured that's how our life would go. He would fall in love, and I would…be there.

"Yeah, well, I panicked and told her to email me for my hours if she needed something when she said hello." He pulls his head back and sucks air through his teeth. "Bethany thought she was being helpful when she told Waylynn we were on a lunch date."

"Jesus," Oz hisses and looks at the door. "You're lucky she didn't claw your eyes out."

"She told us to enjoy the date and excused herself."

"That sounds terrifying," he whispers in awe. "Why does that seem worse?"

"Because she made walking away look easy," I admit, and he nods slowly.

"What happened after that?"

"She ignored me for several hours. I probably have an ulcer. Then I badgered her until she let me come over and explain, then she suggested she shouldn't even talk to me anymore because I'm her teacher. I thought I was losing her, so I admitted I'm pretty much obsessed with her."

"And that worked?" His eyes are wide.

"She actually let me in the house then."

"Wait, she didn't even let you in?"

"No, we sat over there." I point to the bushes.

"Man, you fucked up," he mutters. "Did you tell her about Bethany? About…"

"No, I was fighting for my life."

"Oh shit, I don't think that's good. You should have told her everything. Why were you such a whore?" He shoves my shoulder.

"Don't act like it was just me," I hedge.

"Yeah, well, she hasn't caught me having dinner and lunch with my hookups." His superior tone makes me want to punch him in the balls.

"It's not like I was screwing around or something. They both approached me."

"You need to cut that shit out." He points.

"What should I do? Where a shirt that says, 'Taken, do not speak to me'?"

"No, that would be worse. All the chicks you've blown off for years would try to get with you thinking you were ready to settle down or some shit. I don't know how girls' heads work."

"Any other suggestions?"

"How about you just don't give them a chance? Don't be all aloof and tortured, they love that unavailable shit."

"I'm not tortured," I scoff.

Oswald gives me a blank stare. "Tragic backstory, brooding, too smart for your own good, and handsome as hell because you look just like me and I'm fucking gorgeous."

"Shut the hell up. If anything, you look like me." I can't believe that's my argument. "It doesn't matter. She's not upset anymore." I rein the conversation back in.

"Lucky for you."

"I know," I reply with relief.

"Is she already in bed?"

"She's sleeping on the couch."

"Did you have a chance to get her a shirt or anything?" he asks after walking into the kitchen.

"No, I worked and came here." I just explained my day to him. When would I have had time to shop?

"I'll get her something for next week," he says and walks over to the fridge.

"How early do you need to be at the stadium?" I make sure to keep my voice down.

"Ten. I'm going to sleep in," he singsongs.

"Do you have everything you need with you?"

"Yep, I just need a ride." He has a package of deli meat out and is rolling it up to shove it in his face.

"What should we do with Waylynn?"

"I can think of a lot of things I want to do with her. Be more specific," he mumbles around his mouthful of food.

"Should we wake her up and make her go to bed?"

Oswald walks around me, heading out of the kitchen and into the living room, where Waylynn is still curled up on the couch. "Nah, she looks comfy, and that ass…" He takes another bite from the meat in his hand and makes an exaggerated growling sound.

"I don't know who raised you."

"Oh, that's funny coming from you. What's your name in her phone?"

"It was the first thing that came to mind," I whisper harshly.

"I wonder why." He pulls a face and heads back to the kitchen.

Waylynn

. . .

"This is starting to become a habit," I murmur mostly to myself, because Memphis and Oswald seem to be sleeping. Neither of them stirs when I try to untangle myself from them. Oswald has a hold of my legs again, and his face isn't in my butt, thankfully, but Memphis' hand is woven into my hair. I can turn my head just enough to see the tiniest sliver of light coming in through the curtains. We slept here all night—well, most of the night. It has to be very early.

I rub Memphis' leg, trying to get him to wake up, and he rocks forward a little, but that's it, so I try to pull my leg out from Oswald's grip. He draws in a deep breath that could be called a snore, then shoves my legs right off the couch.

I hit the floor with a thud, but the worst part is Memphis still has a hold of my hair, so I'm the one that ends up with my face in his crotch.

I freeze, praying he's not going to wake up with me like this, like I was trying to take advantage of him, but that was apparently too much to ask. I know the exact second he wakes up, because he stops breathing—it's not a subtle change. I give it another heartbeat, hoping I'm imagining him holding his breath, but when he stays silent, I peek up at him through my hair as the pressure on my hair tightens.

"It's not what it looks like," I say quickly.

"Too bad." He blinks slowly a few times. His sleepy blue eyes seem to be having a hard time focusing. "Why are you on the floor?"

"Could you let go of my hair?"

The relief is instant, but he ends up pulling a few strands of my hair out as he tries to tug his hand free. "Shit, I'm sorry."

I stay on my knees but tilt my head all the way back and push my hair out of my face. "It's okay, it wasn't bad until he pushed me off the couch." I glare over at Oswald. His mouth is open as he breathes deeply without a care. "Sorry about getting so" —*in your junk*— "familiar." That's the only polite way I can think to phrase it.

"Would you get up from the floor?" Memphis directs me, even though he expressed it as a question. When I glance up, he's rubbing both of his hands over his face.

"Sorry if I hurt you." I know guys act like the world is ending if they get hit in the balls, and I just headbutted him.

"You didn't." He pulls his hands away, and I watch his shoulders fall when he sees me standing. "It's early, are you going back to bed?"

"Yeah, I think," I tell him, even though there is no way I'm falling back to sleep after that. Memphis stands up, and I realize he probably wants to lie down too, so I get out of his way and head toward the stairs. I can feel him behind me the entire time. I'm actually curious about which room he's been using. I tried to figure it out earlier today but couldn't.

I know from the sound of his footsteps that he doesn't stop at the first or second room. Maybe he needs the bathroom, but he passes that too, leaving only one option—my room.

My heart is beating crazy fast, but I pretend not to notice

he's right behind me and pull down the covers to my bed.

From the corner of my eye, I see Memphis walk over to the balcony door and test the knob. I deflate a little. He was just checking the locks. I slip into bed and tuck my toes under the covers. "I keep it locked, Memphis. You don't have to worry."

"I know, but I need to make sure. Does it bother you?" My eyes track his movements as he goes around the other side of the bed.

"No, I just don't want you to worry about me so much."

"Is this okay?" He touches the bed, making it clear he's asking if he can sit down.

"Yeah." I pull the covers up over me a little. I don't know why this feels so different than lying on him while I slept on the couch, but it does.

Memphis doesn't pull back the covers, but he does lie down next to me. A small groan leaves his lips, and the hair on my arms stands up.

"Oswald said your beds were made of fairy fucking clouds." He turns to look at me with the corner of his lips quirked up.

I laugh because I can imagine him saying that. "Should we go wake him up? I feel bad that he slept on the couch when he has to play today."

"No. If we wake him up, he'll want to steal my spot, and I'm not giving it up." His eyes meet mine, and I swear there's more meaning in his gaze than just his spot in the bed right now.

"Okay," I agree softly.

"Close your eyes, Waylynn." I snap my eyes shut at his command. Am I making things weird? "If you keep looking at me like that, I'm going to get myself in trouble."

"What kind of trouble?" I surprise myself with my flirty tone.

"Do you really want me to answer that question?" His voice is low, gravelly.

"No, not yet." Apparently, I'm not as brave as I thought when pressed.

"Good girl," he rasps, and I let out a dreamy little sigh. "Now go to sleep."

BATES

I KNOCK on the door again, even though I didn't get an answer the first time. There's no way he left already. It's too early, and we always meet here before the game because parking is a bitch.

When I push out of the apartment door, I scan the lot, not seeing his truck. "I'll be a son of a bitch," I curse, pulling out my phone to call him. I can't believe I didn't notice he wasn't here.

"Where are you?" I ask as soon as he answers.

"Heading home. I just dropped off Oz."

"Oh." I lean against the building. I thought he ditched me for Waylynn, not that I would blame him, but still. "I'm at the apartment."

"Be there in a minute," he tells me before disconnecting.

Within two minutes, the truck is pulling into the small parking lot. When Memphis gets out, he's in khakis and a button-up. *Walk of shame.* I won't give him shit until we're in the house.

He beats me to the punch as he's unlocking the door. "I need a shower."

If he spent the night with Waylynn, I would think he'd be…happier, but he just seems frustrated. "Do I want to know what you were doing?" If Memphis wants something real from Waylynn and he just fucked it up with a hookup, he's going to be an asshole all day.

"I—we spent the night at Waylynn's." He starts unbuttoning his shirt.

I wait for him to add more, but he doesn't, so I prompt, "And?"

"And she smells really fucking good. I should get awarded sainthood for lying next to her and keeping my hands to myself."

I chuckle. "Go rub one out, or I won't be able to deal with your cranky ass today."

"Fuck off," he gripes and slams the bathroom door.

"That's my advice to you."

The bathroom door opens, and he leans against the doorframe. I think he's about to give me shit, but instead, he says, "I can't even take her to the fucking game. I have to meet her at the seat. How stupid is that? That place is packed with idiots, and half of them are drunk by noon, but I'm sending her in alone because I don't want anyone running their mouth about her and me."

"I can meet her at the gate," I offer with a shrug.

Memphis' brows furrow. "You could," he agrees. "Let me shower, and I'll let her know."

"Make it quick. Do you need your phone for material?"

I can hear him mumbling through the door, but I can't make out what he's saying, probably telling me to fuck off again.

By the time Memphis is out and dressed, it's almost time to leave, and Waylynn isn't answering her phone, which is erasing any of the chill he might have had. "Why the hell isn't she answering or responding to my text?" He looks to me.

"Maybe she's already there, or maybe she's walking," I suggest.

"Let's just go, she might be at will call." Memphis shoves his phone and keys into his pocket. He looks like the guy I grew up with, in faded jeans and a worn T-shirt that's a little too small.

Once we're out on the street, we dodge in and out of foot traffic, moving closer to the school. The line to get in is long, as usual, but this time, Memphis is anxious. Oz is supposed to play today, and he's worried about Waylynn.

He was right about people already being shitfaced. The game starts at noon, but I would bet some of them have been drinking since they woke up. Memphis leans close to the window when we reach the front of the line. "Memphis Gravlin and Peter Bates." He hands over our IDs. "Has Waylynn Graff picked up her ticket yet?" he asks as she slides the tickets and our identification back.

The woman behind the glass looks down briefly. "Nope, and I can't give it to anyone else. I need a photo ID," she tells him.

"I just wanted to know where she is," he says but turns around in the middle of speaking so she can't hear what he said.

We both scan the crowd, but I don't spot her. "Try calling her again, see if she responded to your text," I encourage. "Maybe something came up."

He dials her number and brings his phone up to his ear. His nostrils flare before he grates out, "Hello?" There's a short pause before he snaps, "Why didn't you answer? Where are you?"

He covers his other ear to block out some of the noise. "What? Tell me where."

"She's not going to tell you anything if you bark at her like that." I shake my head.

"No, it's not for the best. Tell me where you are. I'll send

Bates to get you. Waylynn?" He looks down at his phone. "Fuck."

"She decided not to come?" I ask, jogging behind him as he gets into an entrance line.

"No, she decided not to sit with us. She doesn't want to risk getting me in trouble." He stops dead in his tracks and turns to look at me. "You know what's fucked up? I don't know if I want to kiss her or fucking spank her for it."

"Both if she's into it."

"Spank her!" a girl next to us yells as her friend drags her away.

"Did she tell you where she's sitting?"

"No," Memphis scoffs. "I'm going to put a tracker on her phone."

"What the hell, man?" He has never been possessive. He's always been protective of Oz and me, but this is beyond that.

"This is the same girl who invited Oz over and allowed him to invite two other people over. She's too nice."

"Do you want to walk around and look for her before the game starts?" I offer, knowing it will be nearly impossible to find her. Even the student section is huge at the Big House.

He looks around but doesn't answer, so I try another option. "Maybe if you call her back and be *nice,* she'll agree to tell you what section she's in, and I'll go find her before the game ends and walk her out."

Memphis' features relax a little, and he nods in agreement. I follow him over to a wall and he makes a call.

"Hello." This time he sounds less *rip your head off.*

"Thanks for picking up." I would kind of like to hear what she's saying to him. Whatever it is, it has his entire focus. "I'm not mad at you. I was worried. I shouldn't have yelled." My eyes are about ready to fall out of my head. Memphis Gravlin is being apologetic and comforting her.

"I still don't think it's necessary, but if that's what you want, I'll deal with it. I just need one thing, Waylynn. I need you to tell me where you are so Bates can come get you and walk you home." His lip curls up in a snarl, but he says, "Fine, do not forget to text me, Waylynn." After one more short pause, he tells her, "Good girl. Call me if you need anything," then he disconnects.

"What the hell was that?" If I didn't see it for myself, I wouldn't believe it. Memphis is in love with this girl *and* he's an utter asshole.

He completely misunderstands my question. "She said she would text me before the game ended."

"Smart girl, I think we all know you would have gone to get her if she told you where she was now."

"Probably," he admits with a shrug of indifference.

"You better watch it. A lot of girls won't put up with that caveman shit," I warn.

Memphis rubs the side of his face. "Caveman, really?"

"Don't pretend you don't know what I'm talking about."

"I'm not, but I can't say I understand it," he confesses. "The first time she spoke to me, she called me Mr. Gravlin, and it re-fucking-wired my brain."

I laugh but smooth my features when he looks over at me with a scowl. "How many times have you been called Mr. Gravlin?"

"A lot," he admits, "but not by her."

"Ah, don't kid yourself. You've always been a controlling bastard."

"She's just so…sweet." He struggles for the word.

I drop down into my seat and look over the players already on the field. "Please don't make me listen to her call you daddy," I tease. If that's what gets them off, I don't care. Hell, it might be fun.

"No, she called me sir," he says with a completely straight face. My expression must clue him in that I don't know if he's being serious or not. "I programmed myself in her phone under sir."

I almost make a smartass comment but decide against it. "Whatever makes you happy."

"She does," is his simple reply.

TOE THE LINE

Waylynn

The bleachers are hard, and my butt's so big I feel like I'm taking up two seats. I've been avoiding Memphis' calls, but now that I'm in my seat, I answer. "Hello."

"Hello. Why didn't you answer? Where are you?" He sounds angry.

"I got my own ticket. I'm not going to get you in trouble," I reason.

"What? Tell me where," he demands.

"No," I mutter softly, even though it's hard to deny him. "I'm still here to watch Oswald, and you can watch the game without worrying anyone would see us. It's for the best."

"No, it's not for the best. Tell me where you are. I'll send Bates to get you."

"I'll talk to you later," I say, then hang up quickly. My stomach is in knots. He sounded mad. I hate that I disappointed him, but I did it for him. I'm not willing to risk getting him in trouble if someone sees us. It's not worth it.

I jump when I feel cold liquid splash against my leg. "Sorry about that." The guy next to me rubs the side of my thigh, trying to get rid of the beer he just spilled on me when he sat down. I pull my leg over, but there's not much room with how packed this place is, so I end up pushing his hand away.

"It's okay." I rub my leg a few more times so he doesn't try again. It's weird he even did it.

"Want my drink?" He offers me the half full cup he spilled on me as if that will make it better.

"No thank you." I wish I could have gotten a seat at the end of the row, but I took what was available.

"I'll be more careful," he tells me with glassy eyes.

I nod so he doesn't feel the need to keep talking.

"Are you here alone?" He looks around me at the couple who's squished together.

"No, my friends are in another section. I bought my ticket late," I explain.

"That sucks. You're welcome to hang out with us," he offers.

"Um… I'm just going to watch the game," I state. How do you hang out at a football game? I don't get it.

"Let me know if you need anything to drink." He lifts his glass before taking a long drink.

I look down when my phone rings and see Sir in bright white letters on the black screen. "Hello," I say softly because I feel like the guy next to me is listening.

"Thanks for picking up," Memphis tells me in a much softer tone than his other call.

"I don't want you to be mad at me, not for this," I admit.

"I'm not mad at you. I was worried. I shouldn't have yelled. I still don't think it's necessary, but if that's what you want, I'll deal with it."

"Thank you."

"I just need one thing, Waylynn. I need you to tell me where you are so Bates can come get you and walk you home." There's a slight edge in his tone, letting me know he's not going to let this go.

"I'll text you before the game ends," I compromise.

His slight pause makes me think he's going to argue, but he finally says, "Fine, do not forget to text me, Waylynn."

"Yes, sir."

"Good girl. Call me if you need anything." I grip the phone tighter against my ear, but he hangs up before I can respond, not that I had actual words to say.

"That your dad?" the guy next to me asks as soon as I pull my phone down from my ear.

I choke on the spit in my mouth and end up coughing hard. "No," I grate out after clearing my throat.

Thankfully, anything he might have said is interrupted when the game announcer starts speaking.

The first quarter goes by fast. There are no time-outs or points scored, but the other team is able to score in the second. I don't boo like the group next to me, but a lot of people from our section do. Right after they kick the ball through the goal, there's a scramble to shift players, and that's when I see number twenty-five run out onto the field.

"Oh god." I cover my mouth with my hands but keep my eyes glued to Oswald as he gets in the line.

The guy next to me misunderstands. "It's okay, there's plenty of time for them to come back."

When the game resumes, Oswald runs away from the line and grabs the ball right out of the air. I was so busy watching him, I didn't realize they were throwing it to him. The second his feet hit the ground, he runs up the field. I'm already on my feet, but when he gets smashed to the ground by someone in a white shirt, I let out a little yelp. I don't think my heart starts beating again until Oswald hops up off the ground and runs back to his team.

People are screaming and yelling, blowing airhorns, but I'm about to pee my pants. I can't believe that guy hit him so hard. I lower myself back into the seat, but I'm only perched on the edge this time.

Thank god they don't throw the ball to him the next play, he just scrambles around with the other players, and someone else gets knocked down.

At the beginning of the fourth quarter, I'm a wreck. Oswald has scored points, but he's also been clobbered a bunch of times. How the heck does he keep getting back up?

"You know him?" the guy next to me asks when they flash a photo of Oswald up on the big monitors.

"He's in my English class," I answer.

"He's good. You're wearing his jersey."

"I know," I reply, addressing both statements.

When there's seven minutes left—I know because I've been watching the clock like a hawk—I text Memphis my section, row, and seat number. I have no idea where they are or how long it will take Bates to find me, but I wanted to keep my promise, and the guy next to me is really starting to get on my nerves. It seems like he's been complaining about Oswald since he asked if I knew him, saying crap to make it seem like he's not playing hard enough or he's messing up.

I'd rather watch the rest of the game from the aisle at this point.

MEMPHIS

. . .

When my phone buzzes, showing Waylynn's number, I get a sense of satisfaction. She listened. There's seven minutes left in the quarter, which is a lifetime in football. "I'm going to get her," I tell Bates.

He looks over at me, clearly not surprised, even though he says, "You told her *I* would go get her."

"You're coming with me, right?"

"Yeah."

"Then I told her the truth," I hedge.

"You're shady." He snorts but stands up. We have to edge by a few people to get out of the row, but it's not too bad.

"She's in thirty-three." I haul ass up the steps, intending to get to her quickly, but I spot a vendor selling hats and decide to do something that might make her feel better about me coming for her.

Thirty bucks later, I'm heading down to her section, scanning the area. I spot the number twenty-five first, then see my name in bold letters between two long braids. The sight causes me to stop on the steps, and Bates runs into my back. "What the hell?"

Waylynn hops out of her seat to stand up, and I see the guy next to her lean back so he can look at her ass. That gets me moving real fast. The row behind her has a few empty seats, so I head down it, pushing past several people, and then I lean forward to cover her up while staring the guy right in the eye.

"Hey!" She swats at me and jumps to the side to get away,

but her face softens when she sees me under the hat. "Memphis?"

"Come on, sweetness." I try to keep my voice level when I extend my hand to her so she knows I'm not angry. I would like to shove the guy's head up his ass though. She was awfully quick to push me away, and it makes me wonder if he's been bothering her.

She looks around and nibbles on her bottom lip. I can tell she's worried someone might see us, but I don't care right now.

"You know I'm not leaving without you," I warn, and she plants her foot on the bench to come to me. I give into the urge to grab her waist and help her down, but I don't move or let go when she stands right in front of me. Our bodies are pressed together, and I bet she can feel how much I like it. "Love the shirt." I smirk. She gets all bashful and lowers her eyes before peeking back up.

"No more sitting by yourself," I tell her when I know I have her attention. Her lips part like she wants to argue, but she doesn't. "Tell me," I order, forgetting all about the guy who was checking her out and why we shouldn't be standing in a stadium full of people who would know at a glance there's more going on between us than teacher and student, or even friends.

"I won't come by myself," she says softly, and my mind goes to an even more dangerous place, thinking about her with her fingers between her legs.

I lean down so my lips are near her ear and whisper, "That's my girl."

Her body sags against me when she melts. I bet I could kiss her right now and she would let me. Knowing I've gotten inside her head and erased those worries that kept her away from me makes me want to do just that.

"Memphis!" Bates calls my name loudly, and it snaps me out of the stupor Waylynn put me into. When I look up, he makes a face that tells me I'm being stupid, and I still don't move. "Waylynn, come on," he says, trying to reason with her since I'm beyond it.

Her chest pushes up against mine as she takes a deep breath, then she shimmies to the side and steps away from me.

Now I just need to pretend I don't have a dick print in my jeans. *Fuck.*

BATES

THE SEXUAL TENSION between the two of them is off the charts the moment Memphis gets his hands on her. They are attracting a hell of a lot of attention from the people sitting around them, and I know that's the last thing they need.

It takes me a second to stop gawking and say, "Memphis." Calling him Gravlin would draw even more interest.

He looks at me but doesn't do jack shit to pry himself

away from Waylynn, so I try her instead. "Waylynn, come on."

She breathes deeply and her chest rises, pushing her tits up even more. I probably shouldn't be noticing that, but then she steps to the side, putting space between her and Memphis. I wave her toward me, and she says, "Pardon me," several times as she passes in front of people to get out of the row.

"Hey, sorry to make you wait," she tells me once she's on the stairs.

"You're good. Have you been enjoying the game?" I ask as Memphis sulks behind her when he gets out of the row.

"Enjoying..." She widens her eyes as if she thinks the question is crazy.

"Don't worry, I won't tell Oz you hate it." I chuckle as we make our way back up to the main deck.

"I don't hate it," she says hurriedly. "It's just...so rough. You can hear it when they hit. Like a car crash. Do you think he's going to be okay?"

That makes me laugh harder. "He'll be fine. He wears pads for a reason."

"I would run the other way if one of them came at me, pads or not, and I don't even run," she says seriously. It's adorable. As soon as the thought strikes me, I look away from her and over at Memphis. He's not glaring at me like he wants to rip my balls off, so I don't think he noticed.

"What's the plan now?" I ask, making sure not to stare at Waylynn too much.

"We can go down and meet him in the athletics hall," he offers, checking in with Waylynn.

"I can—"

"Come with us," Memphis interrupts. "If anyone asks, you're there for my brother, but they won't," he promises.

"As long as we can keep a few feet of space between the two of you, I think it will be fine," I tease. Waylynn's cheeks turn pink with a blush. *Shit.*

Oswald

THE REPEATED slaps on the back are starting to get to me. I'm happy we won, but it wasn't easy. I don't think there's a lot to celebrate with a three-point difference.

Once the coach is done with us on the end of the field, he heads back toward the locker rooms. There are all kinds of people in the hall—press, the athlete heads, and some players' families. It's easy to spot Memphis in the crowd. When I get closer, I realize he's standing behind Waylynn. She's a lot shorter, so it was harder to see her, but the minute I do, a grin splits my lips. She's wearing my number across her chest, and what a fine fucking chest it is. The material is tight over her tits and sits a little looser on her waist where it's gathered up so it's not over her hips. She's in a cute pair of cutoff shorts that are a little longer than what a lot of girls wear, but she looks amazing.

"Look at you, representing." I grab her in a tight hug the moment I'm close enough. When I pull back, I tug a little extra fabric by her shoulder and marvel at the shirt. "Where'd you get this?"

"I know a guy if you need one," she teases, then spins around to show me her back, and I see my name across her shoulders. She peeks around at me, and I wrap her up in my arms again, feeling her butt tucked against me.

"You can tell him to hook you up with one for every day of the week." I sway her from side to side. "Hey, guys," I greet, finally saying hi to Memphis and Bates.

"Officially on the roster." Memphis sends a fist bump my way, and I unhook from Waylynn to return it.

"Just a matter of time."

"See? He's fine," Bates tells Waylynn. "You're going to have to stop taking so many hits, she was worried," he ribs.

"You were?" I peek down at her, and she nods. "I'll see what I can do." My grin is probably too big, but it's nice to have someone worry about me besides my brother.

"This is going to take a little while. What are you guys going to do?"

"I have shit to do at the house," Bates pipes up quickly.

Memphis looks at the side of his face questioningly. He usually hangs out with us on Saturday unless he has a show or something. "We can go home and wait for you. You good if we grab something to eat?"

"Yeah, I need a little while before I stuff my face." If I ate now, I would probably hurl it all back up.

"Okay, go do what you need to do. Let me know when you need a ride," Memphis tells me.

I give Waylynn one last squeeze and kiss the side of her head before heading into the locker room.

HISTORY

Waylynn

MEMPHIS INVITES Bates to eat with us again after we spend half an hour walking around and talking, mostly about the game, but he declines. We end up leaving him at the corner of State Street and walk toward my house.

The sidewalks are filled with people. Memphis has the hat pulled low on his head so it's harder to see his face, and I'm not too worried someone will spot him, but I still can't get over how different he looks in jeans and a T-shirt.

"What?" he asks without even looking over at me. He could tell I was staring.

"You just look different," I admit.

"Do you want me to change?" He peeks at me from the corner of his eye.

"No, of course not. You look…handsome both ways. In jeans or slacks. Whatever you want to wear," I ramble.

"Good to know. Should we see if we can get a table anywhere?" he asks as we walk past packed bars and restaurants.

"We can go home," I offer, not wanting to push our luck any more than we are. If we run into anyone now, he could tell them he was walking his brother's friend home, but eating at a restaurant would be difficult to explain.

"Fine by me. Are you sure we're not imposing?"

"Yes, but all I can promise is some frozen pizza or something. Unless you want to go to the grocery store? I never remember to take anything out of the freezer." I haven't gotten used to cooking dinner for myself.

"Frozen pizza, ramen, I don't care, I'm just hungry," he replies.

"It looks like it's going to take longer than usual to get home," I comment, looking at the people and traffic holding up the streets.

"I used to avoid game days," he mumbles and puts his phone to his ear. "Hey." He pauses. "We haven't even made it home yet. Honestly, you might want to walk or grab a scooter if you can find one. It's probably the quickest option."

Memphis pauses again, I'm assuming to let Oz speak, then

says, "We'll plan better next week. Call if you end up needing us to come." He hangs up a few seconds later.

The foot traffic thins out once we get off State and then tapers off even more when we turn down the street to my neighborhood. When the house comes into view, I sigh. Not only am I looking forward to the air-conditioning, but I also really need to pee.

I do a little speed walking to get to the door faster. "Do you mind getting the alarm so I can run to the bathroom?" I look over my shoulder as I'm unlocking the door.

"No, it's fine." He grins.

Memphis

Waylynn tosses her bag on the counter and dashes out of the room. Her purse falls to the side and some of her things roll out onto the counter. The orange bottle of pills spinning in circles draws my attention more than the other items and brings back bad memories. My mother's bag was always filled with them. Most of the bottles didn't even have her name, or if they did, the pills inside weren't what was prescribed.

I glance toward the doorway to make sure Waylynn isn't returning then pick up the bottle. The pills inside make a soft rattle. The label has been peeled off, leaving a patch of sticky residue in its place. Damn it.

I twist the top to see what's inside, but it's just tiny little circles. I have no idea what they are. The door upstairs closes, and I know I'm out of time unless I want to confront her right now. I tuck the bottle back into her purse, but I'm pissed, and she must read it on my face because she walks into the room slowly, as if she's hesitant.

"Everything okay?" She tugs on the hem of her jersey. What I might have thought was a nervous gesture before feels more like she's hiding something. I look into her eyes. They seem as clear as usual. Is she on something right now?

"Your bag fell." I step to the side, revealing the pens and papers that slipped free along with her unzipped purse. Her eyes widen, and she rushes over to shove everything back inside.

"What a mess." She tries to sound like she's half laughing, but there's something in her voice, a tremor that I might have chalked up to nerves before, but now I can't stop thinking about the pills.

I can't lose someone to addiction again, I won't. I think about walking out the door and never looking back, but my feet feel rooted to the tile. Not only do I not want to walk away from her, but I don't know if Oz would, even if she was using. He doesn't remember things the way I do, and I'm to blame for that. I made sure he had food when I didn't, and I made sure to keep him away from them when they were mad at the world because they couldn't get another hit. I watched Mom waste away until she was nothing but skin and bones, covered in sores and shit I don't even want to think about.

I let my eyes roam over Waylynn. Her full hips and thighs look nothing like my mom's. The small, soft swell of her stomach and breasts are part of what drew me to her. She looks healthy, but not all addicts look the same.

"Um..." Waylynn reaches across her body and grabs the elbow of her other arm.

She's probably wondering why I'm staring at her like she's a stranger. Is she?

"Still hungry?" She rounds the island, putting some distance between us. I note her purse is zipped up and tucked away now.

"Why do you have pills in your purse?" I wasn't ready to ask the question, but it comes out anyway, and my harsh tone makes it sound like an accusation.

"You looked through my purse?" She's defensive, they always are.

"Your bag fell," I point out, but I wouldn't feel guilty if I did. I need to protect my brother and myself. "What are they?" Oswald told me there were a few doctors in her phone contacts, but I didn't think much of it at the time. That should have been a clue right there.

"Mine," she says without any other explanation.

"Clearly, they came from your bag, but what kind of pills are they? Why are you taking them?" I ask slowly, but not because I think she's stupid and doesn't understand the question, I'm just trying to control my anger.

"A lot of people take medicine."

"A lot of people don't carry around bottles of pills with the labels scratched off, but addicts do."

"Addicts?" Her head pulls back a little like she's surprised, but I don't know many users who would admit to themselves or anyone else they have a problem. "You think I'm doing drugs?" She really sells the fact that I'm confusing her.

"You already admitted they were yours," I remind her.

"Admitted it was my medication." She's the one to speak slowly now.

"Then why isn't there a label?"

"Because I know what they are, and it's no one else's business," she snaps.

"If you're around me and my brother, I have the right to know if you're a junkie." As soon as the word is out of my mouth, I regret it, but I don't know how to take it back or if I even should.

"I'm supposed to divulge my full medical history to you because we've hung out a few times?" Waylynn's arms are across her chest, but her shoulders are curled in.

"It's more than that, and you know it." Her glib remark pisses me off, because she knows there's more to this than just hanging out a few times.

"Do I?" She narrows her eyes on me. "I know virtually nothing about you or Oswald besides he could eat half a cow daily and loves football, or at least I'm assuming he does because he works so hard at it, and you're extra bossy with the need to take care of people."

"I'm not hiding something that could be dangerous to myself and you." I hate the way she's looking at me like I'm disappointing her. I haven't done anything wrong.

"I'm not a danger to myself or anyone else." Her back goes ramrod straight.

"You're putting poison in your body," I snap. Why can't she just admit what's going on here? Then we could at least discuss this and get her help.

"I am taking medication prescribed by a doctor," she says slowly through her teeth.

"Yeah, we noticed how many you have in your phone. How many do you have to hit up to get your fix, or do you just bribe them with your parents' money?"

"What the fuck is going on?" Oswald asks, having heard most of my last comment. He's looking at me like he has no idea who I am.

"She's taking pills." I point across the room.

Waylynn takes a deep breath and lets it out slowly before calmly saying, "Prescribed medication."

"Bullshit. If it was something you should have, you wouldn't have scratched off the label," I tell her again.

"Because you decree it so?" Waylynn's eyes are wide, angry, and worst of all, hurt.

"What kind of medication is it? What do you have?" My eyes roam over her from head to toe, but I don't see a damn thing wrong with her.

"Chill out, Memphis," Oz says gently.

"No, you should be the last person to say that. She could get you kicked off the football team. If you're with her and she gets caught or pulled over, you could take the fall."

"I would—I would never let anything like that happen," she defends with complete disbelief.

"How are you going to stop it? Throw money at the problem and hope it goes away? That's probably what your parents did for you."

"Memphis," Oswald says softly, like he's ashamed of me. It's not something I've ever heard from him before.

Waylynn blinks at me several times, but her mouth stays closed, which makes me madder at her and myself. I want her to say something back, to tell me the truth, but she's just looking at me with sad, hurt eyes.

"You need help," I spew at her, but it ends up coming out all wrong, like an insult instead of the assistance I'm trying to suggest.

"You're right—I probably need my head examined again for ever letting you shove your way into my life."

"Examined again?" Oswald questions, whereas I'm too mad to even hear more than the blatant mischaracterization of our relationship.

"I'm not *asking* you to leave this time. I'm telling you to leave, and don't bother coming back!"

"Wait, wait, let's talk about this. Waylynn, are you using?" Oz asks doubtfully.

"No." Her single word response is short and filled with anger.

"Then what is he talking about?" Oswald looks between the two of us, clearly torn.

"He saw my pill bottle, and then this." She gestures to me with a jerky motion. "You know what? I don't need to explain myself to either of you. I told you to leave."

"I'm not going anywhere until I get some fucking answers. I will not watch you waste away like she did."

"She who? Whoever made you believe you're the one to hold ultimate responsibility over everyone?"

"Someone had to do it," I snap, while at the same time Oswald says, "Our mom. We lost our parents when they OD'd."

"She didn't need to know that," I accuse, pissed Oswald is sharing our secrets while she has hers.

"Fucking rich." She spins around and looks at the ceiling.

"I'm trying to explain why you are acting like a complete whack job," Oswald yells, hammering it home.

"She has a bottle of unlabeled pills in her purse. She already admitted they were hers." I point. "I want to help her. I can't do it again." I'm yelling now too.

"This may be hard for you to actually hear, Memphis, but I don't need your help. I don't need anything from you, despite what you may think. I'm not some helpless girl, too dumb not to know when to talk to strangers or take drugs. I chose to let you in because I felt something with both of you I hadn't ever experienced—a connection from the first time you spoke to me. I should have known it was insane, just like everything else." She laughs, but there's no humor in it. "I'm sorry about your mom. Hell, if you would have talked to me and explained your concerns, I probably would have told you what the pills are, but you're not the only one with baggage, and maybe I wasn't ready to spill my secrets to a guy who acts like I don't exist half the time."

"You're in denial. I've seen it a hundred times," I argue, but I can hear the lack of belief in my own tone.

"Okay," she agrees without a fight, and I know I've lost something in that moment. "I want you to leave. Do whatever you need to do—report me, call the cops, whatever—but you need to leave."

"Memphis, go. Let me talk to her," Oswald urges with wide, pleading eyes. It's not just me who hears the finality in her flat tone.

"No, you both need to go. I would never in a million years come between the two of you."

"You're not." He spins to face me. "Tell her she's not," he pleads.

She's smarter than both of us. My face feels funny, all tingly and hot, but I can't force myself to give Oswald the lie he wants. She would never believe it anyway.

"I'll talk to him, and we can talk tomorrow," Oz offers as a latch-ditch effort. He knows there's no way she's going to let him stay.

"Sure," Waylynn agrees again in that light flat tone that tells me she's lying.

Oswald takes two steps back to the door while I'm the one stuck in my spot. I know there won't be a tomorrow, but he's still clinging to hope.

"It was a great game, Oswald. Thank you for inviting me."

"Always, Wavy. I want you there every game."

She gives him a thin smile and a nod that seems to help my brother breathe easier, but I see it for what it is—a goodbye. "Come on, Memphis, let's go." I watch my brother walk out of the door, then turn to look at Waylynn. The anger is gone from her face, but what's left behind is worse. Her expression is indifferent and apathetic. Even her hazel eyes seem flat.

It's on the tip of my tongue to beg her to talk to me, but I'm afraid I'm only going to make the situation worse or find out I was wrong, and I don't know if I can come back from that.

"Waylynn," I try, but she's already shaking her head.

"No. If there was ever anything I needed from you, it's for you to leave now." She can't even look at me. Whatever is happening, it's not just with me. She's fighting her own demons, and I'm the one that brought them to her.

I hear the click of the lock the second I'm out the door, and then the kitchen light shuts off right after.

What have I done?

Continue the story in *Touching Oblivion*, book two of the Tasting Madness series.
Preorder Touching Oblivion

ABOUT THE AUTHOR

Albany lives in Michigan where she's happily married to her high school sweetheart. She spends most of her time juggling her four children's extracurricular activities, with her nose stuck in a book. When not reading you can find her writing her very own book boyfriends. Albany's passion is writing romance with real characters that are far from perfect, but always seem to find their own happily ever afters

If you enjoyed my book, or any other consider leaving a review.

For updates:
Readers Group Albany's Agents
Albanywalkerauthor@gmail.com
www.albanywalker.com

ALSO BY ALBANY WALKER

Coming soon

Touching Oblivion Book Two of Tasting Madness

Tasting Madness Series

Seeing Sound

Completed Monsters Series

Friends With the Monsters

Some Kind of Monster

Completed series Havenfall Harbor

Havenfall Harbor Book One

Havenfall Harbor Book Two

Completed Series Infinity Chronicles

Infinity Chronicles Book One

Infinity Chronicles Book Two

Infinity Chronicles Book three

Infinity Chronicles Book Four

Completed Series Magical Bureau of Investigation

Homecoming Homicide

Creeping it Real

Perfectly Wicked

Dollhouse World can be read as standalone novels

Amusement

Diversion

Standalone novels

Beautiful Deceit

Becoming His

Stone Will Obsidian Angels MC

Printed in Great Britain
by Amazon